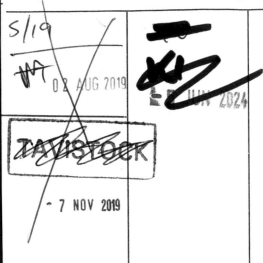

The first part of SPIES AND SAUCERS, "The Fallen Nun", takes place in 1959. Our protagonist, Kyle Black, wakes up one morning to discover a dead nun lying facedown in the marijuana garden in his backyard. Attempting to solve the mystery of how the nun ended up in his garden leads Kyle to strange encounters with an Irish Cyclops named Finn mac Cumhall, a Devil Bat grown to enormous proportions by a dead mad scientist, two homicidal tabloid journalists, and a sickly extraterrestrial abducted by a time travelling mother superior . . . .

In "Communist Town, U.S.A.", a young FBI agent named Philip Trowbridge is sent to Wisconsin in 1955 with orders to infiltrate a small town, reportedly a hotbed of underground Communist activity, in which several previous FBI agents have disappeared without a trace . . . .

"Spies and Saucers" is set three years earlier in 1952 and involves a blacklisted, left-wing Hollywood screenwriter named Curt Adamson. Down on his luck after having been dumped by every studio on the West Coast, Adamson is recruited by a covert spy agency to write a screenplay for an unknown reason—unknown only to Adamson, that is. Adamson's superiors are well aware of the screenplay's purpose. Though consistently told he doesn't have a "need to know", Adamson insists on discovering the truth behind the tale he himself is weaving, and uncovers a plot far more outlandish and ominous than the cheap horror and science fiction B-movies on which he's built his tarnished reputation . . . .

SPIES AND SAUCERS

ROBERT GUFFEY

ANDERS

2014

Jacket art by Emily Hare.
Book design by Pedro Marques.
Text set in MrsEaves and Univers.
Titles set in Belgrad.

Printed in England by T.J. International.

PS Publishing Ltd
Grosvenor House
1 New Road
Hornsea, HU18 1PG
England
E-mail: editor@pspublishing.co.uk
Visit our website at www.pspublishing.co.uk.

TO ALL THE FLYING SAUCERERS OF THE 1950S

(both terrestrial and otherwise): George Adamski, Alan ("a-lawn"), Orfeo Angelucci, Kenneth Arnold, Gray Barker, Albert K. Bender, Truman Bethurum, Leonard G. Cramp, Daniel Fry, Waveney Girvan, Gerald Heard, Karma and Suma, Donald Keyhoe, M.K. Jessup, Carl Jung, Meade Layne, Howard Menger, James Moseley, Orthon, Ray Palmer, Mark Probert, Bryant and Helen Reeve, Captain Aura Rhanes, Solganda, Frank Stranges, Valiant Thor, George Van Tassel, Harold T. Wilkins and any other related entity whose identity has been temporarily wiped from my mind.

SPIES AND SAUCERS

1
THE FALLEN NUN

*"It is better to know some of the questions
than all of the answers."*
James Thurber

1

Kyle Black

THE NUN FELL IN MY BACKYARD at some point between 11:00 p.m. on July 19th and 7:00 a.m. on July 20th, 1959. I recall being in the garden at around ten having a smoke just before going to bed. I know I didn't fall asleep until sometime around eleven. And I didn't hear anything crash in the garden, which was just outside my window. Therefore, the event must have occurred at some point during those eight hours.

When I awoke I put on my robe and wandered out into the garden, as I did every morning. I loved my garden dearly. I'd been tending it for years, even though the crop had been illegal since William Randolph Hearst initiated a campaign to demonize hemp as a "devil weed" so the plant would never be a viable alternative source for paper. The campaign was successful. It was so successful the "satanic" stigma has remained attached to the plant to this very day, years after Hearst's death in 1951.

The nun was lying facedown in the middle of my garden. I'm sure you can imagine my shock. I'd never seen a nun lying facedown before, certainly not in my garden. It didn't take long for me to realize she was dead. I even poked her habit with a long stick just to make sure. She didn't move. Her body lay atop a pile of fallen branches and bright green spring leaves. I glanced up and could see that many of the branches in the overhanging trees had snapped off. I studied the nun again. There was a distinct impression in the ground as if she had fallen from a very great height.

Now you have to understand, I live in an isolated area in the hills above Malibu known as Trail's End. I inherited the house from my father who was something of a recluse and a Luddite. He hated all sounds of radios and televisions and cars and planes. The reason he chose to live in Trail's End was because it was well outside the flight path of anything even remotely resembling an airplane.

From where, then, did the nun fall?

I had no idea. All I knew was that I had a dead woman in my garden, which was filled with illegal substances. How could I alert the police without going to jail—if not for murder, then for possession of marijuana? On the other hand, if I didn't call the police I might be suspected of murder. That is, if the body was ever found.

I kneeled down beside her. Tentatively, I reached out and touched her shoulder with my fingertips. I found myself holding my breath. Her black robe was damp with morning dew. My palm sank into the wetness as I gripped her shoulder and pushed her over onto her back. I tried to regulate my breathing as I studied her face. She seemed to be in her seventies. It was a long, angular face with too many awkwardly sloping planes to be considered attractive in any way. It was a harsh face. The face of a school teacher in the first grade, the one who yelled at you for spilling glue on the floor.

The fact that her face was distorted into a grotesque visage of pure fear didn't help matters any. Her bloody mouth was paralyzed in a distorted "O", her front teeth knocked out by the impact of the fall. Even if there *had* been a plane from which to fall, I didn't believe her injuries jibed with a descent from such a drastic height. If she'd toppled out of a plane she would have been nothing more than a messy red spot, right?

The first word that popped into my mind was *Fort*. Back in college my roommate was into weird paranormal stuff like the Hollow Earth and Atlantis. His hero was some kook from the

1920s named Charles Fort who wrote books about frogs falling from the sky and invented the word "teleportation." Could the nun have somehow been the victim of *spontaneous* teleportation? Perhaps she was wandering around in a convent somewhere when—*bloop!*—she just blinked out and appeared in the sky above my garden. I imagined her having the time to spin her arms and legs like pinwheels before at last plummeting to her absurd death, similar to the coyote in those Road Runner cartoons I used to like as a kid.

Of course, the how and why of the nun's presence in my garden was almost beside the point. The important thing was to act. I grabbed the nun by her ankles and dragged her into the garage. I then went into the house and found a metal chest in the attic I once used for old books. (I had recently built an extra bookshelf in the living room, rendering the chest useless.) I dragged this chest downstairs.

There was an old car in the garage I'd been meaning to get rid of for years. It barely ran. My father had kept it because it was against his genetic make-up to throw anything away, even things he hated. I dropped the chest inside the trunk of the car, then dropped the nun inside the chest. I knew of a lake only a mile away at the bottom of the hill; it was rarely visited by anybody. I figured I'd dump the chest, as well as the nun, into the drink. Simple as that.

Which is when the doorbell rang. My heart began beating fast. Who could it be? Nobody ever visited me, except for my mother five years before. A definite mistake. My mother and I didn't get along at all. She was a religious zealot and didn't approve of my little gardening project. It wasn't pleasant to recall such unfortunate lapses of judgment. I hadn't made that same error in the past five years. Mainly because I hadn't seen anybody in the past five years. Except for this nun.

And . . . in a few seconds, if I managed to get my courage up . . . whoever was knocking at the door.

I wiped my brow of sweat, straightened my clothes, and reentered the house through the door that led into the living room. I opened the front door as casually as possible. Standing on my porch were two middle-aged men wearing cheap black suits. One was short and rumpled and looked like a starving rat with a skinny, turkey-like neck and a wrinkled roadmap of a face; he had a shiny, brand new camera strapped around his scrawny neck. The other was tall and slim with the slick look of an aging actor; deep scratches on his face marred his otherwise handsome features. "FBI", the short one said, holding up his badge. "This is Agent Layton, I'm Agent McGuire. How're you doing today, sir?" The man slipped the badge back into his jacket pocket.

"Uh . . . fine", I said.

"You live here alone?"

"Yes."

"Have you seen anything . . . *strange* lately?"

"Strange?" I glanced back and forth between the pair, trying to read the expressions on their faces. It was impossible. Both were impassive. "What do you mean 'strange'?"

"You know—strange", McGuire said, the loose flesh on his neck vibrating slightly as he spoke. "I dunno, like a nun appearing out of nowhere."

I burst out laughing. "Like *what*?"

McGuire wasn't laughing. Neither was Layton. "You heard him", Layton said. "Like a nun appearing out of fucking nowhere. You know what a nun is, don't you?"

"Sure." I tried to wipe my smile away. "Sure I do. But I've never heard of one appearing out of . . . out of 'fucking' nowhere."

The agents exchanged unreadable glances. McGuire turned back toward me. "Oh, you haven't? Well, I guess we'll just have to take your word for it, won't we?" For the first time he snickered.

I began to get angry. "Are you accusing me of something?"

McGuire acted startled. He spread his fingers out and pressed them against his unimpressive chest. Then he tapped on his chest with his knuckle. A sick, hollow sound echoed somewhere deep inside his lungs. "Who, me? Accuse *you*? Oh my, I'd never do anything like that, now would I?" He elbowed Layton in the ribs.

"Oh no", Layton said, trying to suppress a smile.

The little guy, McGuire, reached into his jacket and pulled out a .38 revolver. He pointed it at my forehead. "Okay, genius, show me where the nun is."

I raised my hands in the air. "I—I—"

He shoved me backwards into the living room, almost toppling me over. "I don't have all day to listen to you stutter. Where is she?"

He lifted up onto his tippy-toes, grabbed me by the collar, and pressed the cold barrel against my left temple. I could barely speak.

"If I were you, I'd tell him", Layton said while digging into a package of Rolaids.

I pointed at the door leading into the garage.

"That's the wisest move you've ever made, white boy", McGuire said while pushing me toward the door. I didn't understand why he was calling me "white boy." McGuire appeared to be white himself, maybe Irish or Scottish. He opened the garage door and scanned the tiny room. "Where?"

"Th—the trunk of the car", I whispered.

McGuire glanced at Layton. "What're you waitin' for?" he said. "Do it."

Layton lifted up the trunk. He seemed surprised when he saw the chest inside. Before he could even ask I said, "She's inside there. The key's in my left pants pocket."

"That's the spirit, white boy", said McGuire. "You're really catching on quick. Cooperation is the key to enlightenment." He reached into my pocket and withdrew the key. He tossed it to Layton, who immediately shoved it into the lock with shaking hands. He seemed anxious, very anxious.

I couldn't see the inside of the trunk from where I was standing, only the look of dismay on Layton's unshaven, tired face. "What the fuck is this?" he said, spreading his hands in the air.

McGuire dragged me toward the car so fast the tips of my shoes scraped the ground. Inside the chest, where I had stuffed the nun only a few minutes before, was an exact duplicate of myself. And I appeared to be unconscious. To be dying, in fact. My torso was covered in blood.

"This some kind of a joke?" Layton said, the tension rising in his voice.

McGuire slapped me upside the head. "You tryin' to hoodwink us? Huh? Is that what you think you're doin'?" He slapped me again, this time even harder.

I allowed myself to fall to the ground. "Please! I *swear* I put her in there. I don't know where she is."

The FBI agents (if that's what they were) just stared at each other for a second, then McGuire grabbed my ear lobe and forced me to my feet. He said, "Okay, if that's the way you want to play it, pigfucker. Get in the trunk."

Layton pulled my dying double out of the chest and dumped him on the concrete floor as if he were nothing more than a sack of garbage.

"What?" I said. "No, I—I really—"

McGuire pumped a single bullet into the wall. "Get into the motherfuckin' trunk!" The sound of the explosion was enough to send me jumping into that little box. I'd always been somewhat claustrophobic, afraid of being buried alive like in that Edgar Allan Poe story. And now here I was, surrounded by darkness. McGuire slammed the lid shut and locked it.

"Okay, genius", said McGuire, his voice muffled, "here's the deal: You're gonna stay in there until you suffocate or you're gonna tell us where her holiness is hiding her wrinkled ass. Which will it be?"

"He means it", Layton said. "Believe me, I don't want to see you die at such a young age, kid. I'd do what he says, and I'd do it pretty soon if I were you."

"Or maybe we should just kill him now", McGuire said. "Shoot him right through the trunk."

"Hey, hey, give the kid a little time", Layton said. "He's confused. He's had a rough day."

I broke in and said, "I can't tell you something I don't know!"

A moment of silence followed. Then Layton said, "Okay, let's just drop the good cop/bad cop routine. Remember that lake we saw about a mile back?"

"Yeah?"

"Dump him in there. At least that way he can't identify us later on."

"Is that absolutely necessary, sir?"

"Don't start with me, I've had a long day!"

"Yes, sir."

Sir? The dynamics between the two seemed to have changed. Now the little rat-faced guy was taking orders from the tall, handsome guy.

"But, sir, how shall we transport him there?"

"Put the damn chest in the trunk of our car. Drive him to the edge of the lake and dump him the fuck in. While you're doing that, I'll stay here and tear the place apart. The bitch has to be here somewhere. If I don't find her, maybe I'll just have to beat this asshole's twin to relieve some tension."

You can't imagine the extent of my fear as I felt them carry me back through the living room and into the driveway where I was deposited in the trunk of another car. The metal lid slammed shut above me. The car pulled away from my house, and I could somehow feel the lake drawing ever nearer. I think I must have blacked out. I don't know.

My next conscious thought was feeling the water pouring into the chest through the thin spaces between the hinges. The liquid filled my mouth and my lungs as I beat feebly against the metal.

Under normal circumstances I would have died right then and there.

Instead I awoke in a convent surrounded by nuns.

"He's coming to", I heard an old woman say.

They were standing around me in a circle. Most of them were very old, well past seventy.

"Excuse me", one of the nuns said, "but do you know where Mother Superior is?"

"What did you *do* with her?" another said and tried to attack me with a cane. The other nuns had to hold her back.

"Please forgive her", said the first nun, who was much younger than the others. "She's very distressed. It's not every day that one of the sisters is, well . . . consumed by a hyper-spatial vortex created by a dying extraterrestrial being, you understand."

I blinked twice. "Excuse me?" I said.

2

Johnny Layton

WE GOT THE CALL AROUND FOUR P.M. Pandolphi, head of the "Weird Desk" at the CIA, told us to check out a possible crash of a spacecraft in Heathville, Wisconsin. Though we had no official ties to the Agency, Pandolphi himself secured our job at *The Midnight Sun*. The tabloid was valuable on many levels. It served as an excellent conduit for disinformation, a convenient leak for classified information that certain officials wished to reveal to the public, and an effective cover for investigating weird phenomena without raising any eyebrows. It was also immensely entertaining—the *Mad Magazine* for spooks, you might say.

It was about ten o'clock the next evening when we found the convent. The dilapidated building lay on the outskirts of what might have been the smallest town in the entire United States of America. On some maps it wasn't even listed.

We had been here nineteen years before when we were just starting out in the biz. That's when me and my partner, photographer "One-Shot" McGuire, broke the story of Dr. Carruthers and his Devil Bat. The story should've made us stars. Instead it landed me the loveless marriage of all loveless marriages and branded my partner and I forever as sensationalistic "monster hunters." Hell, that's the only reason Pandolphi contacted us in the first place. So maybe it all worked out in the end. Yeah, right.

Though we left the motel at dawn, it took us until noon just to find Heathville again. The first place we visited was a gas station tended by an amiable young man with a sunburned face who was more than willing to discuss the weather, or the history of the town, or the best place to go for a cheeseburger, but when we asked him about the rumors he clammed right up. The next place we visited was a small drug store on Cottage Grove Avenue where I bought a Cherry Coke and a ham sandwich, and McGuire bought a Dr. Brown's cream soda and a corned beef on rye. The old man behind the counter was as forthcoming as the gas station attendant . . . until I brought up the rumors.

Perfect. A small town. A big secret. A pair of valiant reporters (i.e., us). All the elements were there for a front cover story. Needless to say, front cover stories pay the most cash and I really needed it. My ex-wife Mary was raking me over the coals. My kid needed some kind of hernia operation, I guess, and she refused to use her *own* money to pay for it even though her family had gotten dirty rich off peddling substandard cold creams to the Great Unwashed. Didn't she know I had more important things to concern myself with than dealing with her petty little grudges?

I had secrets to uncover.

That's how McGuire and I make our living. It may not be your normal nine-to-five existence, but it pays the bills—well, most of them, at any rate. I had to create a whole new word to describe what I do: cryptoscatology, or the study of secret shit. When I'm at a cocktail party, however, I simply say I'm a journalist. More often than not I neglect to mention the fact that I'm a journalist for *The Midnight Sun*, the biggest selling tabloid this side of *Confidential Magazine*. Not because I'm ashamed, mind you. It's just that . . . well, people don't understand. They don't understand that tabloids like *The Midnight Sun* have more truth in them than your average installment of the nightly news.

Though I get paid most for uncovering the sex lives of Hollywood actors and politicians, I also investigate ghosts and UFOs from time to time to break up the monotony. Basically, Pandolphi (or should I say the American taxpayer) gives us a crap load of money to do what we *would* be doing anyway. All he asks in return is that we hand over any information we can dig up about specific names and addresses of what he calls "alien contactees." He told us he was particularly interested in what these contactees know about the interface between the alien pilots and their spacecraft. According to him, headband devices of flexible plastic material that contained electrical conductors were retrieved from the Aztec crash of 1948. These headbands were believed to be connected to the piloting of the craft somehow. Pandolphi and his cohorts in the Aviary (some secret team of eggheads within the U.S. government who've taken it upon themselves to solve the UFO riddle, such as it is) seem most obsessed by this one detail. Who knows why? Certainly not me.

As a well-informed cryptoscatologist, I had heard rumors about a pre-Aztec crash for some time. The gist of the rumor was this: About three years before the UFO crash in Aztec, New Mexico a similar incident occurred in some backwater hick town somewhere in the mid-West. The military descended upon the town and swept up all the wreckage, leaving not a trace behind, etc. etc. I had dismissed the rumors long ago, not thinking it was worth my valuable time, until Pandolphi called me out of the blue with the general location. Leading me and McGuire once more to Nowheresville, U.S.A.

After our non-productive conversation with the old man at the drug store, I knew we would have to handle this the hard way. These rednecks just couldn't bear to give up a single piece of information to city slickers from *HOLLYWOOD*, the playground of Lucifer himself.

We drove on over to the local library, only about four blocks away from the drug store, and proceeded to scour through the 1945 newspapers. Since we knew we couldn't skim through 365 papers in one day, we decided to begin our search early in August. The common assumption among UFOlogists is that the aliens began their up close and personal examination of the human race because of the detonation of the atom bomb. They wanted to see just how dangerous these domesticated primates had become. If true, August 5th would obviously be a good starting point.

We flipped through the headlines so damn fast we almost set the archives on fire. Just after 8:00 p.m. McGuire at last found what we were looking for in Section A at the bottom of the back page. The date was October 23rd. The headline read: GREEN FIREBALL CRASHES TO EARTH. In brief, it stated that a fireball "of monstrous size" had blazed a trail across the twilight sky, impacting in the woods surrounding Heathville at around 6:00 p.m. According to the article, the first person to examine the meteor was a nun named Aimee Machail who lived in a convent nearby. About three hours later, astronomers from the University of Wisconsin arrived on the scene "accompanied by a military envoy" and took the meteor away. That was it. No further questions asked. The naiveté of the article was both charming and scary. It reflected both the innocence and the utter gullibility of 1940s post-war America.

McGuire took notes on the article while I pulled out the most recent telephone book from the rows that were displayed on a shelf across the aisle. I looked up the convent mentioned in the news story, praying it was still in existence and hot damn, sure enough it was. I jotted the exact address down in my notebook, then we hightailed it out of the library. I wanted to get this over with before the day was through. Heathville wasn't a place you wanted to be stuck in for more than a day. Besides, it held bad memories for both of us.

The nuns had found as obscure a location as possible for their little convent. It stood in a clearing within the Heathville woods—a circular clearing accessible only by foot through a wide, winding path. I was a little uncomfortable leaving the car so far away. I felt isolated, unprotected by fluorescent lamps and nearby police sirens. The night was dark, but somehow the woods were darker. The only sounds were those of crickets. The trees loomed over us like shadowy demons with long, spidery talons. No doubt about it, this was the ideal setting for Something Very Bad To Happen.

As we continued walking an overwhelming sensation of fear swept over me with the force of a storm-wracked ocean wave. It was so powerful, it stopped me in my tracks. I glanced at McGuire. "You feel that?"

McGuire nodded. "Zone of fear. Just like what Keel told us about a couple of years ago."

I took a deep breath. "Okay, we have to calm down. It's just ultrasonic waves, nothing more."

"Keep tellin' yourself that", McGuire whispered.

For a moment I considered turning back, but the rationalist investigator (to say nothing of the tapped-out, ne'er-do-well dad with enormous child support bills to pay) in me shrugged off such silliness and kept moving forward.

The Cyclops emerged from the woods with a gnarled club in its hairy fist. It had to be at least eighteen feet high, perhaps even taller. It was naked except for a furry loincloth wrapped around its waist. It had teeth that curved upward like the tusks of a mastodon. It snarled and charged down the path right toward us. McGuire, always prepared, whipped out his camera and took a few pics before screeching in terror, almost pushing me off the path, and fleeing in the direction from which we'd come. I was right behind him. The Cyclops' clawed feet made the ground quake beneath us. It let out a terrifying roar like a dozen lions screaming at once. I swear I could feel its hot breath on the back of my neck.

The thing's fist wrapped around my torso and lifted me high into the air. I yelled out McGuire's name. To my surprise, he didn't jump off the path and dash into the woods. He took one picture of me trapped in the giant's fist, let the camera dangle from his neck, whipped a revolver from his belt, and aimed at the giant's head. I was scared . . . of both the giant *and* McGuire. I knew what a terrible shot McGuire was. I felt the bullet whiz past my skull. The Cyclops roared in agony as McGuire's bullet blew off its ear lobe. But that wasn't enough to make him drop me. I craned my neck downwards and bit the bastard's hand. This had no effect whatsoever, except making me want to gag. His hand tasted like dirt and worse.

McGuire aimed again, pulled the trigger, and got the son of a bitch right in its dark brown pupil. The thing howled in pain, tossed me onto the ground, knocking the wind out of me, and began thrashing around, pushing whole trees to the ground. McGuire bent down, grabbed me by the back of my collar, and helped me get to my feet.

"Can you run?" he said.

I didn't even respond. I just took off, McGuire trailing right behind me.

We'd seen a lot of weird crap in our lives, but never anything like this. The Cyclops was now blindly running down the middle of the path, striking out at everything around him. Flocks of birds squawked with fear and flew away in order to put as much distance between themselves and this horrible beast. I wished I could fly away as well. I knew we couldn't outrun this thing. Its stride was impossibly long.

I turned around, grabbed McGuire by the shoulders, and pushed him off the path. We went tumbling down a small hill, through the prickly branches and the muddy dirt, landing at last in a shallow puddle. The Cyclops continued running down the path, its club swinging back and forth like the scythe of the Grim Reaper. A tree flew down the hill and began rolling toward us. McGuire and I just sat there in the puddle for a second, watching it roll right toward us. I don't think either of us could believe our luck (bad, *again*).

Then I grabbed McGuire by the shoulder and shook him out of it. We panicked and went running in opposite directions. The tree crashed into the mud puddle only seconds later, finally coming to rest against an older and much stronger tree.

The edge of the tree had missed my spine by mere inches. I just stood there in the dark for a few moments, rail straight, trying to catch my breath. I felt as if even my breathing were too loud. What the hell else was lurking in this weird forest?

I turned around slowly, wishing I had the eyes of a cat. The darkness was so impenetrable I could see nothing, certainly not McGuire. I didn't want to call out McGuire's name for fear of alerting the Cyclops. I could still hear him screaming in pain somewhere up there at the top of the hill and didn't want to take the chance that his hearing was far better than his eyesight at the moment.

So I started walking in the direction where I had last seen McGuire. I had to step over the fallen tree. Every branch that broke beneath my feet seemed to sound like whole armies clashing in the night. I walked for several minutes, growing more anxious the farther I wandered from the spot where I thought McGuire had been. Then it began to rain. Jesus, I thought, how could this situation get any worse? Cursing and wheezing and wincing from the serious bruises the Cyclops had left on my torso, I eventually came to a cave. At first I wondered if this was the home of the dreaded Cyclops. The entrance to the cave was large, but it didn't seem large enough to accommodate that monster's considerable girth. Perhaps McGuire had entered the cave to get away from the rain?

I tried to peer into the darkness within, but could see nothing. All I knew was that it felt very warm inside. That was enough for me.

The Devil Bat swooped out of the cave right at me, screeching like a horde of demons from Hell. Hell? Is *that* where this cave led to? Perhaps this whole damn forest was located in one of the inner rings of Hades.

I dropped into the dirt, clasping my hands behind my neck. I knew what kind of damage those bat talons could cause. I'd seen this thing before, almost twenty years earlier.

This was Dr. Carruther's Devil Bat, returned from the dead.

The thing had a wing span of about eighteen feet. It was enormous. It wasn't as big as that damn Cyclops, but neither was it a normal flying rodent. Could this possibly be the same beast McGuire and I had encountered so many years before? If so, it had once been a normal, everyday bat, one that had been enlarged to enormous proportions by a mad scientist who had used this thing to kill the business associates he felt had betrayed him.

I glanced behind me and saw the bat arcing around to make another dive with its claws. I wasn't going to give it another chance to try and kill me. For a second I considered running into the cave, but what good would that do? It no doubt knew every crack and crevice in that dark pit. No, the best move would be to dive into the tangled bushes and hope the prickly vegetation would prevent its diving claws from reaching me. I hit the dirt, sliding across the muddy grass, all the while screaming as loud as possible. I wasn't screaming because I was scared. I was screaming on purpose, to attract help.

The wind from the Devil Bat's passage blew across the back of my neck. It screeched at me in anger and frustration. I glanced over my shoulder and saw it preparing to make another dive. I popped up from the brush and screamed again, then leaped as the thing's fangs drew nearer and nearer. This time its frustrated cries were drowned out by the booming sound of the giant's approach. I could hear the Cyclops dashing down the hill, causing a slight landslide as he did so. His mighty club sent more trees shattering into tiny splinters. The sound of its club slamming against the bark was like lightning hitting the earth. It seemed as if the giant were running to and fro, so eager to kill me that he couldn't stop and listen for the exact source of my screams. So I had to help him out again. I crept out of the bushes and saw the Devil Bat perched on a branch only a few feet away, staring at me. I screamed again, a short one this time, then jumped back down. Now its talons ripped into my scalp. Blood trickled down my neck. I had to worry about that later. The *thud thud thud* of the giant's strides made the hard dirt beneath me quake once more. I flipped over onto my back and watched as the Cyclops came into view. The Devil Bat saw it too and screamed and attacked, diving at the giant's bleeding eye. The Cyclops had no time to prepare. The Devil Bat sank its claws into his throat. The Cyclops dropped his club and reached out and grabbed the thing by its leathery wings. He tried to tear it apart, but the bat stabbed him in the throat with his claws. The Cyclops bellowed and let it go. The bat flew away, spiraled upward into the night, then swooped back down and sliced the giant across his hairy chest. The Cyclops punched the flying rodent in the head, sending the winged beast twirling into a nearby tree and hitting the ground only about twenty feet from where I now lay. The bat righted itself and launched another attack at the furious Cyclops.

I didn't want to see anymore. I jumped up and dashed away from that crazy, nightmarish scene as fast as my tired feet could manage, almost slamming right into good ol' One-Shot McGuire.

"Hey, boss", McGuire said casually, "I thought you were dead."

"You almost gave me a heart attack. You see that?" I shoved my thumb over my shoulder.

"Jesus", McGuire said, laughing, "I haven't gotten photos as good as this since we were trapped in that sewer with those giant rats in Sumatra. When Pandolphi called us I never thought—"

"Would you just take the damn pictures so we can get the hell out of here?"

"I hope this flash works", McGuire said and snapped several photos, the flash advertising our presence like a neon billboard. Fortunately, the two beasts were so busy fighting each other they didn't even seem to notice. The Cyclops had gotten the upper hand and was now beating the Devil Bat into the ground like a sack of flour, the bat's legs gripped tightly in its gnarled fist.

"Hey, isn't that thing the Devil Bat?" McGuire said.

I just stared at him for a second. "What does it *look* like?"

"That son of a bitch died years ago. How could it still be alive now?"

"It *couldn't*."

"What do you mean?"

"Forget it. Let's talk and run."

"Let's just run", he said. I didn't argue with him. I took off through the woods, not even looking behind me to see if McGuire was following. We ran for about ten or fifteen minutes, the shrieks of the Devil Bat mingling with the violent grunts of the Cyclops.

Finally, we leaned up against a tree and tried to catch our breaths. I had never realized, until now, how out of shape I was.

"Those things aren't real", I said between gasps, "they can't be."

"They seemed real enough to me", McGuire said.

"It's the zone of fear, I think . . . or maybe some other environmental influence toying with us, playing with our minds."

"But why the Devil Bat?"

"That's what tipped me off. That thing almost killed us the last time we were here. What are the chances of us encountering something *exactly* like it all the way out here in the woods? To tell you the truth, I was dreading this assignment. I didn't want to come back here. It reminds me of Mary. And it reminds me of that flying nightmare. And I don't want to be reminded of either of them at all."

22

"The Cyclops", McGuire said softly, almost to himself. "Now I know where I've seen that thing before. My mom was Irish on both sides and she used to tell me folktales from the old country before I went to bed. The one that always scared me the most was the story of Finn mac Cumhall and the giant Angus. The picture book she showed me had very realistic looking illustrations inside. And they looked almost exactly like that thing."

I nodded. "Something's going on in these woods beyond a crashed saucer. Something's playing with our minds. I don't know about you . . . but my mind doesn't like that at all."

"So what's your mind going to do about it?"

I thought about it for a moment, then whispered, "It's gonna find Aimee Machail and give her a talking to. Let's get the hell out of this place before some other nightmare shows up."

McGuire chuckled. "If it's *your* nightmare, it'll be Mary's lawyer appearing in a puff of smoke with a court summons in its claws."

I didn't even respond. I wasn't in the mood.

At that moment we heard a scream rip through the night: " . . . please, where are you? No, please, no!" It sounded like the voice of a man. It was coming from the general area where the Cyclops and the Devil Bat were still locked in combat. I thought, *Let the poor fool, whoever the hell he is, deal with his* own *nightmare.* We picked up the pace even faster than before.

We managed to find the main road again, and started back toward the convent. Get thee to a nunnery? You bet, Willy S., I certainly will.

You see? Despite the fact that I wrote for a trashy tabloid, I knew my Shakespeare.

At last we reached the end of the path and the convent came into view. It was a modest one-story building, its only elaborate feature being the arch-shaped stained glass window above the wooden double doors that were shut tight against a strong, cool wind that had begun to whip through the leaves and branches. The building seemed to be painted a pale yellow color, though it was difficult to tell in the dark. The paint was peeling in unseemly patches.

The second we began ascending the three creaking steps that led up to the porch, the fear dissipated. This isn't unusual in UFO flap areas. Such "zones of fear" are limited in circumference, and this one was no different.

"Should we . . . whip out . . . the FBI badges?" McGuire said, still out of breath from our panicked flight.

"No", I said. We'd bought the badges from an old junkie in San Diego a long time ago, before we'd even hooked up with Pandolphi. Sometimes they came in handy when we needed entrance into obscure places where journalists—particularly tabloid journalists—aren't welcome. "Let's just lay off the badges." I, too, was out of breath. "I think it'd be wise to try the straightforward approach first."

I knocked on the door. I waited. Nobody answered.

"The wind's blowing pretty hard", McGuire said. He was slowly getting his breath back. "They probably didn't hear it."

As I lifted my fist in the air to knock a second time, the doors swung open to reveal an emaciated old woman in flowing black robes. She planted her hands on either side of the doorway. The sleeves were very wide and drooped down low enough to reveal long bony arms and varicose veins like a transparent chart of the human body one might find hanging on the wall of an Anatomy class.

"What do you want?" she snapped.

Gee, I thought, real comforting nun. This gargoyle would be more at home on the *ledge* of a cathedral than inside it.

"Uh, hello, Miss", I began, "I don't mean to disturb you—"

"Well, then, why are you?"

I nodded. Okay. So it was going to be this kind of an interview. No use beating around the burning bush with this chick. "Listen, I'm Johnny Layton and this is my colleague. You can call him 'One-Shot' McGuire. We're investigative journalists. Right now we're looking into certain . . . rumors we've been hearing for years. You wouldn't happen to know anything about a Cyclops and a Devil Bat haunting these woods, would you?"

Her brow furrowed. "What? What're you talkin' about?"

"Okay, maybe not. But what about *this*?" I reached into my pocket and pulled out a torn piece of newsprint: the 1945 newspaper article. (McGuire's "note-taking" more often than not involved filching reference materials from the library.) I held it up to her face.

She squinted as she scanned the headline, then laughed loudly. The laughter soon turned into a rasping cough that continued for a few minutes before at last dying down. "You're the first person to bring that up in . . . " She rolled her eyes. "Oh, in years."

"Since 1945?" McGuire said.

"No. Some fella asked me about it a couple of years back. Some reporter in a black coat with a goatee goin' by the name of Keel. He looked like the devil, he did." The old woman laughed as McGuire and I exchanged knowing glances. "Heck, maybe he was. The devil delights in trickery."

"Is that so? Well, I doubt the devil had anything to do with this incident." I tapped the article with my fingernail.

"I do believe you'd be right. The devil has little to do with meteorites."

"Is that what it was?"

The old woman glared at me like a haughty school marm. "That's what the newspaper says, don't it?"

"Newspapers aren't always right."

The old woman looked affronted. "Why would you say that?"

I laughed. "Because I've written for them all my life!"

"Am I hearin' you right? Are you admitting you print *lies*?"

I elbowed McGuire in the ribs. I had a hunch this was our woman, and I wasn't about to let her off the hook. "Yeah, sure", I said casually. "Not all the time, though."

She crossed her willowy arms over her flat chest. "Is that considered ethical nowadays?"

I shrugged. "Depends on the situation. I'm sure you've had to lie from time to time. To comfort God's children, make them feel more at ease with the state of earthly affairs? If it's the will of God it can't be wrong, even if it is lying. Isn't that right?"

"I ain't never told a lie in my life."

"Oh, is that so? What do you call it when you 'misidentify' a crashed alien spacecraft as a meteorite?"

She seemed flustered for a moment. "I won't have that sort of talk here!" She was about to slam the door shut, but before she could do so I planted my hand on the rough, uneven surface and held it in place.

"And why is that?" I said.

Her eyes were wild with a mixture of rage and fear. "There ain't no such thing as aliens!"

"What proof do you have to back up that statement?" I knew I was committing a logical fallacy (*argumentum ad ignorantiam*), but went with it anyway just to annoy her.

For a few seconds the old woman tried to push the door closed, then gave up when she realized it was a futile effort. "How'm I supposed to prove something *ain't* real?" I said nothing. She sighed. "If I answer your question, will you go?"

"Cross my heart."

She glared at me with penetrating blue eyes, as if trying to gauge my sincerity. For some reason she seemed skeptical. Perhaps, I thought, I shouldn't have admitted to being a habitual liar. That tends to make people suspicious.

"Because", the old woman said, "the Bible don't mention nothin' about space aliens, so therefore . . . ." She spread her hands in the air and allowed the sentence to trail off, as if the answer was self-evident.

"The Bible doesn't mention a lot of things", I said. "It doesn't mention the IRS or Barbie dolls or LSD or dinosaur fossils. But they all exist, right?"

"Dinosaur fossils", she said with tight, bloodless lips, "were placed in the Earth by God to test our faith."

"Wait a second, wait a second, by extension are . . . are you saying that *aliens* were placed here to test our faith?"

The old woman's lips tightened even further into a straight line. Then she whispered, "Ain't it obvious? These extraterrestrials aren't necessarily demons. They're not necessarily the work of the devil. They might have been placed here *on purpose* by God to see how easily our faith could be shattered. It could be God's way of separating the wheat from the chaff."

"It sounds like you've thought a lot about this. Have you ever *seen* an alien?"

The old woman's eyes darkened. "If I had, I wouldn't tell no lyin' newspaper reporter about it."

"Why? Why not spread God's Holy Disinformation and see how many people's beliefs are destroyed?" The old woman didn't answer this time. "Are you scared there wouldn't be anyone left but you, maybe?"

She grumbled, "Leave my doorstep before I'm forced to call the authorities."

Still smirking, I held my hands in the air and backed off. She began to close the door. Then at the last second I grabbed it again. I placed my hand on her bony shoulder, surreptitiously planting a tracer on her robe. The tracer was the size of a flea and looked like a metallic piece of lint. Pandolphi had given me a whole slew of keen devices, just one of the perks that went along with being an auxiliary member of the Aviary.

"Oh, one last question", I said. "By any chance, would your name happen to be . . . Miss Aimee Machail?"

The old woman seemed more offended by these words than by anything else I'd said. Strangely, as her anger grew more and more severe her backwoods accent seemed to fade away. "Certainly not! My proper name is *Mother Superior* Aimee Machail and I expect to be addressed as such in the event that our paths ever cross again, though the possibility of that happening is—thankfully—very low indeed. Now please remove your unwelcome appendage from my shoulder before I'm forced to *lop it off!*"

Needless to say, I backed away and the door slammed shut immediately. "So it's going to be this kind of an interview", I repeated beneath my breath.

McGuire reached inside his jacket pocket. "Let's just blow this bitch away", he said.

I grabbed his elbow. "No! She's hiding something and I want to know what it is."

"But—"

"We're going back to the car! Now c'mon."

McGuire sighed and removed his hand from inside his jacket. "Yes, sir", he said, the bitter sarcasm creeping back into his voice. He was just jealous that Pandolphi considered me the superior member of this team, which was only natural. After all, I had always been more cool-headed. McGuire tended to be somewhat overzealous.

We hurried back to the car, climbed inside, flicked on the heater, and listened to an AM radio station broadcast out of nearby Madison. I sat and listened to the radio host babble on about his petty terrestrial affairs as my imagination ran wild with substantial front-page-worthy images: photographs of small, jagged pieces from an otherworldly spacecraft stored away for over a decade in the basement of a dilapidated church. Or perhaps we could even get our hands on the *pieces* themselves.

We waited two hours, then hiked back up the path. We followed the perimeter of the clearing, making sure we couldn't be seen from the windows of the convent, and snuck up on the building from behind. After some careful snooping we came upon a rectangular basement window obscured by overgrown weeds. I pulled out my scanner to check on Machail's location; the tracer indicated she was on the third floor near the back of the building. I told McGuire to go to work. He crouched down, reached into his pocket and removed a pair of pencil-thin lock picks. He eased them into the window frame. With a mere flick of the wrist he unhooked the latch and pulled the window open. I slipped through the window feet first. I managed to balance myself on a stack of wooden crates that threatened to topple over the second I placed my feet on them. Fortunately, this didn't happen. *Instead* I slipped on a pool of water that had collected on the top crate from a leaking pipe above and fell flat on my face. *Then* the crates came toppling down. Right on top of me, in fact. Yes, it had definitely evolved into one of those kind of interviews.

Groaning, fearful that I would soon be discovered, I planted my scraped palms on the cold concrete and pushed myself up onto my knees as quickly as possible. I called myself a jackass for even coming to Heathville in the first place. I glanced around at the fallen crates that surrounded me. Some of them had cracked open upon impact, spilling pinto beans all across the floor. That's when I looked beyond the scattered mess . . . and saw it.

Curled up against the corner of the room.

In the fetal position.

Chained to the wall.

The creature had the head of a white snake; its body was covered in a shock of snow-white feathers. It was bipedal. If it had been standing, it would've been about five feet tall. A long, thin tail was coiled around its right leg. It had a pale, sickly pallor and seemed emaciated, like a corpse in a concentration camp. Of course, I had no way of knowing if this was its proper skin tone, but somehow I doubted it. The reptilian lifted its shaking head and stared at me with pleading, mucous-covered yellow eyes. I had never seen such a look, not even in a human being. It wanted only to be free.

How long? Had the creature been sitting there for eleven years? Imprisoned and alone? Waiting for his people to come? Why had he been left behind? Did they assume he was dead? Or was he an acceptable loss, just as hundreds of American POWs were considered "acceptable losses" when we pulled out of North Korea? It was difficult to feel indignant toward them, if indeed this was the case, knowing our species had done far worse.

Suddenly, I realized I was already thinking of the alien as "he." Hell, I wasn't even sure it was a "he." From where I was standing I could see no evidence of genitalia. But either way I knew it was more of a "he" than an "it." I could see that just by looking into his eyes. Where I saw humanity, Mother Superior Aimee Machail saw Satan. What might very well have been the very first human/alien contact was twisted and perverted by religious fanaticism. I suppose I shouldn't have been surprised.

And yet I was. I was so surprised and disgusted and overwhelmed I couldn't move. I watched while the alien bobbed his head up and down over and over again, as if trying to tell me something.

"Johnny", McGuire whispered harshly from the window. "What's going on down there? You all right?"

I looked up at him to respond. That's when I saw the headband. Dangling from the ceiling on a single piece of thread so thin the object almost appeared to be suspended in space. It was shaped like an egg, and clearly meant to be worn over the reptilian's forehead. I could think only of Pandolphi's comment about the headbands retrieved from the Aztec crash and his belief that they were connected to the piloting of the ship. This was it: the Holy Grail Pandolphi and his pals had been looking for.

Machail hadn't just imprisoned the alien, but had purposely tortured him for over a decade by placing his salvation only a few feet from his grasp. Like Tantalus in the Greek myth, forever punished in Hades by being chained to a tree with water just below his chin and fresh fruit dangling from the branches above his head.

McGuire whispered my name again. I was surprised, and even a little pleased, to hear a hint of concern in his voice.

"You better get down here", I said.

McGuire dropped into the rectangular patch of moonlight streaming in through the window. You should've seen the expression on his wrinkled face when he turned and caught his first glimpse of the alien. It was the only time I'd ever seen him speechless.

"You think you can unlock those chains?" I said.

He seemed dismayed. "Are you sure you want me to?"

"Trust me, he can't hurt us."

McGuire nodded and pulled the lock pick from his belt. Before he could do anything with it, however, I grabbed his wrist and told him to wait.

"Look at this", I said, pointing at a massive pile of what looked like pale reptilian skin stacked up against the black furnace that stood in the corner of the basement. The furnace was in operation, the flames flickering deep within its ancient, dark belly. Whatever was burning inside had turned to smoke and was now being coughed up into the otherwise pristine Heathville air.

"Do you realize what's going on here?" I said. "He's been molting. All these years, molting."

"So what of it?" McGuire said. Then it struck him. He shook his head in disgust. "They're dumping all his extra skin into the furnace?"

"This is it . . . one of the rarest aliens of all, the type Pandolphi's always going on about, the ones that have skin like certain frogs in South America. Psychedelic skin."

"I thought that whole bit was another one of Pandolphi's weird fantasies."

"Apparently not. The nuns burn the skin in the furnace, send the smoke up into the night air, and *voila*: instant psychedelic gas. It's been permeating this entire forest for decades. Who knows what kind of paranormal affect it's had on the local wildlife and the vegetation and all of Heathville?"

"That explains the fear zone."

"And your Cyclops."

"And the Devil Bat."

"Jesus, this is quite a find. We better document this." I gestured for him to hand over his camera. I snapped dozens of photos in a row while McGuire went to work on the lock.

"This thing's pretty rusty", McGuire said. "Crude too. The window was harder to break into." I heard a distinct *click*, and the lock fell away from the central link. The chains were wrapped around his entire body. McGuire slowly began unspooling them. The alien just sat there, not even helping with his own escape.

I snapped a few more photos. Perhaps it was the flash that gave us away, or maybe it had been the sound of the falling crates. Either way, the result was the same.

About twenty feet behind me a wooden stairway led up to a door . . . a door that abruptly swung open, spilling fluorescent light into the shadowy room. Framed in the doorway were half a dozen nuns armed with shotguns and revolvers. Mother Superior led the lot. She aimed a sawed-off shotgun at us.

"I told you somebody was down here!" she shrieked. "They're tryin' to let the devil free!"

"Get behind those crates!" I called to McGuire. He was already two steps ahead of me. Both of us leaped behind the stacks of crates as bullets ricocheted off the walls. The alien was about eight feet to the right of us, still staring off into space. The crates made pretty good cover. I didn't have to tell McGuire to pull out his gun. I clipped one nun on the shoulder, making her drop her pistol to the floor. (Too bad I was aiming for her forehead.) McGuire got one of 'em in the chest. She let out a scream, toppled over the railing, and fell to the concrete floor with a sickening *crack*.

The other nuns descended the stairs, still firing away. Mother Superior couldn't stop shrieking. I didn't recognize a single word that emerged from her mouth. It was all gibberish mixed in with snippets of Scripture. Perhaps that's a distinction without a difference.

The bullets were coming so fast McGuire and I were forced to stay down. We took the opportunity to reload our guns. Fortunately, the second Mother Superior reached the floor of the basement she slipped on the pinto beans and went crashing backwards into the nun behind her. The sisters fell like dominos, accidentally firing into the air. Bullets embedded themselves in the ceiling. I watched, amazed, as one bullet severed the thread hanging from the ceiling, sending the headband into the alien's lap.

The headband began to glow. The alien's haggard, quaking arms reached out for the oval band. He lifted it upwards and placed it on his forehead.

Mother Superior screamed, "NO!" and scrambled to her feet, half-running, half-crawling toward the alien. I leaped up and aimed at her head—surprised to find that the damn gun had jammed. I abandoned the safety of the crates and intercepted her while McGuire covered me. I tackled Mother Superior. We fell to the floor as she raked at my face with her fingernails. I screamed. She grabbed at the camera and ripped it off my neck, then slammed it into my head. The room spun and I found myself back on the floor. Mother Superior continued her attack. I could only watch as distorted, wavy bands of rainbow-colored lights erupted from the alien's head, coiled about his body like insubstantial chains. The hair on my head and arms stood on end, the air smelled like ozone. A weird geometric pattern resembling a Persian rug spread out from the alien's solar plexus and engulfed him. His body disappeared into—or perhaps *transformed* into—a paisley, tentacled formation hovering in midair. The sprouts and tendrils spiraling off from the formation caught Mother Superior in their grasp and drew her deep inside. She vanished. Then the portal collapsed in upon itself and blinked out like the image on a television screen. The alien and the nun were gone.

The remaining nuns panicked, fled back up the stairs. McGuire raised his gun and aimed at their backs.

"No!" I screamed at McGuire as I jumped to my feet. He lowered his gun, an exasperated look on his face. I said, "That's not necessary."

"They would've killed us, man!"

"Well, they're not going to now. We're getting out of here."

"This whole trip was a big waste of fuckin' time."

"What do you mean?"

"We didn't even get any photos!"

I frantically scanned the floor. McGuire was right. The camera was nowhere to be seen. "She took it with her", I whispered, disbelieving.

McGuire threw his hands in the air. "I've had that camera for years! It's got *sentimental* value! Now I've gotta buy a new one! I guess we'll just have to chalk this fiasco up to experience, right?" He shook his head, clearly annoyed.

"We're getting those photos back", I said.

"How?"

I reached into my coat and pulled out the scanner. "We're gonna track down the cenobitic bitch."

3

Kyle Black

"THAT'S . . . PRETTY UNBELIEVABLE", I said.

I was now sitting up in bed. All the nuns had left except for one. Her name was Sister Marina Wilson Riley. She was the youngest nun in the convent, still in her early twenties. She'd been left on the steps of the convent at age two.

"I suppose so", she said, "but then again you weren't there. I've been studying quantum physics for quite awhile now. Some physicists believe that alternate universes do indeed exist. In fact, I believe it's possible to travel backwards and forwards in time *into* these alternate dimensions. Perhaps the residual energy of what I choose to call a 'wormhole,' a tunnel linking two stretched-out singularities, somehow infects the people it comes in contact with like a virus. From the alien to Mother Superior to you. Causing all manner of disruptions in the space-time continuum. That's probably how you ended up here. You see?"

I nodded. "Uh . . . I didn't know nuns studied physics."

"They don't, at least not the ones here. I'm something of an exception, I'm afraid. Of course, I haven't been studying it *formally*, you understand. My knowledge is rudimentary, gleaned from science journals and the like. I'm just an amateur."

"You referred to the thing in the basement as an 'alien.' Does that mean you don't believe it was . . . well, you know . . . "

"Satan?" Riley laughed and waved her hand in the air. "It was obviously an alien. I tried to tell them that for years, but they wouldn't listen." She sighed. "Doesn't matter now, though, I'm happy to say. The alien's no doubt gone back to his home planet and Mother Superior . . . well, who knows where she is? Maybe on Venus." Riley laughed. "She'd probably think it was Hell."

"Could you show me where the alien was kept?"

"Sure, if you feel up to walking."

I threw the sheets aside and stood up. "Oh, I do, believe me. I don't like enclosed spaces, and this room's just a little cramped for my taste."

"I know what you mean. I've always wanted to leave here and experience the real world." She sighed. "The other sisters shouldn't mind if I show you the basement. After all, there's nothing to hide anymore."

She led me through the flimsy wooden door and across the hall where a flight of stairs led down to the first floor. Since it was well past ten o'clock, the whole place was quiet and dark. In the back of the kitchen was a heavy oaken door bolted on the outside. Riley removed the bolt and pulled the door open slowly; it creaked like the entrance to a haunted house in an old Hollywood movie. We descended the stairs in darkness.

"Watch out for the railing", Riley said. "It broke when Sister Athenacea went over the side."

When we reached the bottom of the stairs she flicked a switch on the wall that cast a dim fluorescence across the room. I was startled to see a dead nun lying at my feet—the second in one day. I jumped back and let out a little gasp.

"What's that?"

"Sister Athenacea", Riley said, stepping over the body. The floor was covered in dried blood and pinto beans. "One of those men got her right in the heart. He was a pretty good shot."

"Aren't you . . . alarmed?"

Riley waved her hand again in that nonchalant way she had. "Oh, it was the will of God. Besides, she used to whack my head with a ruler when I couldn't memorize *Revelations* fast enough. I was kind of glad to see her go. Here's where we kept the alien."

She gestured toward the corner of the room. Behind a pile of broken crates I saw a tangled web of steel chains. I didn't know what I was expecting to find. Perhaps some evidence of the alien's existence. Perhaps I thought I could just *feel* its recent presence by standing in the same spot it had once occupied. I felt nothing except cold.

I spotted a dark shape in the abandoned nest; it was so thin and translucent, I might very well have missed it. But something told me to kneel down and study the nest closely. Have you ever seen a snake when it sheds its skin? Imagine the same thing except five feet long and in the shape of a human being. It lay silently on the floor in the corner of the room, almost as if it were asleep, waiting to strike. I reached out—with some hesitation—and touched it. It wasn't slimy or disgusting in any way. It felt dry, fragile, like an ancient parchment hidden away for a thousand years in a cavern beneath the Dead Sea Desert.

"Look at this", I said.

I heard Riley approaching from behind. "Hm? Oh, that's just its skin. We had to remove that every month or so."

"What would you do with it?"

"We'd burn it."

I winced. "Where?"

"In the furnace." She gestured toward the other side of the room. "It would give off a weird smell. Sometimes I would come down here and smell the fumes just for fun. It would make me feel relaxed and put me in the right frame of mind to think about things like wormholes and alternate timelines and quantum foam. It would, I don't know, put me in tune with the universe. You know what I mean?"

I rose to my feet. "Have you ever heard of the South American toad that induces psychedelic hallucinations when you lick its skin?"

Riley wrinkled her nose. "Who'd want to do something like that?"

"The same kind of person who'd want to think about quantum foam, whatever that is." I reached into my pocket and pulled out a pipe. Ever since I had started tending my garden I'd kept at least one pipe on me at all times—usually two, in fact, just in case I lost one. You never knew when you might have an emergency. I thought this would definitely qualify as one of those.

"What're you doing?" Riley said.

I ripped off a strip of dried skin and stuffed it in the bowl. Then, as an afterthought, I ripped off some more, rolled it up, and slipped it into my pocket for later. Who knew if I'd ever get access to this stuff again? "I suspect there's some kind of psychedelic component to the alien's skin. That's why you were in such a relaxed state when you ingested the fumes."

Riley's skin turned ashen. "You . . . you mean I . . . I was *high*?"

"Do you realize you're probably the only person on the planet who's experienced an alien high? If this stuff can turn a nun into a quantum physicist just from a contact high, imagine what would happen if you inhaled it directly into your lungs."

"I wouldn't like to think I . . . you really think I was *high*?" She held her hand to her lips and giggled. "How exciting."

"It's gonna get even more exciting in a couple of seconds." I pulled out a cheap lighter and held it to the skin in the bowl.

"Why do you carry a pipe and a lighter around with you?" Riley said. "Do you smoke often?"

"Every chance I get. Don't believe what the media and those old crows who raised you say about marijuana. It's a sacred herb with healing properties. The only reason it's been demonized is because of—"

"William Randolph Hearst and his plan to maintain a monopoly on the paper industries?"

I just stared at her for a second. "How'd you know that?"

"I read it in an article called, um . . . 'The Emperor's Invisible Clothes' by Hieronymus M. Stone. It was in an issue of *The Realist Magazine*. I found it at the local library."

I beamed. "That's me! I wrote that under a pseudonym about a year ago."

"Really? Are you joking?"

"No, no. I worked the research on that thing for about five years before I sat down to write it. I'm surprised it was even in the local library."

"I took notes on it, but I had to hide them from the other sisters. My, this is an honor to be in the presence of a real author."

I waved my hand in the air, just like her. "Oh, it's nothing." The pipe began to heat up in my hand. "Ouch!" I almost dropped the pipe. I couldn't help but laugh. "I think the stuff's getting impatient. It *wants* me to smoke it!"

Riley laughed too, then grew quite somber as I lifted the pipe to my lips and inhaled. She studied the pipe with scholarly fascination, her brown eyes widening as the bowl glowed cherry red. "Wh-what do you feel?" she said.

I held the pipe out to her. "You want to try?"

"Oh no, I don't think I—"

She didn't have time to finish. Or rather, I didn't have time to *hear* her finish. The space surrounding me warped into an infinite pattern of pulsating snowflakes and I found myself in a dark forest I didn't recognize. Beside me was a giant with one bleeding eye locked in mortal combat with what looked like an immense bat. The Cyclops was crushing the bat in his grip, trying to hold the flying demon at bay while it stretched its wings as far as they could possibly go, as if the Cyclops were attempting to rip the thing in half. I was standing only five feet away from the giant's ankle. The ankle was bigger than my head. I didn't know what was happening. Was this real? The bat managed to free one wing and swatted the Cyclops' wounded eye. The Cyclops screamed in pain and stepped back, almost crushing me. I leaped out of the way. The rank odor of his leathery brown foot made me understand how real this whole situation was. I wasn't dreaming. I could die. I began to panic.

I looked around for Marina. "Marina!" I screamed. "Marina, please, where are you?" That did it. The Cyclops clobbered the Devil Bat into the dust like a dirty carpet, bashing its skull in several times, then spun around and snatched me up in his fist.

"No, please, no!" I screamed.

"What's wrong?" the Cyclops said, lifting me up to his bloody eye. "I'm not *your* nightmare, am I?"

"*What*?" I said, shocked that I wasn't dead yet. "Who . . . who *are* you?"

"Finn mac Cumhall. What's your name?"

"Kyle. Uh . . . I'm, like, totally stoned, dude." I started to laugh. The panic was doing weird things to my mind.

Finn turned his head to one side. "What is 'stoned'?" he said.

"That's where you inhale smoke from a sacred herb into your lungs. It makes you happy. It makes you feel better and heals things."

"Like my eye?" Finn said.

"Yes, even your eye", I said.

"My eye . . . ." He whimpered as he dabbed at the blood trickling down his face. He almost seemed to be on the verge of crying.

"Hey, Finn . . . you want to get stoned?"

"Can you heal my eye with this 'stoned'?"

"I can certainly try. I know it's not going to make it any worse. What do you have to lose?"

Finn thought about it for a moment. "Nothing at all. Let's go into my cave here and try this 'stoned.'"

"Right on", I said.

"I love this . . . this 'stoned,'" Finn said.

"Me too", I said. "It's the most beautiful thing in the world."

Me and Finn sat cross-legged in front of a fire in Finn's dark cave. "That bat's been trying to steal my cave for years", Finn said. "But I showed it."

"You sure did. How long have you lived in this groovy cave, Finn?"

Finn shrugged. "Only for a few minutes now. But to me it seems like a lifetime. You see, I'm not real. I'm a tulpa, a spirit given three dimensions by the palpable fear generated by a human being. The human's not here right now, though. He's gone to the convent in the woods. He's breaking through a basement window right now."

"Right on", I said, vaguely aware that he might be talking about Marina's convent but not really caring. "Hey, don't bogart that thing, dude. Oh, wait, we each have a different pipe. I'm such a dope." Fortunately, Finn owned a pipe large enough for him. I used my own pipe. It was in my mouth right now. In fact, it had been in my mouth when I told Finn not to bogart his pipe. This made me laugh. I started to laugh so much that Finn got the giggles too. There we were, two happy idiots.

Finn lay down on the ground and put his hands behind his head. Above us a circular hole in the cave roof looked out upon the distant, crater-pocked face of the full moon.

"I feel so good", Finn said. "This is the best I've felt in years."

I stretched out beside him. "What's it like being a nightmare?" I said.

"Oh, it's not that bad", Finn said. "You're not needed all the time. You come and you go. But I really don't like scaring people. You know how hard it is when people put too many expectations on you."

"I understand. Boy, do I ever. My mother expects way too much from me. She's a complete bitch, let me tell you."

"Hey, don't talk about your mother that way. That's not what a gentleman would do. I'm Irish. We don't put up with that kind of behavior."

"Oh, I forgot you were Irish. Sorry. I just met a girl who's Irish, I think. Or at least she's got a super-Irish name. She's cute. I think I want to marry her."

"Then don't waste any time, my friend. Tell her how you feel right now. There's no time like the present."

I lifted up onto my elbow. "You know, you're right. There *is* no time like the present. I want that girl to have my babies."

"There's no reason why she shouldn't. She probably loves you, friend."

"It doesn't matter what mother says about it. What does she know? She thinks I'm not an adult, just because I grow weed for a living. What's wrong with that?"

"Nothin', my man, nothin'", Finn said, sat up, and took another long hit off his pipe. "This shit's gooooood", he said, drawing out the word as long as possible.

"I only grow the best shit in California. That's why the government wants to get their hands on it."

"Fuck the government", Finn said. "I piss on the United States government."

"Damn straight", I said. "You and me both, pal. Hey, what if you come live with me up in the hills? My house is on the highest peak of Trail's End, in Malibu. You can't miss it. The doors are always open to you—you *and* yours. You could help protect my marijuana garden. If the FBI shows up, you could just crush 'em all into dirt."

"Fuck the cops", Finn said. "I'd rip 'em in two and eat the fuckers."

"All right. Let's *do* it."

"You, me and Marina could live together. And your baby."

"And my baby. That's right. What should we name it?"

Finn thought about it for a moment. "McGuire."

"McGuire? Why?"

"He's the man who gave birth to me."

"Okay. Well, that doesn't really have any connection to me and Marina."

"That's true. What's your name?"

"Kyle."

"Hi, Kyle. I'm Finn." Finn reached out and shook my hand, being careful not to crush it.

"Hey, Finn, what's up?"

"Not much. Just sittin' here. Hey, is that the moon way up there?"

"I think it is."

"I always wanted to go there", he said.

"Really? So did I."

"Yeah? How funny. You want to go?"

"Right now?"

"Sure. Why not?"

"That'd be a dream come true. Hey, this shit in the pipe, man . . . it turns nightmares into dreams . . . nightmares into dreams . . . ."

"And how could that be bad? Why is it illegal?"

"Because of Hearst and his paper monopoly."

"Damn Hearst! Let's go to the moon, dude."

"Let's go!"

"Okay, follow me."

"I will", I said.

We lay there for another hour before Finn finally rose to his knees . . . then after twenty minutes he rose to his feet . . . then after five minutes he strolled out of the cave and into the cool night air. The bleeding had stopped and his wound seemed to be almost completely healed now. Finn leaned down and performed something that looked exactly like the Heimlich Maneuver on the Devil Bat. After a few moments the bat coughed and said, "Hey, is it true? Are we going to the moon?"

"You're flyin' us there, buddy", Finn said. Finn picked me up and placed me on his hairy shoulder, then the gentle

Cyclops climbed onto the Devil Bat's back and we flew up, up into the air.

Up.

Up through the misty interior of a tall and multilayered cumulonimbus cloud that appeared to ascend forever and ever.

Up.

Up into the storms of the troposphere; up through the clear, sunny skies of the stratosphere; up into the coolness of the mesosphere; up into the blazing heat of the exosphere; up out of the Earth's atmosphere, into the airlessness of outer space. I was surprised to see that the stars didn't twinkle way out here. The sunlight that reflected off the surface of the Earth glared at us from far below. Ahead of us lay the magnificent desolation of the moon's surface . . . or, rather, that's what I *expected* to see based on everything I had ever read about outer space when I was a kid, back when I thought visiting other planets would be cool, until it hit me one day that all a space pilot could ever be is a trained monkey who simply sits in a garage in space for years on end while pushing the buttons he's told to push by his militaristic masters back on Earth. I hoped the Soviet Union reached the surface of the moon before the United Snakes. Besides, I knew you'd need military training if you were going to be an astronaut. There was no way I was ever going to join the military, no matter what mother said. Why should I be an astronaut when I can stay on Earth and get blasted out of my mind way more than touching the stars could ever accomplish? At least, that's what I thought until I saw what the moon *really* looked like. Man, it was a trip. A thirty-mile-high crystalline dome loomed up from the canal-scarred surface like a tattered fragment of a forgotten myth. The dome was a truncated icosaheron pocked by massive holes. Years past, the abandoned domes were no doubt ripped asunder by ferocious meteor showers. We now flew toward one of these holes. Once we'd flown within a distance that enabled us to study the ashy gray deadness of the lunar surface with some amount of clarity, we saw a series of castle-like structures located miles past the dome. They too seemed to be in badly need of repair. With the heightened curiosity of a school boy, I decided to explore the millennia-old ruins.

The touchdown was gentle. I slid off the Devil Bat and pressed my palms against the rock fragments littering the desolate landscape. I planted my extra pipe into the soil, claiming the moon for potheads everywhere. I glanced left and right, backwards and forwards, seeing only a horizon that dropped away on all sides. Then I turned my attention toward the sky. It was strangely fuzzy, as if I were looking back at the blue globe of Earth through dust-smeared glass.

Finn, the Devil Bat and I travelled across the surreal landscape without speaking, too stunned by the sights, until we reached the edge of one of the empty canals that slashed its way across the surface. It was so massive. We couldn't possibly travel around it, so we had to either fly over it or scale down into its depths. The Devil Bat was curious and wanted to see what the canals looked like way down below. So he flew us down there. The inner edges of the canal were smooth and glimmered like black glass. The bottom of the canal was much the same. Finn and I climbed off the Devil Bat and tried to walk across, but this was almost impossible. We kept slipping as if we were trying to dance across a frozen lake without skates. The Devil Bat laughed at our pratfalls, but we didn't mind. We laughed along with him. We were all having so much fun.

A lunarian insect the size of a '57 Chevy emerged from a circular storm drain and tried to eat us with grayish pincers that looked like onyx, but Finn clubbed him to death with his fists and the Devil Bat ate him. The insect—which somewhat look like a cross between a spider and a kangaroo—was the only form of life we encountered on the moon until we reached the interior of the castle. Once the Devil Bat had completely digested the insect, we flew once more into the air and headed toward the distant parapets.

It took us about an hour to reach the transparent crystalline double doors that stood wide open at the base of the 1,000-foot tower. I was reluctant to touch the walls, out of fear that they might crumble to fine dust. We passed through the doorway and entered a massive hall consisting of strange angles and mysterious protuberances that seemed to serve no useful purpose. I glanced at the opaque ceiling and was fascinated that I could see up into the floors above. It looked as if the upper floors were paralyzed in free fall, trapped in time. The hall made me feel disorientated, but not lost or alone. After all, I was with friends. Finn and I helped each other move across the slippery glass floor of the grand hall, at the far end of which stood a spiral glass staircase. Our feet made no sound against the smooth, ice-cold floor, not even Finn's. Tentatively, I pressed the tip of my foot against the first step; it did not break. Then I placed both feet on the step. I kept my eyes on the stairs as I ascended, watching the floor drop out beneath me. It was as if we were walking on the air itself.

We wound our way up the glass spiral, occasionally glancing to our right or left in order to take in the sights. To my surprise, lush lunar jungles could be seen only a few miles away, far off in the distance. No doubt, there was life there. That would be our next destination, I thought, if Finn and the Devil Bat were amenable. We approached the highest landing. From two stories down I was able to discern a dark mass moving about along the floor above like a shark, but I felt no fear.

The dark mass became more distinctive as I neared the highest landing. It was only a man in a dark robe pacing before a narrow window devoid of glass. At last I reached the landing and placed my shaking hand on the knob. It turned before I even applied pressure to it, and the door swung inward. Thankfully, the door was massive enough to accommodate even Finn.

The room beyond was rather expansive. It was completely empty except for its lone occupant. The tall man turned and beckoned his guests forward.

I took only two steps, then paused. "Who—who are you?" I whispered.

"I am the Bringer-of-Ecstasy", the man replied, "and you are needed elsewhere now. Finn and the friendly bat will stay here with me for the time being."

"But . . . but I want more crazy adventures", I whined like a child.

"And you shall have them", said the man, waving his gloved hand through the air. "By the way, you're much kinder than the other ones who will arrive here precisely ten years from now. I just wanted you to know that."

Then he snapped his fingers. Finn only had enough time to wave at me sadly before the white light subsumed me once more and deposited me on a crowded city street in the middle of 110-degree weather. Almost everyone surrounding me wore black robes from head to toe—but these robes were far different from those worn by the old man on the moon. These people were mostly dark-skinned women who appeared to be buying fruit from a series of wooden carts set up along the wide thoroughfare. The only people with their faces uncovered were the men selling the fruit; they had brown skin and appeared to be Middle Eastern. They stared at me with expressions of intense shock and fear.

At that moment something disturbed my peripheral vision. I glanced upwards and saw far above the buildings something that looked like a cross between a metallic insect and a helicopter devoid of rotor blades sailing through the cloudless blue sky without a sound. It was wholly unnerving for some inexplicable reason and instilled a queasy feeling in the center of my stomach. Perhaps most odd was the fact that the people around me barely took any notice of it whatsoever. They seemed far more disturbed by *my* presence.

One of the fruit vendors held his hand up to his face as if he were miming the act of talking on the phone. Abruptly, a silver antenna sprouted out of his thumb as he yelled into his pinky in a foreign language I couldn't understand.

I began to run, pushing women out of the way. I was so panicked I fled into a dead end alley. Where was Finn? Where was the Devil Bat? Were they still thousands of miles above my head? A sleek lenticular craft that hovered only inches off the ground followed me. The mirrored dome on top collapsed into the body of the vehicle and a half-human/half-robotic creature emerged. It was about seven feet tall and appeared to be a weird conglomeration of scrap metal and discarded human remains. It pointed its arm at me. Instead of a hand it had two silver prongs with blue flashes of electricity that arced between them.

First it spoke in Spanish. Then in English: "We request your immediate surrender. Please comply to Section II of Article II of the International Laws Pertaining to the Capture of Prisoners of War. Please identify your name, rank, serial number, and Genetic Index Code. If you do not comply to these protocols, we will be required by law to apply a humane level of non-lethal force in order to properly adjust your behavioral deficiencies. We expect a reply within ten seconds after the tone." Then it began speaking in French.

I never got to hear if the thing was proficient in Russian, Chinese, and Esperanto as well. Instead the endlessly replicating snowflakes returned, swept over me, and I found myself once again standing in front of Marina in the basement of the convent. Her eyes were as wide as flying saucers. "What happened?" she said.

I grabbed her shoulder in order to steady myself, but it didn't quite work and I stumbled forward. She wrapped her arms around me. I had become light-headed all of a sudden. "How long was I gone?"

"About a minute. Where did you go?"

"You don't want to know." I managed to pull away and steady myself.

"Oh, but I *do*."

I shrugged. "The Moon? The Middle East? Sometime in the future, I guess?"

She tapped her chin thoughtfully, looking very cute as she did so. "Or perhaps it was the present in an alternate universe."

"I suppose." I reached out and gently stroked her cheek. Marina didn't pull away. She looked so beautiful. "It's . . . it's like part of me is still *there* somehow", I said. "I have a feeling this isn't over . . . like I'm going to disappear again—"

The noise came from behind me. I turned and saw a lean, familiar-looking man leaping into the basement from the ground level window. When he saw us he said, "What the *fuck*?" Agent Layton.

A second man landed next to him. Agent McGuire. He panicked when he saw Marina. "Oh, shit! It's one of those fuckin' nuns!" He whipped out his .38.

"Forget the nun!" Layton said. "What about him? I thought you got rid of that pigfucker!"

McGuire squinted at me through the dim lighting. "Well, I-I *thought* I had—"

"You idiot!" Layton slapped McGuire upside the head. "You want him to blow the lid off this whole operation? No more tracers! No more pen-cameras! Is that what you want?"

"Don't sweat it, sir. I'll just have to get rid of him again."

McGuire aimed the .38 at me. Marina jumped in front of me and spread her arms out like . . . like Christ on the cross. "No, please, don't!" she screamed.

Instinct took over. I pushed her out of the way. An explosion ripped through the small basement. I grew lightheaded again. The weird snowflakes returned. The bullet got me right in the—

4

Johnny Layton

I JUST WANTED THIS to be over with.

I shoved the key into the lock with shaking hands. I hadn't had any sleep in forty-eight hours. I was operating on coffee and adrenaline alone. Well, and a few bennies.

I swung open the trunk, expecting to find the bitch stuffed inside. Instead I see the nebbish who gave me the key, the very same asshole who was now standing in the doorway in McGuire's grasp.

"What the fuck is this?" I said, spreading my hands in the air.

I can't imagine the look of utter dismay that must've been on my face. What had to be the guy's identical twin was stuffed in the trunk with what looked like a bullet hole in his chest. Had we stumbled upon an attempted murder in progress? At one time I would've been excited, but compared to the first genuine extraterrestrial contact this was just soap opera stuff. I was getting angrier and angrier by the second. (Those bennies were really workin' on me.)

McGuire dragged the asshole toward the car so fast the tips of his shoes scraped the ground. I glanced back and forth between the body and his twin. They were even wearing the same exact clothes. "What is this, some kind of a joke?" I said.

McGuire slapped the guy upside the head. "You tryin' to hoodwink us? Huh? Is that what you think you're doin'?" The asshole said nothing so McGuire slapped him again, this time even harder.

The dude fell to the ground. He was on the verge of crying. "Please!" he whined. "I *swear* I put her in there. I don't know where she is."

McGuire and I just stared at each other for a second. I was at the end of my rope, and McGuire knew it. He grabbed the asshole's ear lobe and forced him to his feet. He said, "Okay, if that's the way you want to play it, pigfucker. Get in the trunk."

Without even thinking about it, I pulled the twin out of the trunk and dumped him on the concrete floor as if he were nothing more than a sack of garbage.

"What?" the asshole said. "No, I-I really—"

McGuire pumped a single bullet into the wall. "Get into the motherfuckin' trunk!" The sound of the explosion was enough to send him jumping into that little box. McGuire slammed the lid shut and locked it. We tried the good cop/bad cop routine for a bit, but that didn't work. The asshole maintained his innocence. Well, I was too pumped up to deal with that nonsense for long. I told McGuire to dump the crybaby in the lake at the foot of the hill just to get rid of him. McGuire was more than happy to comply.

Meanwhile, I tore the house apart looking for the slightest evidence that the nun had been there. We *knew* she had been. Pandolphi's tracer, which was linked to a covert satellite in orbit, had pinpointed her exact location. The tracer led us to this asshole's driveway. Unfortunately, I think I popped one or two or three bennies too many and my hands weren't so steady and I dropped the scanner as we got out of our car and it bounced twice and rolled right past McGuire and he dove for it and tried to catch it before it went over the edge of the cliff but . . . well, that was the last we saw of the scanner. We decided to resort to the junkie's FBI badges. And when *that* didn't work we switched to Plan C: Operation Bare Knuckles. Sometimes the old-fashioned way works best.

McGuire had been gone for almost an hour before I decided to check the back yard. It's a good thing I did too. I discovered the impression in the ground where she hit. Beside it the sun was glinting off the tiny circular tracer, where it must've fallen upon impact. About two yards from the tracer I found the camera. It was smashed into a dozen or so serrated pieces, all totally useless. Pulitzer-Prize-level photographs destroyed by a mad nun and a dimensional rift in space. Needless to say I was depressed.

That's when I heard a grating noise above me. I glanced up just in time to see the cornerstone plummeting toward my skull. I leaped out of the way seconds before the projectile crashed into the earth, splitting into smaller sections. I landed against a tree with a thud, then glanced upwards once more. I saw the barest wisp of a black robe retreating from the edge of the rooftop.

I was on my feet again. I considered rushing into the house and up to the second floor to find the entrance to the roof, but what if there wasn't one? That might waste valuable time. Despite my extra weight, I was still a Boy Scout at heart. I skinnied up the tree and from its branches saw Mother Superior Machail darting across the roof. I vaulted from the thickest branch to the gaping hole in the ledge where the cornerstone had once sat. My hands touched the roof first, scraping the skin off as I slid across the concrete. Then my knees hit, *bang*! For a second I thought I might've busted something, but I kept moving anyway. I wasn't about to let that bitch out of my sight now.

"Stop!" I yelled, though I had very little breath inside me. I whipped out my gun, hoping she would see it and stop.

Stop she did. Right on the far edge of the roof. She was still ten feet away from me, but I was close enough to see the blood and scratches on her face. Sticky redness dripped from her nose and mouth. She'd no doubt fallen from tree level and was knocked unconscious; Mr. Asshole thought she was dead and stuffed her in the trunk for some stupid reason I couldn't possibly fathom.

Machail raised her quaking arms in the air and yelled, "Please, God, forgive me for allowing Satan to go free! Give me another chance. Strike this man down with lightning so I may live to hunt Satan and return Him to his rightful imprisonment beneath—!"

Suddenly, the edge of the roof gave way and Mother Superior plummeted to her bloody death two stories below. Again. This time, however, I imagined the fall was final.

I tiptoed over to the edge and peered downwards. She had landed about two feet from McGuire, who stood in the driveway looking up at me with a dismayed expression on his face. "What the hell?" he said. "Are you trying to kill me? Where the fuck did *she* come from?"

"Nowhere! Which is exactly where she's going!"

"Huh?"

"Nothin', forget it! Listen, I've got some good news and some bad news!"

"Oh, shit. Give me the good news first!"

"You're not dead!"

"Yeah, okay, and the bad news?"

"The film was destroyed!"

McGuire threw his hands in the air and sighed. "So this shit's been another big waste of time then!"

"I refuse to accept that! We're going back to that convent and wring a story out of those nuns if it takes all week and a bushel of bamboo slips under their ancient claws!"

McGuire pointed at Mother Superior. "What about her?"

"Let God take care of her. We've got a plane to catch."

5

Finn mac Cumhall

TO THIS DAY I CHERISH the sacred herb my old friend Kyle gave me so long ago. The Devil Bat loves it too. We partake of it often. In fact, the two of us introduced the Bringer-of-Ecstasy to its wonders, then convinced him to guide us to the jungles of the moon where we met many friends and experienced so many wonderful adventures. Out of lunarian sand we built a statue of Kyle in honor of his memory and placed it on a high peak in Mons Apenninus. I once asked the Bringer-of-Ecstasy if we would ever see Kyle again, and he said, "That is not for me to say, my son. That is for the Universe to decide."

The Devil Bat and I spent ten years exploring the various metropolises on the moon. We particularly enjoyed their system of gambling, which involved games of chance based on precise, strategic moves. (It's hard to explain.)

After ten years had passed the Devil Bat and I were lounging out on the lunar landscape in Mare Vaporum soaking up some Earth Rays when my companion turned to me all of a sudden and said, "I wonder where Kyle is now."

"I wonder the same thing from time to time. Remember when you saved him from that weird insect thing?"

"Yes." He laughed. "It looked like a cross between a spider and a kangaroo."

"That was some weird shit", I said. "An ugly motherfucker, too."

"The only thing uglier is your face in the morning."

"Ha", I said and punched him slightly on his left wing, but just hard enough to let him know I could rip him in two again if I really wanted to. The Devil Bat was a little passive aggressive. He'd never really forgiven me for killing him that one time, but nonetheless we had more in common than not and so we stuck by each other. We'd been through a whole war together—that time when the Venusians attacked the moon several years ago—and he had saved my life more times than I could count. So whatever bad blood there was between us never got in the way of our friendship.

The Sea of Tranquility was filled with thousands of dead Venusians, by the way. The two of us were considered war heroes on the moon. We could have anything we wanted. Perhaps it was all becoming a little bit too boring for us.

"You know what I'm thinking?" said the Devil Bat.

"What's that?" I asked, already knowing what he would say.

"I was thinking of going back to Earth."

I sighed. Yes, the unspeakable had been spoken. Now we would have to choose. Would we both go together or would one of us stay behind?

"You don't want to go, do you?" the Devil Bat said.

"No, no, I do", I said. "It's just that . . . ."

"It's just what?"

"It's just that I've become so *comfortable* here."

"Maybe that's why we have to leave."

I sighed again. "I suppose you're right. When're you planning on leaving?"

"Right now."

"You always have to be so god damn spontaneous?"

"It's just my nature."

I got up out of my lawn chair and said, "Okay, well, there's no time like the present."

"You're coming with me? You know you don't have to . . . not for me. I'll come back and visit. Really I will."

I sighed. "I know you won't. You'll find someone else. There, on Earth."

"That's not true."

I nodded sadly. "It's true."

There was an awkward moment of silence. Then he said, "Okay, maybe it *is* true. Maybe you *should* keep an eye on me."

"Okay, then I will." I straddled his back once more.

The Devil Bat pretended to groan—an old joke. Then he whispered, somewhat fearfully, "But where on Earth are we going to go?"

"Don't you remember?" I said. "Kyle told us his home in Malibu is always open to us. He said you couldn't miss it. It's at the top of Trail's End."

"Then that's where we'll go", said the Devil Bat and we lifted up from the lunar surface. We didn't want to stay and say goodbye to all the friends we had made on the moon. It would just be too sad.

Coincidentally, on the way up, we passed a primitive look- ing white capsule with an American flag painted on the side. It was descending. So, I thought, the Earthmen have finally done it. We wondered if they would find Kyle's pipe planted in the dust and understand that other Earthmen had been there before them. We circled their landing module for awhile and even let them take photos of us. What would they think of that? Would they show the photos to the boys back home or keep it to themselves? Would they venture past the bor- ders of the Venusian graveyard in the Sea of Tranquility and visit the bright and colorful cities that lay beyond? Would they even be allowed to see what we had been so privileged to see? If they were deemed worthy, perhaps they would. Maybe not these Earthmen, but others. Earthmen who might come later in a more seemly vehicle than a portable garage with primitive retro rockets welded to its bottom. (If some stranger broke down outside your house in a beat-up jalopy, would you be so eager to come out and make his acquaintance? I didn't think so.)

And so eventually we tired of these Earthmen and soared upward toward that familiar, shining blue oblate spheroid hanging high in the sky. It took us awhile, as we opted for the scenic route around Mercury, but eventually we reentered the Earth's atmosphere, avoiding the artillery fire of circling fighter jets, and found Kyle's house tucked away in the beautiful mountain peaks of Malibu, California. It felt odd being on the blue planet again, but not as odd as what happened next.

As we hovered over what I was certain to be Kyle's home a gunshot rang out. A bullet almost hit the Devil Bat in the head. Only a swift dive prevented his sudden death. I bellowed in rage and managed to deflect two more shots with my club. As we neared Trail's End we spotted Kyle, looking a little older but no less like Kyle, standing on his roof aiming a high-powered rifle at us.

I waved at him and shouted, "Ho there, Kyle, it is I! Finn mac Cumhall!"

"And I", the Devil Bat cried, "Finn mac Cumhall's companion, the Devil Bat!"

Even from so far in the air I could see the grin spread out across Kyle's face. "It *is* you!" he said. "I never thought I would see you two again!"

"Fortunately for all of us, you were wrong!" I shouted. "Where should we land?"

"Right here!" Kyle said and waved us down. The Devil Bat alighted upon Kyle's roof. I dismounted and picked up my old friend, without whom I never would have left the Earth in the first place, and hugged him so hard I almost crushed his ribs. Kyle laughed and returned the hug, then wrapped his arms around the hairy neck of the Devil Bat.

"Where have you two been?" he said.

"We just left the moon", the Devil Bat said.

"So you've been there all these years?" Kyle said.

"Yes, we've had many grand adventures", I said, "but it was time to go. We passed some Earthmen on the way here, by the way."

"Earthmen?" Kyle said, furrowing his brow. Then a look of recognition flared in his eyes. "Oh, *them!*" he said and laughed, shaking his head derisively. "Let's go down to the sun deck below and you can tell me all your wonderful stories."

"I would be more than willing to do so", I said, "after you've explained why your initial greeting took the form of a gunshot."

"I apologize", Kyle said. "I haven't been myself lately. I'm getting more and more paranoid. My enemies are closing in. Unfortunately my crop is becoming more and more demonized in this country. I thought you were the Feds closing in under some sort of clever disguise."

I laughed. "That would be a rather peculiar disguise", I said. "But I forgive your rash behavior. Let us move to the refreshments. Do you have lemonade?"

So the three of us sat in comfortable lawn chairs, not unlike the ones we had just left on the moon (I was amazed that he had such large ones ready for us, as if a part of him knew—despite his pessimism—that we would indeed be reunited in the future) out on Kyle's beautiful sun deck and exchanged strange stories while drinking lemonade. Kyle seemed much sadder than the last time I had seen him. This was, it turned out, because he had lost his one true love many years before. The woman he had once been determined to wed.

"Tell me", I said, "what happened to that little lass?"

"I took a bullet for her, right in the chest." He opened his paisley shirt and showed us the scar. It was a bad one. "I'm not exactly sure what happened after that. But I do know I eventually teleported into an emergency room in the future. The doctors of 2029 were able to save me with some kind of weird wand-like device, and then I teleported again, to here. A full five years had passed. I came to in a country I didn't recognize. A new President had come and gone—assassinated by a nobody. A faceless loser. And the United States was now entrenched in a senseless war that continues to this day. The country's not getting better, it's getting worse. I hitchhiked back to Wisconsin, but by that time the nunnery had been closed and that whole area in Heathville had been bought up by the government and quarantined. I haven't seen Marina since." He reached out in front of him, as if to embrace a ghost. "Sometimes, I think I can almost feel her cheeks . . . ." He stared intently at nothing, shook his head, glanced down at the ground and sighed. Then locked eyes with mine once more and said, "Do you think she's dead?"

"I doubt it, my boy", I said, patting him on the knee, "not if this is truly a just and righteous universe."

The Devil Bat held out his empty glass and said, "So, do you have any *pink* lemonade?"

6

Marina Wilson Riley

KYLE DISAPPEARED ONCE MORE, right after jumping in front of the bullet that would have taken my useless, oh-so-holy life.

While the two thugs were hypnotized by the pulsing, shifting geometric patterns that consumed Kyle's body I withdrew the .32 from my robe and shot the little Irishman in the stomach and chest and neck. The tall, slender gentleman I hit in the groin—just like Mother Superior taught me when I first reached puberty.

I left them like that, half-alive, half-dead.

Lying on the floor was the final remnant of Kyle's existence: the pipe and lighter. Kyle's kind offer echoed inside my head: *You want to try*? I bent down and scooped the objects into my palm. I cradled them against my chest and prayed to God to help me find the strength, the courage, to go through with what I had in mind. I rolled up the alien's discarded skin into a compact bundle and stuffed it under my robe.

That's when the other sisters came rushing down the stairs. Sister Beatrice, the one who had found me on the steps twenty-one years before, said, "We . . . we heard gunshots. What happened?"

"Nothing", I said calmly. "Nothing at all." I lit the pipe, drew it to my lips, and inhaled.

My last image of them was the horrified expressions on their wretched, aged faces.

Then the gentle caress of rainbow bands and the penetration of geometric patterns into every pore of my sanctified body and the blinding illumination of pure white light and the disease-ravaged prostitutes of the Cimarron Strip seen from a horse-driven covered wagon and a fleeting glimpse of shining turrets in Kashmir and watching a convoy of UN soldiers in gun-mounted jeeps retreating from mass death in Sierra Leone and the sweet scent of cotton candy at Disneyland in August and the breathtaking sight of a geodesic dome beneath the perpetual noon of the Antarctic wastes and the feel of my heart beating in my throat as I descend into the caverns beneath Death Valley and the smell of burning flesh in snow-covered Donner Pass and the press of desperate bodies as two hundred living skeletons line up for poisoned soft drinks and the sound of massive engines lifting up from the moons of Mars and communing mind-to-mind with a mad dolphin on Europa and climbing the slopes of Mt. Everest to touch the matted fur of a yeti and the sun reflecting off the glass skyscrapers of San Francisco at twilight and the stench of human sweat in the oil rigs of Texas and rowing slowly beneath the bridges of Venice and hacking an escape path through the jungles of Mato Grosso and—

O, what wonders I saw, what trials I experienced, from that day forward.

Imagine, imagine, imagine unending illumination, unending stimulation, unending ecstasy.

I can only pray that God forgives me for my sins.

2

COMMUNIST TOWN, USA

PHILIP TROWBRIDGE FIRST SAW the town at night. He arrived in Middlesburg at the bus station at around six P.M., just as the sun was setting. It was a small town in the middle of Wisconsin, one of the smallest in the state. It looked like the kind of town he'd always wanted to settle down in. Growing up in the middle of a slum in Los Angeles hadn't endeared him to life in the city. He was only twenty-five, but felt far older. He'd had to sacrifice a lot to work his way up this far in the Bureau. This was his first major assignment, and he wasn't going to blow it.

When he was a teenager his dream had been to join the Army so he could fight the Japs and the Krauts in Europe. He even tried to join once, but the recruiter knew right off that this scrawny, underfed kid couldn't be more than fifteen. Ten years later, in 1955, there was a new enemy abroad and not thousands of miles away in the alien landscape of Germany or Japan. The new enemy had infiltrated the core of American society. Right here in the heartland. Philip's goal was to help stop the disease from spreading any further.

He followed his orders and strolled over to the Potter Boarding House on Brandywine Street, five blocks away from the bus station. He had a suitcase in his hand, his only luggage. The uniform lamps that lined the broad street seemed comforting somehow as they blinked on one by one, the orange twilight sky spread out behind their fluorescent eyes like marmalade. It almost seemed as if they were turning on for his benefit alone.

There were others on the street, typical mid-Americans with pleasant smiles on their rugged faces. Even though he was new in town, almost all of them were polite enough to tip his hat or flash a red-lipstick-lined smile. Such pleasant people. It was hard to believe that an enemy worse than the Nazis had taken root here. It was even harder to believe that a dozen special agents like himself had disappeared from this idyllic town, leaving not even a trace of themselves behind.

Philip spotted the quaint sign hanging outside the two-story house. The sign read POTTER'S BOARDING HOME and was ringed with images of interlinked circus animals carved into the wood. A smaller sign affixed to the bottom read VACANCY. The house looked old and perfect and dream-like, like something out of a Sherwood Anderson novel, the kind of home Philip had always dreamed about while trapped with his disintegrating parents in a disintegrating apartment building at the top of a disintegrating Bunker Hill in Los Angeles.

He walked up the steps and pulled aside the screen door. The wooden door beyond was wide open. Inside lay an anteroom that contained a staircase leading upwards. Lining the flowery wallpaper was a series of paintings depicting generations of what Philip assumed was the Potter family.

In a room to his left he saw about a half-dozen people sitting around a long table, as if they were just about to begin eating supper. A tall, thin woman in her early seventies sat at the head of the table. "Yes, may I help you?" she said, rising, then turned to the men at the table and said, almost as if annoyed, "Oh, please, *stay*." Some of them had begun to rise with her. "You don't want your potato pancakes to get cold, do you?"

Each of them nodded as they lowered themselves back into their chairs.

Philip sat his suitcase on the carpeted floor, then took his hat off. "Sorry to disturb you, ma'am", he said. "I'm just looking for a room. I saw the vacancy sign outside."

"It's forty dollars a month", said Mrs. Potter. "It's a big room. Can you afford that?" She glanced at the single suitcase on the floor.

"I can afford it for a month", Philip said, smiling. "I expect to have a job before then. And if I don't . . . well, trust me, you won't have to tell me to leave."

"I want to get one thing straight right now", Potter said, "I can't afford to give you a job. We already have enough . . . 'tenants' like that already." Potter flashed an annoyed glance at a young obese man sitting to her left. He continued to stare at his potato pancakes, as if ashamed.

"I wasn't planning on asking you for a job, ma'am", Philip said. "I have a lot of skills. I'm sure I can be of use to somebody around here."

"Ridge is lookin' for a clerk at the grocery store", said an old man sitting across from Potter. He had a thick Hungarian accent. "Isn't that right?" he said to a muscular man with short red hair sitting beside him. This man, no older than thirty, seemed completely disinterested in the question. He was too busy shoveling food into his mouth. "Mm", and a shrug was his only reply.

"That's 'cause no one else wants the job", said a middle-aged man sitting beside the redhead. He had wavy black hair and a bony face and eyes that twinkled with merriment. He emitted a high-pitched laugh and turned toward Philip. "Old man Ridge is kinda... well, he's almost blind. And you know what W.C. Fields said."

Philip just stared at him, slightly confused. "No . . . what did he say?"

"'I never met a blind man who wasn't a son of a bitch!'" The man tilted his head back and burst into laughter. Everyone else at the table looked uncomfortable. "So I guess Ridge is just *almost* a son of a bitch."

"Harry!" the old woman yelled. "How many times have I told you to watch your language at the table? By God, I swear I'll toss you out onto the street and give the dog your room. You've got the biggest room in the house and it's wasted on you. You don't do anything but sit around and stare at the wall!"

Harry rolled his eyes. "I'm a writer", he said. "The old woman thinks that translates into the word 'bum.'"

"Well, it does", the old woman said. "Honestly. The kind of things you write . . . ." She just let the sentence trail off, then her face darkened, as if she were embarrassed. She turned back to Philip and said, "Mr. Ridge was stricken nearly blind during the war, and might be given to outbursts due to simple and understandable frustration, but by no means is he a bad man. I'm sure he would give you a chance in his store. It's not a glamorous job like being a hack writer, but it's an honest living."

Harry just kept eating his potato pancakes. His grin faltered only slightly.

"It sounds good to me", Philip said. "If you know where I can find this Ridge, I'll go talk to him right now."

Potter shook her head. "No, no. It can wait until morning. Right now you can sit down right next to Mr. Biriescu here." She gestured toward the thin old man.

"Thank you", Philip said. He sat down while the old woman introduced the other people at the table: Harry Mason (the writer), Nicholaus Biriescu (the old man), Marcus Potter (the obese young man, Mrs. Potter's grandson), Rust Bebe (a muscular man, a policeman, who hadn't uttered more than a syllable since Philip had entered the place), and Mrs. Potter herself.

"You may call me Emily", Mrs. Potter said. "What's your name?"

"Me?" Philip said as he picked up a fork and eyed the potato pancake that Emily slipped onto his plate. "I'm Herbert O'Leary. I'm just a guy tryin' to find his way." He smiled sheepishly as he dug in.

He didn't know when or where the contact would occur, but he had been told to wait for it. He had gone down to Ridge's Grocery Store well before 8:00 a.m., before the man's store even opened, and asked the man nervously if he could please have a job. The old blind man refused at first, saying he didn't trust Philip's voice, but after some more pleading he relented, threw him a dark green smock, and told him he could get started by opening some boxes and stocking the shelves.

Philip was kneeling on the ground unpacking cans of peas when a pair of shapely, nylon-covered legs caught his attention. "Excuse me", said a soft, musical voice. He looked up at a pretty young woman whose short dark hair was obscured by a sheer yellow scarf, her eyes invisible behind a pair of large dark sunglasses. She removed the glasses and said, "Do you work here?"

He had the urge to say, "What does it *look* like?" He thought he'd left his days of lower-class menial labor far behind when he fled from his boyhood home in L.A.'s Bunker Hill. He understood this was just a part he was playing, but still. It was deep cover. He had to *become* that lowly person all over again, and he didn't like it. Didn't like it at all. Only the thought of being rewarded by J. Edgar himself kept him going through this strange hell.

So he swallowed his pride and said, "Yes, ma'am, I just started. I'm just getting used to all this." Philip flashed her a weak smile, then glanced around. The old man could probably answer her questions better, but he'd gone out back to help bring in another delivery. "I'll try to help you if I can, ma'am."

"Do you know if you carry organic foods?"

Philip furrowed his brow. "*Organic* foods? What's that?" He'd never even heard the term. It sounded like something out of an outer space movie.

The woman smiled. "It's okay. You probably don't. It's not really urgent. You sell matches?"

"Sure. Up at the counter." He pointed toward the plastic bowl that contained the matches.

"Oh, I don't need them. I don't smoke. But I hear that cigarette you like is coming back in style."

Philip did a double take. No, he wasn't expecting a woman. He wasn't expecting a woman at all. Now the words came to him automatically, as if a robot were saying them. "I . . . can't enjoy a cup of joe in the morning without a cigarette."

"Are you an Arab?" the woman said, smiling.

"Only on my best days."

The woman nodded three times. "Clickety-click, handsome. Perhaps you'd like to meet later, talk about the Middle East."

"I've always wanted to go back there." Now he strayed from the script. "My name's Herb O'Leary. I . . . don't have a phone."

The woman reached into her purse and jotted down a phone number on the inside of a full book of matches. "Fine. You call me, Herbert. Around six o'clock."

Now he strayed even further from the script. "Maybe we can go out for a drink."

The woman arched one painted eyebrow. Her smile wasn't fake this time. "Maybe." She turned on her heel and began to leave the store.

"Wait. Ma'am. What do I call you?"

She turned slightly and glanced over her shoulder. "My name, of course. It's on the matches."

He glanced back down at the phone number. He pulled back the matches and saw a name written in black ink: EVA. It was only three tiny letters, but for Philip they were magical. They contained his entire future.

A voice from behind him broke him out of his reverie: "See you've made a start at gettin' to know this town." The old man was chuckling.

"Do you know her?" Philip said.

"She's been here for a couple of years. A school teacher. Quite a catch. She's pretty standoffish. I'm surprised she gave you her number. Yep, she's a real knockout."

Philip was confused. "How . . . how do you know she's . . . ?" He didn't know how to ask the question without being rude.

"I may not have eyes, son, but I ain't stupid. I hear how everyone talks about her. Lotta guys have asked her for her phone number and haven't gotten it. Only a real knockout can cause that much disappointment in the world. Lord, I wish I were your age again, son."

"Oh, yeah? Why?"

The old man shook his head back and forth. "Are you kiddin'?" He laughed to himself and shuffled back outside again. "Only a young man can really appreciate disappointment. When you're old . . . well, you just come to expect it. Yes, sir. You've got a lotta disappointment ahead of you. Don't take it for granted. Milk it for all it's worth."

"That sounds . . . I don't know, kind of cynical."

The old man didn't even turn around. "It's not cynical. It's the total opposite. If you can still get hurt bad, and I mean *really* bad, then that just means you've still got some feeling left. Enjoy it while you can. Enjoy *feeling* something. All of it goes away after awhile, the good and the bad. Now . . . get those peas stacked on the shelves or I'll kick you back out on the street."

Philip nodded and went back to work, thinking about Eva's smile.

Philip sat on a stool at Sonny's Bar located three blocks away from the grocery store. It was almost seven o'clock. He had made the call from a phone booth the second he got off work.

She had told him to meet her here. She explained to him that she had never visited this bar before now, so it would appear to the casual observer as if he had invited *her* there. Philip thought this was odd for her to mention, since he *had* invited her there.

Philip sat nursing a Scotch, thinking about what the old man had said about disappointment, when he felt a hand on his shoulder. The hand was dainty and covered in a white lace glove. "Hey, Herbert Without A Phone. Funny meeting you here. You bring all your girls here?" She laughed as she eased herself onto the stool beside him.

Philip's laugh was tinged with nervousness once more. It was only half an act. "Nah, I just got into town. The old man recommended this place."

"Ridge? Really?" She pursed her lips and raised her eyebrows in surprise. "Maybe it was a lucky place for him, back during the Pleistocene."

Philip didn't know what that last word meant, so he decided to let it go. "What're you having?"

"The same as you."

Philip glanced up at the bartender, a thirtyish burly man with a yin/yang symbol tattooed on his arm. The bartender took the opportunity to give Eva the once-over as he placed the drink in front of her. Then he lumbered over to the other side of the bar to settle down a drunk man and his even drunker wife.

Eva cocked her head to the right. "Let's go grab a booth. I'm starved. How about you?"

Philip shrugged. "I could go for a bite of something." He hadn't intended the double entendre, and the second it came out he winced.

Eva smiled. "Don't get ahead of yourself, Herbert Without A Phone. Let's just see what the kitchen can do for us first."

He followed her to a booth in the back of the room, kicking himself mentally. How could she be so unphased by his stupid insult? She seemed to take everything in stride, even this cloak and dagger business. How long had she been doing it? At least for two years. Isn't that how long the old man had said she'd been living in Middlesburg? He wondered how long she'd been working for the Bureau in an official capacity. He didn't even think women were allowed to be on the payroll. Was that just a dodge for public consumption? Since being promoted, Philip had seen so much that wasn't what it appeared to be on the surface. He felt as if he'd been wearing blinders for the first twenty-five years of his life.

The second they slipped into the booth Eva nudged up next to him—not obscenely close, but they would definitely seem intimate to anyone observing them from afar. Eva placed her elbow on the red and white checkered tablecloth and leaned in close to him, her mouth half-agape, as if fascinated by every imperfection in his face. She whispered, "Call the waiter over here and order something to eat and then we'll get down to business, OK? Oh, and ask him to put the jukebox on. We don't want anyone accidentally overhearing what we have to say, do we?"

Philip nodded. "Of course." He held his hand in the air, motioning for the bartender to come over.

"Are you new at this?" she asked through a smile.

He didn't want to admit the truth, but what the hell. "This is my first."

"That's good. You don't have any preconceived notions or prejudices. That's what we need here. We'll ease you into the job slowly."

"It all seems fast to me."

Eva placed her hand on his knee, just for a second. "It gets faster."

The bartender came over and said, "The kitchen's going to be closed soon, folks."

"I think we know what we want", Eva said. Philip had no idea what he wanted. He had no idea what she wanted either.

Philip nodded. "The special for both of us", he said as authoritatively as possible. He didn't even know if they offered specials here. "Oh, and turn on the jukebox will you?" He slid a nickel across the tabletop. "Nat King Cole. 'Answer Me, My Love.'"

"Comin' right up", the bartender said, snatching up the nickel, and walked away toward the kitchen, leaving Philip and Eva alone except for a few drunken couples scattered around the bar, all of them lost in their own personal dramas.

"Good choice", Eva said. "Now let's get down to it." She reached into her purse and pulled out . . . something. Several somethings? He couldn't quite tell what they were at first. She slipped the objects into his lap beneath the table. "Look down at them", she whispered, still smiling, "casually."

He glanced down at his lap and saw two or three black and white photos depicting an old man with a wide bulge around the middle. He had a salt and pepper beard and a full, red face. Broken capillaries stood out on his bulbous nose. He clearly had a love for the grape. He looked familiar.

"This man is named Almos Biriescu", she continued to whisper, leaning toward him and giggling as if they were sharing some kind of intimate joke. Philip could feel himself growing excited, not just because of the nearness of her soft white skin but because of the importance of the information being imparted to him. "He's the one who started the Communist Party here in Middlesburg eight years ago, right after the war. Since then it's grown immeasurably, faster than in any other town in the entire country. You're not smiling."

He tried to keep an amused grin on his face, though it was difficult. "Sorry", he said. "It's just that there's an old man in the boarding house where I'm staying with the same last name as this man."

"Nicholaus? That's Almos's brother. Jesus, you're still not smiling. You look like your mother just died."

74

"I'm sorry."

"Get closer to me and relax. Consider it an order . . . from Jedgar himself."

OK. He decided to get into character more, if that's really what she wanted. He slid closer to her, put his hand on her thigh. It felt both soft and firm through her dress. He could feel the smoothness of her nylon stocking through the cotton material. She didn't move away from him. She slid her hand on top of his and pressed it down even harder. He could feel an erection forming in his slacks.

"Nicholaus won't be of any help to you", she said. "He hates his brother. They're both Hungarians. They came over here back in the late 1920s during the Revolution. They were forced to flee the country. Something happened between them."

They were interrupted by a cute young waitress who brought them two specials. "Careful", the girl said, "the plates are hot." Cute, yes, but not anywhere near as striking as Eva.

"Thank you", Philip said. Eva didn't pull away from him, even as the waitress was putting the plates down in front of them. Eva ignored the food and acted as if she had eyes only for him. She looked at him adoringly and brushed a lock of hair out of Philip's face.

He said, "Are you like this with all your contacts?" He leaned in and brushed her rouged cheek with the back of his hand.

Her smile faltered for a second. Then she leaned in close as well, brushed her lips against his ear lobe, and whispered, "That's none of your business, is it? Nicholaus knows that Almos is an ardent communist and hates him because of it. Nicholaus used to be a communist, but the American lifestyle changed him. We won him over with . . . ." She glanced down at the dinner in front of him and waved her hands slowly over the plates of hamburgers and French fries and coleslaw. (Until only a few years ago, hamburgers had been called "Patriot

Sandwiches" and coleslaw "Victory Lettuce" so as not to disturb loyal Americans with their overtly German names. The war was still a sensitive subject with a lot of people.) Eva looked like a high end fashion model advertising a unique product manufactured in limited editions for the elite, as seen only on television. "Cheeseburgers and French fries", she said. "Even though they live in the same town, Nicholaus hasn't spoken to Almos in years. There are better ways to approach Almos than through his brother."

She grabbed the photos and slipped them back into a manila envelope sitting on her lap. She then pulled out another snapshot and placed this one in his lap as well. Eva gave him one last pat on the knee, then pulled away, for which he was grateful. He wasn't certain how much more of her closeness he could stand. He'd been dedicated to his career for so long that he hadn't even gone on a date—not a serious one—in a couple of years. Eva was the kind of woman you wouldn't mind getting serious over.

She began nibbling on a French fry. "Study that one closely. She's your entrance into the Party. Her name's Sophia."

He glanced down. The photo depicted a glum young woman in her early twenties. She wore black rimmed glasses, her brunette hair pulled back in a ponytail. There was something hardened and girlish about her at the same time. She looked like a pseudo-intellectual, the kind of girl who wore black berets and turtleneck sweaters, the kind of misguided bohemian he'd sometimes seen standing on a soap box in the middle of Pershing Square in Los Angeles passing out copies of *The Communist Manifesto* and preaching about Utopia, never realizing she was standing in the middle of one. Or at least as close as any country had ever gotten.

"Where can I find her?" he said.

"Go to the Mosler Safe Building on Main Street tomorrow morning, right before you go to work. They don't open their office until eight, but she's usually there at seven. She's dedicated to her job. Knock on the door. She'll open it. Tell her you're interested in picking up some information on the Middlesburg Youth Council, ostensibly an anti-war organization composed of young college students from the University of Wisconsin. They want to prevent any future Koreas, or so they say. It's just a front organization. It's red through and through. She'll start to give you a sales pitch. I want you to begin talking to her about the problems in this country, how the minorities are enslaved, the workers exploited by the fat cats, the soldiers brainwashed by the military, all the typical communist rhetoric, all the screeds you've presumably been studying this entire time. Right?" For the first time he saw a very serious expression wash over her pretty face.

"Of course", he said.

Eva patted him on the knee again. "Excellent. Launch into a tirade in front of her. Again, don't be too obvious about it. It has to be casual. She can't get suspicious, not this early in the game or it's all over. If you're convincing enough, she might ask you to join a book club, a little coffee klatch where a dozen or so of her closest friends study the 'classics,' books like *Das Kapital* and *The Holy Family*. Get my drift? Once you're in on the book club, you're one step closer to being in all the way depending on how you conduct yourself. You can't blow it. Get as close to this girl as possible. Your job is to win her confidence. She's the conduit. If you blow it you're packing up and going back home. You'll end up behind a desk somewhere. You want that?"

He wasn't quite sure what to say. There was such a coldness in her voice now. She had transformed into a different person. He felt like he was getting a talking-to from Miss Cloister, his 9th grade English teacher. He felt like saying, "No, ma'am. I promise to do better, ma'am."

Instead he felt himself growing angry and said, "Would I really come all the way to the backend of nowhere if I wanted to settle for a desk job? I wasn't able to fight in World War II because I was too young. I couldn't fight in Korea because I had flat feet. This is the closest thing I'm ever going to be to a soldier in the Army fighting the good fight for my country. I'm not easily confused or flustered, though you've been doing a nice job of trying to make me that way for the past twenty minutes."

Eva smiled. "Good boy. Feisty. I like it. Feistiness can come in handy, but remember that losing your temper can get you killed. Keep that firmly in mind, Mr. O'Leary. What do the kids say these days? Be cool. Just be cool. Now get your hand off my leg."

He'd totally forgotten it was there. But he remained cool. He continued to stare into her violet eyes for a few moments until at last withdrawing his hand gradually, very gradually, using the opportunity to get one last slow feel of the firmness of her legs. She raised one eyebrow at him, a slight smile playing at the edge of her painted lips. She didn't bother to comment on the gesture. She reached into her purse for a cigarette and offered him one without uttering a word. He nodded once. She slipped the cigarette between his fingers and lit it for him.

She said, "Call me again at the same exact time tomorrow night. Tell me how it goes with Sophia. Now that we've been seen in public we can meet somewhere more private next time."

"Sounds promising. Consider it a date."

"Consider it what you want, lover." Eva slipped Sophia's photo back into her purse. "It's as much of a date as O'Leary's your real name. Or Eva's mine. Be seeing you." She leaned in and kissed him on the cheek. Then just as suddenly she was out of the booth and walking towards the door. He watched her go, the contours of her heart-shaped butt just barely visible beneath that respectable looking dress. He saw some of the other men in the bar watching her go as well, and felt a little proud. This was developing into a far more interesting assignment than he'd ever imagined when he walked onto that Greyhound bus in Los Angeles the day before.

He stayed behind for awhile and listened to Eddie Fisher on the jukebox singing "Dungaree Doll" and finished his Patriot Sandwich. Trying to be cool.

The next morning at 7:15 a.m. Philip walked into the Mosler Safe Building on Main Street and located the office for The Middlesburg Youth Council on the directory. He rode the elevator to the third floor, practicing his lines in his head.

The headquarters for The Middlesburg Youth Council looked like any other antiseptic office, and the girl behind the counter might have been a secretary for a chartered accountant. This Sophia certainly didn't look like a subversive revolutionary. She looked like a teenager who spent too much time reading books.

He glanced around the office, looking confused. That's what he wanted to look like.

"May I help you?" Sophia said.

"Um, yes", he said. "I saw this flyer about The Middlesburg Youth Council. They're an anti-war group, yes?"

She smiled, but there was something strained about it, as if it were a purely muscular movement with little or no emotion behind it. "We prefer to say a 'pro-peace group.' The other appellation is far too negative. There's something slightly paradoxical about working *against* war. Can one *hate* war? No, of course not. We here at the Council promote only non-violent civil disobedience. Are you pro-peace as well?"

"No doubt about it. My father died in World War II." Nothing could be further from the truth, but it made a good cover. Philip walked over to Sophia and planted his hands on the counter. "I was against the war in . . . or rather, I was *for* peace in Korea."

"So sad to hear about your father." She tilted her head to one side and pursed her lips as she said this, as if she were imitating a look of sadness she had once seen on an actress in a stage play. A bad one. "But perhaps there was a reason for your loss, if it made you realize how important it is to work for peace. Almost everyone who's on the council now worked hard to try to keep the United States out of Korea. You've found . . . soul mates here."

He acted embarrassed. "Well, I didn't actually *do* anything to try to keep us out of Korea. I was just against it, that's all. I guess I was a little too scared to do anything about it, what with people's attitudes and all. If you're for peace people immediately think you're some kind of coward. But that's not the case at all. I'm no coward."

"I'm sure you're not", Sophia said. "I'd say you're rather brave, coming in here like this. It's never too late to take action. Everyone can do his part." Sophia reached under the counter and pulled out a piece of mimeographed paper. "How long have you lived in Middlesburg?"

Philip laughed. "I've only lived here for three days. I've had a streak of bad luck lately, but all that's going to change now. I already found a job at a grocery store, Ridge's place on Pike Street, and I'm living over at The Potter Boarding House on Brandywine."

She nodded. "I didn't think you looked familiar. Would you like an application?" She pushed the form towards him. "It costs nothing to join the council. It's a volunteer organization. We always need help passing out flyers and, if you want, even more important duties can be yours as well when you feel you're up to it."

Philip picked up the form and glanced over it. It required the standard information, age, phone number, address. There were also some oddball questions thrown in here and there. What was the last book you read? What role should The

United Nations play in foreign wars? If PEACE was an animal, what kind would it be? What would it look like? What would you name it?

Philip took it all in stride, nodded, and said, "Important duties? I don't know how ready I am for that much responsibility. I just want to check out one of your meetings, see what the people are like, if I'm even comfortable . . . ."

Sophia held her hand in the air. "Of course, of course. You don't need to make a decision now. Why don't you drop by our meeting tonight, if you're not busy?"

"Oh, no, I'm not busy. I barely know anyone in town. I wouldn't mind getting to know some people who . . . well, think the same way I do about things. It's hard sometimes, expressing yourself to strangers when you know you're in the minority. I mean, not that I'm a minority . . . ." He chuckled awkwardly. "Well, you know what I mean. You never know how they're going to react to you is what I mean."

Sophia leaned over the counter and patted Philip on the back of the hand. "If you believe in peace in the United States of America, then you *are* a minority. Just as much as a Negro in Mississippi or Arkansas. Or a Gypsy or a Jew in Nazi Germany. Oh, of course, we can hide our minority status more easily than the coloreds. But that doesn't mean we're in any less danger from violent reprisals. Why, many of our members have been harassed here in town. They've had stones with notes attached thrown through their windows, the word 'COMMIE' scrawled across the notes in blood."

"Commie?" Philip said. "They equate peace activism with communism here?"

Sophia nodded. "They do. In many ways this is a very backwards town. Even though we're so close to Madison, a university town, sometimes I think we're living in the Dark Ages here. This is a very conservative town you've wandered into, despite our activities on the council. How did you happen to end up here?"

Philip shrugged. "Luck? Happenstance? An accident? I lost my job in Chicago and had to leave. Not because anybody was making me leave, but because I was fed up with my life, my job, my girlfriend. I was writing little jingles for greeting cards. Can you believe it? Little lies that rhymed." He laughed bitterly. "I guess you might say I was pretty fed up with this whole country in general. In a lot of ways we're just a bunch of hypocrites, preaching peace in our Sunday sermons while blessing bombs to drop on the faceless masses, the ones actually making this world run through their sweat and their blood and their honest labor. I was tired of being used by the big drones above me. How was I any different than a slave?"

Philip sighed. "My job didn't leave me, I left my job. Heck, I was living from paycheck to paycheck anyway. Since it was the end of the month, I had just enough money for a ticket to Wisconsin. I picked Middlesburg as my destination, totally at random. I'd never even heard of it. Maybe that's why I picked it. No expectations. I couldn't be disappointed, could I?"

Sophia laughed. This time it seemed as if the smile were genuine. "I like you. I think the other members of the council might like you as well. What's your name?"

"Herbert O'Leary."

Sophia held out her pale hand. "Pleased to meet you, Mr. O'Leary. I'm Sophia Fenton. Our meeting tonight will be about promoting civil rights in the South, about drawing connections between our foreign policies and the human rights problems here on the home front. A local scholar named Robert Bingham will be delivering a lecture on the topic at six o'clock, and a discussion will follow."

"Do I need to bring anything?"

"Just yourself, and your mind, and that application. Oh, and a pen, so you can sign the form at the end of the evening."

Her smile had grown wider and warmer in the past ten minutes. She seemed far more attractive, less of an ice queen, when she allowed herself to express a genuine emotion.

"You're that confident I'm going to approve?"

"Oh, yes, I am. You'll see."

At exactly 6:00 p.m. Philip arrived at the address. It was just somebody's house with a nice little white picket fence surrounding it. There didn't seem to be anything ominous or special about it.

Philip strolled over to a tiny convenience store down the street and bought a pack of gum. He also asked for some change for the phone.

Outside the convenience store stood a phone booth. He slipped inside, closed the doors behind him, and dialed Eva's number. As the phone rang he glanced at his watch: 6:05. Then he heard Eva's voice: "Hello?"

"Sorry I'm late. My conversation with Sophia went better than expected. She invited me to some kind of discussion group. It's at a house on Caroldale and Dunfield. I'm just about to go inside."

"Good", Eva said. "Try not to go overboard at the meeting. Keep it at an even keel. Be enthusiastic, but not *too* enthusiastic. You understand what I mean?"

"I think so. I guess this means we can't see each other tonight."

"I'm kind of disappointed in that." He could hear the smile in her voice. He could hear her settling back and getting comfortable. He imagined her in bed, wearing a diaphanous nightgown. "It's been awhile since I met someone in this town I could really talk to. Imagine how difficult that's been for me. It's been . . . lonely sometimes. Maybe more

83

times than not." Was she saying all of this for the phone, in case someone was listening? Or was it genuine?

"Well, I guess we'll have to get together tomorrow night so I can give you an update. We can meet at that private place you mentioned."

"That sounds promising", she said. "Unless something more important comes up for you, if the meeting takes an unexpected direction let's say, we'll meet at six and then I'll drive you to a little spot I know just outside town. How does that sound?"

"Sounds . . . fantastic."

"But if an opportunity crops up during the meeting then take it. Don't bow out on my account. Understand?"

"Understood."

"I'll be seeing you, O'Leary."

"Be seeing you."

He hung up, wondering if he'd really pass up an opportunity like that just to hang out with a bunch of socialists two nights in a row. He had to stop a moment and tell himself he was being stupid. He wasn't a teenager. This was serious business. His obligation to the FBI was far more important than a "date" with a female, no matter how stunning she was.

He arrived at 7712 Caroldale Street at 6:15. A young woman, cute but no Eva, greeted him at the door. "You must be Herb", she said. "Sophia told us we might have a neophyte in our midst tonight. May I take your coat?"

"Oh, of course." He handed her the coat, and as she hung it on a wooden rack near the door she said, "Would you like something to drink?"

He found himself standing in a spacious living room that had been transformed into a low scale meeting hall. A little over a dozen people were grouped around a coffee table. Each person had a different drink in their hands. They were all laughing and talking excitedly. Sophia sat in between two middle-aged men, one of whom was puffing on a pipe. Outside that dreary office, with some color in her cheeks and laughter in her eyes, surrounded by people she liked, Sophia managed to look halfway decent.

"I'll have a Scotch", he said.

"My name's Lucy", the young woman said. She took him by the hand and guided him into the room, as if to make him as comfortable as possible. "This is my husband Donovan."

Donovan saluted him with his smoking pipe. "Always encouraging to see a new face around here", Donovan said. He seemed to be a full ten years older than his wife.

Lucy, that enthused smiled frozen on her face, introduced him to everyone else in the room. They seemed to be in the middle of a discussion regarding civil rights for Negroes.

"Let's face it", Donovan said. "It's hypocritical for us to pretend to be freedom fighters in these other countries when we have slaves right here at home that still need to be freed."

A redheaded man named Townsend, sitting on the other side of Sophia, crossed his left leg over his right, leaned back in his chair calmly, and said, "Aren't you exaggerating a little bit? After all, they're not literally 'slaves.'"

"I'm talking *literally*", Donovan said, "not metaphorically."

"See here", Townsend said, "it's this kind of talk that prevents our message from getting out to the common man on the street. The average joe doesn't want to be accused of being a slave owner when he knows he's not. We might actually be able to get some of these people on our side if we just softened the rhetoric a little bit."

"No, no, no", Donovan said. "We gain nothing by cow-towing to the lowest common denominator. That's just going to water our message down until there's nothing left. Pretty soon we're just all talk, no action. Which is what we're doing tonight."

"What would you have us do", Townsend said, laughing, "storm the Bastille?"

"A violent revolution would just blow back in our face *right now*", Donovan said. He emphasized those last two words. "There's a time and a place for everything. Right now we have to focus on getting the truth out to those who want to hear it, not sugar-coated lies for the robots who couldn't give a crap in the first place."

During this whole back-and-forth, Sophia's eyes never left Herb. He took a seat in the chair right across from her. He smiled and nodded at her politely. Then he turned his attention to Townsend and the others. In his peripheral vision, however, he could tell that her gaze was fixed on him, almost as if she were studying him, waiting for him to speak.

It's now or never, he thought.

"I agree with *you*", Philip said, gesturing toward Donovan. "The first thing all of us can do to facilitate change in this country is to not waste our time talking to people who have no interest in hearing what we have to say."

Everyone laughed at this line, even Townsend. They nodded in agreement. Lucy offered him a cigarette. He took it, lit it as Lucy placed another ash tray on the coffee table in front of him. There were already four or five ash trays sitting on the table. They were all overflowing with sad, discarded buds.

"Despite what most people assume", Philip said, "it's actually better to have less people on your side than more."

Townsend furrowed his brow, leaned back in the couch, and crossed his left leg over his right. "How so?"

"It's self-evident", Philip said. "Quality over quantity. Most organizations, no matter how noble their cause, are brought down by the incompetence of the people who run it. No organization, not even one devoted to bringing about social justice, is immune to this. The more people you have, the more stupid people you have. That's just pure statistics talking. Mathematics. Twelve truly devoted agents of change are far more effective than three thousand *semi*-devoted agents of change. Think about it. If you're only semi-devoted, you're no longer an agent of change, are you? You're an agent of the status quo, even if you believe or say otherwise. Anyone who wants to change the world just a *little bit* will be ineffective. If we want to bring social justice to the oppressed minorities in this country, we can't settle for just a little change. We need a big change. A very big change. The kind of change that happens slowly at first, through discussions like this. We're facilitating change just by having this discussion, I really believe that. However, there will come a time when far more drastic measures will be necessary. But the time's just not right for it."

"I agree with you there", Donovan said.

"What are you saying?" Townsend said. "Are you advocating a violent revolution?"

"Not necessarily", Philip said. "Let's call it . . . a *punctuated violent revolution*, okay? Strategic bursts of activity over the course of many years. In and out, real quick. You don't want to burn out all your resources on a single violent action. That won't change anything in the long run. You have to stretch it out over decades, keep the power structure on their toes. Instill fear in them. When they're too busy being afraid, they stop thinking. And when they stop thinking, they let their guard down. And that's when you sneak in one night and finish off all the fat cats right where they sleep." Philip leaned back in the chair, blew some smoke through his nose, and added, "Because as Thomas Kuhn once said, 'No change occurs in science until the old scientists die off.' The same is true with the social climate of a country. The people in power will never listen to reason. The best you can do is unbalance them and win tiny victories against them here and there. They'll use up *all* of their resources to prevent the minorities from getting even a small slice of their pie." Philip shrugged. "So you wait them out, but not passively. In the meantime these punctuated violent actions will serve to educate the right people, the receptive people, just a few here and there, as the decades roll by. As H.G. Wells once said, 'The future is a race between education and disaster.' Those enlightened few will rise to positions of power and make the necessary changes, weaken the structure from within, until the day comes when the whole structure is ready to fall with one last *push*." Philip took one last puff, then flicked the used up cigarette into the empty ash tray. It was a slam dunk. Philip smiled to himself, satisfied.

A brief moment of silence pervaded the room. Donovan glanced around and said, "What did you say this guy did for a living?"

"I didn't", Sophia said. "Go ahead and tell them, Herb. I think everyone will be amused."

For a second Philip was confused. After all, why would they be amused? "I used to write greeting cards", he said.

There was a delayed reaction, then everyone in the room burst into laughter.

Philip smiled along with them, not exactly knowing what the joke was.

He added feebly, "I just quit though."

Donovan reached across the coffee table and slapped him on the shoulder. "Their loss and our gain, Herb! Greeting cards! Jesus, what a monumental waste of talent!"

"Well . . . that's what I thought", Philip said. "That's why I came here."

"Listen", Donovan said, "we were just talking about how we need someone who's good with words to fashion slogans for our organization. Could you do work like that? You know, dream up snappy little rhymes that people can chant on a protest line or maybe paint on a sign. Stuff that's catchy, you know, but relevant, bon mots that'll catch people's hearts and eyes and minds. You know what I mean?"

Philip's eyes lit up as he realized how deeply this would anchor him into the organization. "Sure, yeah, I can do that."

"We have a protest planned in Alabama a month from now", Sophia said. "Can you have the lines written in a couple of weeks so we can have all the signs done before then?"

He shook his head back and forth and laughed.

"What's wrong?" Sophia said. "Is that too soon?"

"No, no, that's fine. It's just ironic is all. I quit the greeting card game because I thought I was wasting my time. Nothing I was doing was having an effect on the world, at least not for the better. Hell, if anything I was making it worse. But now I can actually use that training to do something worthwhile. How strange is that?"

"That's not strange at all", Sophia said. "It makes perfect sense to me. When we live our lives with the intent to change it for the better of our fellow man, then doors open for us and we find ourselves in the right place at the right time. Nothing could make more sense."

"I suppose you're right", Philip said. "Cheers." He held up his glass of Scotch.

"Cheers", Sophia said. They leaned towards each other and clinked glasses over the ash-strewn coffee table.

The next night he and Eva met at Sonny's Bar just as they had planned. She was wearing a stunning yellow dress with spaghetti straps that showed off her olive-toned, smooth shoulders—shoulders he very much wanted to kiss when he slid into the passenger seat of her Packard convertible.

She drove him to an isolated spot up in the hills just outside Middlesburg. From this vantage you could see the lights of the small town.

"The little place looks charming from up here", Philip said, "nothing like L.A. at all. L.A.'s too scattershot, sprawled out all over the place. This place, you feel like you could slip it into your back pocket. I think I kind of like the whole small town life."

Eva pulled a cigarette out of a thin silver case and offered one to Philip. "Sure", he said, and took one. She lit it for him as she smiled.

"You like doing that, don't you?" he said.

"Doing what?"

"Lighting *my* cigarette instead of the other way around."

She raised an eyebrow. "Is that backwards in your view?"

He laughed and shook his head. "No, not at all. It's refreshing. Say, how did you get into this business?"

She shrugged and blew smoke out the open window. The cloud drifted up out the window and into the starry Wisconsin sky. "I don't think we're supposed to get into personal information, Agent O'Leary."

"Don't give me any of that crap." He shifted in his seat and turned towards her. "We didn't have to meet all the way out here just so I could give you a five-minute update."

"Can you think of a safer place?"

"No. Don't get me wrong, I approve of the view." He reached out and stroked her cheek with the back of his hand. She let him go on for a half a second before lightly pushing his hand away. "Give me your thoughts", she said.

"Back in high school a girlfriend and I drove up Mulholland Drive one night. It's this curvy, dark road that snakes all the way up into the Hollywood Hills. You can see all of Los Angeles below you. There were some houses up there. Real fancy houses, the homes of actors and directors, etc." He glanced back out the window at the view. "I remember thinking, 'This must be what Zeus and the other gods felt like when they looked down on Greece from the top of Mount Olympus, as if you could just reach down and crush it all in your fist.'"

"I meant your thoughts about the case."

He smiled. "Yeah, I know."

"So is that what you want to do, reach down and crush it all?"

"Los Angeles, yes. But not this place. I want to preserve it. Save it."

"Maybe you'll have the opportunity to do that if you get on with your report."

"You haven't answered my question yet. How did you get involved in all this?"

Eva sighed, took a few more puffs on her cigarette, then said, "It's a long story, so I'll try to give you the compressed version. I don't want to bore you."

"I don't think that's possible."

"I got married when I was twenty-two, right after college. We met in a journalism class at NYU. Everything was fine for about three months, then Steve was drafted into the war. He had to go overseas to some godforsaken hellhole I'd never even heard of. He never came back. I was very angry. I was angry at everybody. I was angry at the entire United States. I hated it. Hated everything it stood for."

"But the United States didn't kill your husband, it was . . . ."

"I know, but that's not the way I saw it. Anyway, some of my college friends had become members of the Communist Party. They said it was the answer to end all this nonsense, all these endless wars. And I believed them. I was a sincere member for several years. My major was journalism, so I was able to help them write articles and such. They really liked me, or at least they seemed to, so they wanted me to leave New York and set up cells in various small towns throughout the Midwest. I started the cell in Madison, which is still there, but I'm convinced it's really low level stuff these days. There's a glass ceiling I can't get past for some reason. They won't let me rise above a certain level. Maybe it's because I'm a woman, or maybe they suspect the truth about me. I don't know. Since I'm trying to keep this short, just know that I had a revelation one day that the Party wasn't about ending wars, it was about starting them. All over the world. Their promised Utopia was a bunch of lies, and if I kept working for them I was going to get someone else's husband killed just like mine had been. So I offered my services to the FBI and now here I am. I've been one of their major liaisons here and in neighboring towns, like Madison, for awhile now."

"That's . . . that's an incredible story. But I don't understand. If you're here, why do you need me to infiltrate the Youth Group in Middlesburg? Everyone in the group must already know you and trust you, right? Why don't—?"

"They have no idea I'm a communist. That's how cells work. There could be six people in one cell, a different six people in a second cell, and if they're both located in the same city they could interact with each other every day and not know they're all communists. If one of them is caught and they squeal, only one cell is brought down and not two. Besides, I could never join the Youth Group. You have to be under thirty to join."

"Wait a minute. Earlier, when you said your husband was drafted into the war, did you mean World War II?"

Eva nodded.

"Jeez, I thought you were talking about Korea. I don't want to be rude but can I ask . . . "

Eva laughed. "Let's just say I'm not thirty-three yet. Surprised?"

Philip shook his head back and forth. "I'm floored. I thought you were ten years younger. Honestly, you don't look like you're—"

"I get that a lot. My mother was the same exact way. She looked twenty until she was forty-something. Have you decided to change your mind yet?"

"About what?"

"Well, if you decided *not* to be attracted to me anymore that would make this whole thing easier on both of us."

92

"Are you kiddin'? Now you're looking even better than before."

"I see. Just my luck."

"Hey, let me ask you something." He shifted his position and edged toward her. "Do you have a boyfriend, anyone you're seeing in town?"

"I've only dated one guy while I've been living here, but I broke it off just after it started. I live a double life, Herb. It's just not fair for me to build a relationship with someone when they don't even know who I really am. And I could never let them know."

"But you don't have to worry about that with me. I already know who you really are."

She flashed him a devilish smile. "Do you?"

"I'm sure you still have some surprises left for me." He leaned closer towards her, slipped his arm around her shoulders. She didn't tell him to remove it.

"You look like him", she said. Her smile had disappeared.

He just stared at her deep violet eyes for a second. "How so?"

"You have his smile."

"Is that good or bad?"

"I haven't decided yet. Steve only smiled when he was up to no good."

"Steve's not here." He slid his hand up her dress and felt the firmness of her nylon-covered thighs. "I am." He kissed her neck.

"Operatives aren't supposed to act this way", she said as she ran her fingers through his hair.

"So sue me. I didn't read the fine print." He nibbled on her ear lobe.

"We barely know each other."

"C'mon. Sometimes knowing each other *too* well just gets in the way, don't you think?" He leaned in for a kiss on the lips.

She pressed two fingertips against his mouth and pushed him away. "No, O'Leary. I don't think that at all. Give me

93

your report regarding your meeting at the Council." The Ice Queen act again.

"I'll give you one piece of information with each kiss. How about it?" Philip leaned towards her again.

She reared back and slammed her fist into his nose.

"Holy—!" His head snapped back and hit the window in the passenger seat door. "—*shit!*" he cried. He covered his nose with his hand. "Jesus Christ, you didn't have to do that, did you?"

"This has gotten way out of hand. Just give me your report and we'll go home."

"Fuck, am I bleeding?" He removed his hand from his nose and saw spots of blood on his fingers. "I'm *bleeding!*"

Eva gripped the steering wheel and turned the key in the ignition. "You can give me the report on the way back to town."

"Can't you at least give me a handkerchief or something?"

"No." Just as she was about to turn the key in the ignition, a light shone in their face. A flashlight. Someone was walking toward the car.

"Who the fuck is this now?" Philip said.

"I don't know", Eva said. There was a definite hint of nervousness in her voice. He watched as she reached into her purse and placed her hand on a snub-nosed .22 tucked into the inner flap of the purse.

"I didn't know you had one of *those* on you", Philip said.

"*Shh*", Eva whispered harshly.

"What's going on here?" said the voice outside. The dark, looming figure wore a policeman's uniform. "How many times have I told you kids—?"

The figure leaned down and peered into the car. "Oh", he said when he got a good look at the two of them. He seemed surprised. So did Eva, though Philip noticed that her grip relaxed on the hilt of the gun. She removed her hand from the purse and placed it on the steering wheel.

"Eva", the policeman said. "I didn't recognize your car."

"Good evening, Chuck. You really scared me. You came out of nowhere."

"Well, I've had a lot of practice. The high school kids like to come up here and do a lot of things they shouldn't be doing, if you get my meaning. I guess I don't have to spell it out to you two."

"No, you don't", Eva said. "We were just leaving."

The policeman was a middle-aged man, rugged, built like a bear. He squinted his eyes at Philip. "Is your nose bleeding?"

Philip said, "Just a little bit."

Chuck turned toward Eva. "Are you in any trouble?"

"No."

"Do you need to be escorted home?"

"Really, no. I'm fine. We have everything under control."

"If anyone's in danger here, officer", Philip said, "it's me. You should be offering *me* an escort."

"Who the hell are you? I ain't never seen you in town before."

"I just arrived a few days ago. My name is Herbert O'Leary. I work over at Ridge's grocery store."

"The grocery store? What the hell, Eva? Do you know this guy?"

"Of course I know him! Why else would he be in my car?"

"How long have you known him?"

"About three days."

"Three days? And you're already alone with him up here? Who knows who he is? *I* don't know this guy."

"You don't have to know him. I'm a big girl. I can take care of him myself."

"I can vouch for that", Philip said.

"If this guy has done anything to you, Eva, why I'll drag him out of the car right now and—"

"That won't be necessary", Eva said. "As I said, we were just leaving."

"Well, see that you do." The policeman stood up, nervously tapped his billy club against his thigh for a few seconds, then leaned down again and said, "Honestly, Eva, I can't believe you're carrying on with this guy all the way up here after only three god damn days when you refused to even—"

"What the hell is this?" Eva said. "Did you follow me up here? Was this really just a coincidence, or are you stalking me again?"

"I swear to God, it was a *coincidence*. This is my beat. I'm up here all the time. I just don't want to see you waste yourself on some drifter, that's all. Is that so wrong?"

"Herb's not a drifter. He lives here now. And since when is it the province of the local police to comment on my relationship choices? Is that *your* beat too?"

"No. No, ma'am."

"Now you want me to complain to the Captain again?"

"No, ma'am."

"I swear to God I've got a snub-nosed .22 in my purse and I won't hesitate to plug a hole in your skull if you don't get in your patrol car and leave me alone once and for all."

"Now you listen here, *I* don't have to leave! This is *my* beat. Why don't *you* leave like you said you were going to? I'm staying right here and doing my job. I'm not moving from this spot until my job is done here."

"Whatever, Chuck. See you around." Eva pressed her foot on the gas and sped down the winding road that led back into the city below.

"Now give me your report", Eva said tersely.

"Is *that* the guy you—?"

"Are you going to give me the report or do I have to contact my superiors at the Bureau and suggest we need a replacement here in Middlesburg? That wouldn't look good on your record, would it?"

Philip wiped the rest of the blood off with the back of his sleeve and said, "No, ma'am, it wouldn't. Okay. This is what happened." He leaned back in his seat and watched the pleasant countryside speed by. He even saw cows grazing on the side of the road. You never saw that in Los Angeles. He gave a detailed description of everyone at the meeting: their names, their ages, their styles of dress. He repeated almost everything they said verbatim without once referring to notes. He didn't need them. He'd had eidetic memory since he was a child. That was one reason he rose up through the Bureau so fast after having joined the white collar crime detail in L.A.

Philip was very proud as he repeated the extemporaneous diatribe that had so impressed the assembled council members. He expected Eva to give him a gold star, several of them.

Instead she said, "You're an idiot."

"What's wrong?"

"I told you to take it slow. I expressly told you not to overdo it, and instead you waltz in and have to dazzle them with your theatrics. What is this, a high school play for you? You want the applause all for yourself? You need to listen to me and take orders if you want to survive. This isn't a game. There's a reason why I carry a gun. We could be killed at any moment if we break character for even a second. What on earth were you thinking?"

"I . . . just wanted to impress them."

"Maybe you did, maybe you didn't. Maybe your little grandstanding stunt tipped them off and now they're leading you into a trap. Ever thought of that?"

"No. I thought you would be pleased. Honestly, Eva, I don't think they suspected a thing."

"You can't know that. I want you to pull back a bit. Go easy on the scintillating suggestions and the diatribes. If you keep it up, you're going to seem too good to be true. And you *are*. You can't let that kind of doubt creep into their mind. Be helpful, but don't take over the god damn meeting. You understand? Do I need to pin it to your chest?"

"Hey, are you just angry because of what happened up on the hill? Listen, I didn't take advantage of you. You seemed perfectly willing at first, lady. Don't give me mixed signals then expect me to know when you *really* want me to stop. I'm not a fucking mind reader."

Eva pulled off to the side of the road. She took a deep breath then said, "What you are is too young. This is crazy. I'm sorry I led you on. You reminded me of someone I used to love very much and I just wasn't thinking. It was stupid of me. I've been acting unusually stupid since I first met you. You're a nice kid and you're sincere. I don't want to hurt you."

"You should've thought of that before you slammed your fist into my face."

Eva burst out laughing. When Philip didn't laugh as well, she tried to stifle it. "We have a job to do and we just need to focus on that. Agreed?"

"I don't agree that I'm too young."

She nodded. "Of course you don't."

"I understand what you're saying, though. You're right. This is serious. People's lives are at risk, and I'm acting like a fraternity kid out on a date. I'm sorry."

"We both got carried away. It won't happen again. Listen, we still have to meet regularly. It's best to be public about it as much as possible. That's far less suspicious than the clandestine act. Naturally, people are going to assume we're an item. That's fine. That's going to be our cover. But you have to understand something: It's *just* a cover. It's not real. When we're alone, it's just business. It can never be anything more than that, okay?"

Philip nodded.

"When I say it can never be more than that, I don't mean that it *might* be more if you wait until the right moment to make your move. You're not courting me. For your safety and mine and for the integrity of this mission it can never be more than a ruse. As long as you're stationed here, I'm your superior. You'll follow my orders to the letter. Am I clear? Has it sunk in yet?"

"It's sunk in."

"Good." She held out her hand. "Welcome to Middleburg, Agent O'Leary."

He reached out and they shook hands.

"To the letter", he said.

Five days later, in the quiet darkness of her bedroom, he entered her slowly as she wrapped her legs around his thighs and caressed his shoulder blades with her soft hands. He buried his face into her neck and sank his teeth into her flesh. She whispered his fake name then said, "Don't leave any marks. Wait, don't stop what you're doing. Keep going . . . keep going." It was a paradox, and he didn't bother to reconcile it. He decided the last request took precedent over the first. So he dug his teeth in deeper. She didn't protest this time. He tried to remain motionless inside her. No thrusting, not yet. He wanted to commit every inch of her body to his memory. He didn't want to do this fast, not at all. He wanted to remember their time together as accurately as possible. With his eidetic memory, he'd be able to run the details of the evening through his mind over and over again, just in case this perfect moment never happened again. She sucked air through her teeth and clawed his spine with her painted nails. She lifted her legs up even higher and placed her feet on his butt cheeks and gyrated her hips against his pelvis, urging him into motion. "What're you waiting for?" she said. "Let's get to work, sweetie."

He started thrusting.

She demanded he go faster.

And he went faster.

He did everything she told him to do throughout that entire evening and into the dawn as well.

He kept his promise. He followed her orders.

To the letter.

The next morning, after only a few hours sleep, they lay in bed staring up at the ceiling, holding hands and laughing about nonsense.

"So . . . what happened to separating work and pleasure?" Philip said, smiling.

"I still think it can work", Eva said, suddenly adopting her more official sounding tone. "When we're working, and out in public, we won't be lovers."

"But we have to act like we are because that's our Bureau cover."

"Exactly", Eva said. "But when we're alone, like now—"

"We can drop the cover of being *fake* lovers—"

"And we can just be who we are." She turned to smile at him.

"That makes some kind of cockeyed sense." Philip leaned over and kissed her on the lips.

Pretty soon, they were at it again.

"I'm curious", Eva said, gasping for breath, "how many women have you been with before me?"

They lay side by side, spent at last. It was almost noon.

"Not many. It was hard getting girls to give you the time of day when I was growing up because I was so damn poor. I didn't have anything to offer them. So I had to win them over with my stunning personality instead. I did all right. I could count them all on one hand, though. Why do you ask?"

She cuddled up next to him. "Curious."

"I probably shouldn't be asking this, but since you started it: How many people have you been with?"

"Just my husband."

"Really? What about that cop, Officer Friendly?"

"We dated for awhile, but it never led to anything serious. It almost did. One night, in this very bed, in fact. But I changed my mind at the last second. And I told him to go. He was confused and angry. It was horrible of me, the way I did it. He's *still* confused and angry. I tried to explain it to him, but there was only so much I could say. I don't think he ever got over it."

"*Coitus interruptus.* That'll drive any man over the edge, especially a crazy cop. If you pulled that with me, I think I might've gone a little crazy myself."

He leaned over her, planted kisses all the way down to her flat stomach. As she ran her fingers through his hair he knew he couldn't give it another go, no way, but what the hell, at least he could show her a good time while he got his energy back. He planted his head between her legs and thought about that insane thick-necked cop and laughed to himself. Growing up in Bunker Hill, he hadn't developed a friendly relationship with cops. In high school he had been voted Most Likely To End Up In Jail, what with all those delinquent pranks he liked to pull. The idea of him becoming a Federal Agent would have been as likely as rocketing to fame as a movie star. And the cops in his neighborhood would have pegged him as a dropout by age sixteen. They treated him and everyone else in that neighborhood like shit.

They treated his parents worse. But of course, they deserved it. They deserved every bit of what they got.

As he slid his tongue between Eva's legs, as she shuddered with pleasure at his merest touch and clutched at the back of his head and moaned his name, he felt like he was secretly getting back at every cop who'd ever hassled him. In his mind

Officer Friendly became a symbol for the bullshit that was his past and Eva became a symbol for the brightness that would be his future.

⚡

Later that afternoon Eva sat on the edge of the bed slipping her panties and nylons back on and grilling him with all the questions they should've gotten to the previous night.

Philip lay back in bed with his hands behind his head and watched her get dressed. He liked to watch women get dressed just as much as he liked to watch them undress.

"What's the progress with the sloganeering campaign?" she said. The tone of her voice indicated that they had now switched over to the work mode of their relationship.

"They're impressed by my talent", Philip said. "Sophia asked for a whole slew of slogans for the upcoming bus boycott. She seems to be the de facto leader of the group. I'm due to turn in the new batch this Monday night at the next meeting. I can make a political point with a simple one-sentence rhyme better than they can do with a whole book. Simplicity is beyond them. That's the problem with the intelligentsia. They always take the long way around."

"Give me an example."

"We Shall Not *Buy*", Philip shouted, "Where We Cannot *Ride!*" He shrugged.

Eva laughed and nodded. "Simple but effective."

"Imagine a thousand people shouting it over and over again. The thing about me writing greeting cards wasn't just a cover. That's how I worked my way through college. It came easy and I could do it in my spare time."

"But writing greeting cards is a little bit different than writing political slogans." Eva slipped on her bra, then pulled her blouse over her head.

"Not really. It's exactly the same. I just thought to myself, 'How would Dr. Seuss do it if he were a commie agent instead of a children's writer?'"

Eva laughed again. "I like you better every minute."

Philip said, "You're not regretting making love to me yet? That's always a good sign. One girl started crying the second it was over. Imagine how uncomfortable that was."

"Tears of joy, perhaps?"

Philip shrugged. "She was Roman Catholic. Her parents were really heavy into the whole scene. Y'know the deal."

Eva nodded. "I see. I was raised Roman Catholic."

"Oh? I didn't mean to . . . ."

"No, no. It's okay. I stopped believing when my husband died." She finished buttoning her blouse, then slipped on her skirt.

"Well, that's kind of extreme. I mean, I *believe*, I just don't go off the deep end like some people. I don't think God cares if you and me . . . ."

"God doesn't exist", Eva said. "Not for me. That's just the way I feel about it."

"God brought the two of us together."

Eva crawled across the bed toward him and kissed him on the cheek. "We brought *ourselves* together. We can take at least that much credit, hm?"

"Sure", Philip said and they kissed again.

Eva nuzzled her head against his bare shoulder. "Have you ever read *Letters to the Earth* by Mark Twain?" Eva said.

"No", Philip said, "not that one."

"Read it when you get the chance. That'll explain how I feel about God."

"Why, what did Twain say?"

"'God is a malign thug.'"

Philip nodded. "I used to feel that way."

"Really? Why?"

"I wonder if Samuel Clemens had parents like mine." Philip reached out for the pack of Marlboros on the nightstand and pulled out a cigarette. Eva held two fingers up in a V, waiting. Philip slipped the cigarette between her fingers and lit it. Then he slipped one into his own mouth, lit it, took a few puffs. "This isn't something I talk about. The only reason I'm telling you is because . . . well, I guess that should be obvious. My parents were executed by the government. For treason. They were communists. Their trial made all the papers. They were no Rosenbergs, but they made quite a splash in California. They were part of a communist cell in L.A. that specialized in trafficking military secrets down into Mexico and from there to Moscow. The government convicted them on really flimsy evidence. All the liberals were up in arms about it. They should've been. The truth is, the government didn't really have a case. In fact, I think the FBI made up evidence against my parents just to get them convicted."

Eva stared at him aghast, "My God, that's horrible."

"No, it's not." Philip took a few more puffs off the cigarette. "Because they were guilty. I *knew* they were guilty. I was there during all their meetings. I heard what they were saying. Heard their plans. They had done exactly what the government accused them of doing. The Bureau just provided the evidence that they knew was true but couldn't prove. Faked documents and the like. You know how it goes."

"No, I *don't* know how it goes. The Bureau isn't supposed to pull crap like that. We're supposed to be—"

Philip held his hand in the air. "Please. I got over it a long time ago. I'm not bitter. I'm grateful. My parents were guilty and they got what was coming to them. They knew the consequences. They knew what might happen if they were caught. They were misguided. They thought they were fighting for peace on Earth, kind of like you when you joined, I guess. But in reality they weren't fighting for anything except a dictatorship."

"I'm surprised the Bureau hired you with a background like that."

"That's *why* they hired me. I never hid it from them. I turned a weakness into a strength. I told them that I knew better than anyone else how a communist thinks. I heard the rhetoric every day and night from the time I was old enough to think all the way until my parents were taken away from me when I was fourteen. Who better to infiltrate the commies? They checked out my background. They knew I was on the level. The only communists I had ever associated with were my parents, that's it. Well, and now you."

Eva smiled. "*Ex*-communist."

"I thought by joining the FBI I'd be making up for what my parents did. After a few months, though, I don't know . . . I realized it wasn't what I thought it was. But it's the only game in town, so I intend on sticking around."

"What do you mean, it wasn't what you thought it was?"

Philip shrugged. He reached out and caressed the back of her cheek. "Everything we say here stays under these sheets, right?"

"Do you really need to ask?"

Philip nodded tersely. "Okay. It's just that . . . when I first joined I thought the Soviet Union represented the worst dictatorship on the planet. And it does. But sometimes, now that I see how the government works from the inside, I don't know . . . it's as if the United States is a more subtle form of dictatorship. It commands your every move subtly, without ever having to slam a boot in your face like in *1984*. It just weighs you down with bureaucracy upon bureaucracy upon bureaucracy until you don't even have the strength to protest all the damn nonsense you have to deal with on a daily basis. Filling out forms and staying in the white lines and background checks and psychological screenings and loyalty oaths and blah blah blah. The best dictatorship would be the one that camouflaged itself as a democracy. Or a republic. Whatever. Sometimes I think the difference between the Soviet Union and the United States is the same difference between the Dodgers and the Angels. The difference between turquoise and blue."

"Wow, I . . . I didn't know you felt that way at all."

"Don't get me wrong. I still love this country, but sometimes I wonder if it's just because I was conditioned to, you know?"

Eva ran her hands over the hair on his chest. "I think I know exactly what you mean", she whispered.

"Sometimes", Philip said, "I think I'd like to go to a desert island somewhere, some place that's not owned by either side. Some neutral territory in the shade where you could just relax for a couple of minutes without having to worry about ideology. But then I guess we'd have to leave that hefty Bureau paycheck behind, and we certainly can't afford to do that, can we?"

Eva's smile had transformed into a frown. She looked like she was a million miles from Earth. "I guess not, no."

"Hey, did I say anything wrong? Don't go thinking strange thoughts about me. I'm a loyal American. I would never do anything to—"

"Oh no, it's not that. What you said just started me thinking about things . . . about Steve and the war and—"

"Hey. Just because your husband was taken from you, just because my parents were taken away from me, that doesn't mean God's not out there. I realized I couldn't just sit around blaming my parents for the rest of my life and so I got up and did something about it."

"You give God credit for that?"

"I don't know. Maybe. Maybe not." He laughed. "You know, at one point I became Roman Catholic just because it represented everything my parents hated. Now I don't know what the hell I am. The point is, you can't live in the past, not when the future's right here next to you."

"You're right", Eva said, "of course you're right." They embraced and kissed again. "Hey, let's get some coffee down at Morrie's and take in a show. How about it?"

"Sounds great. Just let me get my pants. Now that our work is done, we can start on some much needed playtime."

They both laughed as Philip pushed her out of bed and onto the carpet. Eva reached up and grabbed his wrist and pulled him down on top of her. They kissed, and pretty soon Philip's parents were once more nothing more than what they had always been.

A pair of electrocuted ghosts.

In the car on the way to Morrie's Eva put her hand on Herb's knee and said, "Herb, do you think any of them suspect?"

He glanced at the townspeople through the window of the car, the ones who were out for a Sunday stroll along Parsons Street.

"About you and me? I hope so."

"You know that's not what I mean. The communists. Do they suspect you?'

"They might. I think they've been putting me through the paces, subtly. I think Sophia suspects me most of all."

"Why do you say that?"

"I don't know. She's always staring at me, as if sizing me up for a meat locker. At the meetings, if I happen to glance around the room for a moment, I'll catch her doing it. It's like she's *studying* me."

Eva sighed. "That's hardly a good sign."

"She's just on her guard, for good reason." Philip reached into his shirt pocket and pulled out an object. He casually took Eva's hand into his and spread her palm open. He slipped the object into her grip. It was smooth and metallic, shaped like a rectangle. It wasn't pristine. Scuff marks stained its golden surface. It looked liked a cigarette lighter. "You know what that is?" Philip said.

Eva tossed the lighter into the air once or twice, catching it each time. "Well, something tells me it's not a cigarette lighter. Is it a camera?"

"I've seen other agents use devices like this in the field", Philip said. "The Bureau gave it to me before I left. If there's someone standing next to you they won't even hear a click. If Sophia ever invites me into a meeting more sensitive than the Youth Group, I'm going to document everyone who's there."

"I guess even *your* memory is no match for photos", Eva said, slipping the lighter back into his shirt pocket. "Did the Bureau tell you how many agents were sent here before you?"

Philip just nodded.

"Be careful, Herb. The first agent disappeared in 1947, eight years ago. You understand?"

He patted her on the knee. "Eva . . . I appreciate what you're doing, but I knew what I was—."

"Of course you did. I just want you to be especially careful around this Sophia. Never let your guard down around her. Never allow yourself to believe that this woman is . . . I don't know, your friend."

"Why would I think that?"

"It's just based on what you've said about her. I don't like her at all."

"She's just some smart ass girl who happens to be in a minor position of power."

"Sometimes minor positions of power can be more dangerous than major ones. Call it my professional instinct. Or call it woman's intuition. Just be on guard around her, okay?"

He spread his hands and said, "Okay."

The next day, around 4:30 p.m., he received a call at the grocery store from Sophia herself. That was a first.

"There's a meeting tonight at my apartment at 5:00 p.m. It's important that you be there."

Philip glanced at his watch. That didn't leave him much time. "Nobody mentioned that at the last meeting", he said.

"It's . . . sort of an emergency meeting. You *need* to be there."

"Okay. I'll try to get off early and head on over. What's your address?" Sophia told him and he jotted it on the back of a receipt. "I might be a little late."

"I'll be expecting you", Sophia said and hung up.

Philip tried to call Eva from the phone booth across the street from the grocery store, but her line was busy. She preferred to have him tell her exactly where he was at all times in regard to these meetings. But there was no time.

Philip arrived at Sophia's apartment at ten minutes after five. It was the first time he'd ever been there.

She opened the door and smiled at him and said, "You took forever."

"I know how you like promptness."

"Get in here."

He entered the apartment, and was surprised to see a dinner table set for two. With candles burning in the middle.

"I have a surprise for you", Sophia said.

"Where's the meeting?" Philip said.

Sophia closed the door behind him. "This is the meeting. Just you and me." She pulled a chair out for him. "Do you mind?"

"Of course not." He took a seat. "Why would I?

"Wine?" Before he could respond, she had already begun pouring it into his glass.

"That's . . . no, that's fine", he said. "No more, please."

She set the bottle down on the tablecloth, knelt in front of him, placed her hands on his knee and said, "You've been doing excellent work for the council. I've had a little talk with my superiors at the main headquarters and they wanted me to extend an invitation to you. We have a kind of . . . discussion group that occurs separate from the meetings. Would you like to join?"

"A discussion group? How does that differ from what we do normally?"

"It's only for a select few. I was very pleased when headquarters told me I could approach you with this . . . with this proposal." She rubbed her hand up and down his leg. "You've really impressed me with what you've had to say at the meetings. You have genuine solutions, real ideas on how to make this country better. I can see you're not all talk. You genuinely want to change things."

Philip nodded. "I want to change things."

"Let's change things tonight . . . between you and me."

She leaned toward him and kissed him on the lips. He hadn't expected that she was even capable of behaving this way. He was too surprised to do anything but let it happen. Just for a few moments. He had to assess the situation. The Bureau had ordered him to get as close to the leader as possible. Any opportunity to win her trust, they said, should be taken without hesitation.

"Sophia." He grabbed both of her hands and gently pushed them away. "I don't know if this is a good idea. For the council, I mean." He stared into her hazel eyes through her glasses and suddenly wondered what she looked like beneath that librarian outfit.

"This is entirely separate from the work we do for the council", Sophia said. "The two halves never need to touch. Except behind closed doors. Like now."

"I . . . listen, I have a girlfriend, Sophia."

"I've seen you with her. I'm a little . . . disturbed by your choice. She's quite bourgeois, isn't she? I don't think she's right for you. With a mind like yours, you think you can just settle down and raise 2.2 children in the suburbs behind a white picket fence? Please. I'm saving you from a living death." She straddled his legs, wrapped her arms around his neck, and leaned towards him again.

"I'm in love with her."

"That's ridiculous. And even if it were true, so what? I'm not going to tell her what happens here. I have no interest in marrying you. I have no interest in stealing you away from her. Nobody owns you. I just want to fuck you, that's all. You can keep her. Feel free to do what you want with her. But when you meet me here, you're mine. At least for a little while." She ran her hands up and down his chest. "Just long enough to get your face out of my god damn head. I don't want you there but you are and I need to do something to get you out. I decided this is the only way. That's fair, isn't it?" With that last sentence, the iciness in her voice broke at last and he could hear the desperate tone that hid just beneath her carefully built façade.

Philip knew exactly what it was like to need release from one's own head.

He stared into her pleading eyes for what seemed like a very long time.

He met up with Eva later that evening. She picked him up outside Morrie's.

"You're late", she said as he slid into the passenger seat of her convertible.

"I had an emergency meeting. With Sophia."

"Oh? And what happened?"

"She invited me to join an ancillary organization called The Orpheum Solutions Group. We meet tomorrow at eight o'clock."

"Who else was at this meeting?"

"Just Sophia. And me."

"That's the first time that happened."

"I thought it was unusual", Philip said.

"She was trying to get your guard down. Did you . . . remember what I said?"

Philip nodded. "I was careful."

"Good. This is good. This means she's trusting you more and more. She's the one who's letting her guard down, not the other way around."

Eva placed her hand on his knee and tightened her grip. "This is exactly what we've been waiting for. No agent has ever gotten as high as the Solutions Group. If you make a good splash there, who knows? We might be close to figuring out who Sophia takes her orders from."

"That's great." He tried to smile, but it was difficult.

"You sound sad."

"Oh . . . it's nothing. I was just thinking, if we actually bust this ring then . . . you know . . . I'll have to move on to another case. I'll never see you again."

Eva smiled. He didn't think he'd ever seen a more angelic face. She was truly an angel, an angel who didn't deserve to be betrayed. She reached out and stroked his cheek. "That's so sweet", she said. She leaned toward him and they kissed.

"Who knows?" she said. "Perhaps this case will go on forever. They're so many layers within layers. Maybe if we're lucky . . . it'll never end."

"I want it to end", Philip said, "so you and me can leave this place together."

Eva glanced down at her lap.

"I . . . I don't know about that, Herb."

"What? Why?"

"This . . . this is my life. I've never known anything else. Just . . . Steve. Grieving for Steve, and then working for the

Bureau. Trying to bring these people down. I have to stay here and see it through till the end."

"But what if it doesn't end?"

Eva sighed. She stroked his cheek once more. "Let's not think about that. Let's just think about right now." She planted small kisses on his neck and whispered, "About you and me and my bedroom tonight and the sun rising in the morning and the sounds you make when you . . . ." She wrapped her arms around him and hugged him. He hugged her tight.

When they arrived at her apartment he told her he was tired from working all day and needed to take a shower. She wanted to take the shower with him, but he begged off and said he was going to be real quick about it. He desperately washed Sophia's scent off every part of his body.

Their sex was rough that night, rougher than ever before, as Philip tried to expunge his guilt by giving Eva everything he had to give and more.

Afterwards, she told him it was the best ever.

Sophia grew bored with his performance in bed. She told him so.

"Don't get me wrong, you're still cute, but you desperately need a deeper education." Sophia's extracurricular interests were far more esoteric than Eva's. At first Philip didn't know how to react when she began tying his wrists to her bed posts with leather straps, but she reassured him he would not be harmed. He did not refuse. Her peccadilloes began to interest him more and more. Each time he visited her apartment, she peeled back another layer and revealed a kink stranger and deeper than the last.

And each time he collaborated with her in this way, he learned another vital piece of information that he could pass on to Eva . . . who then passed it on to her superiors back at the Bureau.

Sophia finally told him exactly what she was one day while she had him strapped to the bed. She straddled his cock, placed a pair of metal clamps on his left nipple and twisted. He didn't even cry out this time. He was getting more and more used to her punishment. In fact, he was beginning to . . . .

"We both know what we are", she said, "why don't we both admit it?"

"What're you talking about?" he said. He felt stupid and ashamed. He'd allowed her to humiliate him like this and now . . . he'd compromised the entire operation. Sophia had never wanted him sexually at all. This was all just a game to lure him into a position where she would torture him until he admitted his Bureau affiliations. He girded himself for the worst. He didn't care how much she tortured him. He would never tell.

Never.

"You know god damn well what I'm talking about." Sophia twisted the clamps again.

"God damn it!" he cried and tried to push her off him but the straps were too tight. He glanced at his wrists. They were growing white from lack of blood flow.

"You're no bleeding heart ex-college-kid looking to free the niggers and you know it", she whispered. She twisted the clamps again. "You care about the pickaninnies as much as I do." She twisted the clamps again, harder this time. He bit his bottom lip to keep from screaming. "I'm going to ask a question and you're going to answer it, my little comrade. Without hesitation." She pulled out another pair of clamps and attached them to his right nipple. "Are you now or have you ever been a member of the Communist Party?"

He didn't now what to say, so he remained silent.

"That's exactly what I wanted to hear", she said and twisted both clamps at the same time. He grunted in anger and frustration as blood began to trickle down his chest. She reached under his pillow and pulled out a copy of a little hardcover book. She covered the title with one hand while she read the line, "'During the lifetime of great revolutionaries, the oppressing classes relentlessly pursue them, and treat their teachings with malicious hostility, the most furious hatred and the most unscrupulous campaign of lies and slanders.' Who wrote that?"

"Vladimir Ulyanov", he said, "of course. It's from his book *State and Revolution,* written in 1917. What the hell is this, a fucking quiz show?"

"I knew it!" Sophia said and started thrusting against him fast and hard. "A fellow traveler. I could smell it on you the second you walked in the door. The Leninist tendencies were evident, hidden between every syllable that came floating out of your mouth. You were far too intelligent to be a mere capitalist. I understand, Herb. You had to keep the truth close to your vest, just in case. Just in case we weren't who you hoped we were. But now you don't have to hide. You've found the right place, lover." She leaned over him and sank her teeth into his neck while still riding him. His penis bent backwards so far he could almost feel it beginning to snap. She reared back and began bouncing down on top of him so enthusiastically he could feel the bruises already forming on his thighs while she held the book out in front of her and read Lenin's twenty-eight-year-old proclamations in between animalistic grunts:

"The overthrow of bourgeois rule can be accomplished only by the proletariat, the particular class whose economic conditions of existence prepare it for this task and provide it with the possibility and the power to perform it. While the bourgeoisie break up and disintegrate the peasantry and all the petty-bourgeois groups, they weld together, unite and organize the proletariat. Only the proletariat—by virtue of the economic role it plays in large-scale production—is capable of being the leader of all the working and exploited people, whom the bourgeoisie exploit, oppress and crush, often not less but more than they do the proletarians, but who are incapable of waging an independent struggle for their emancipation."

Sophia slowed to a halt, the musty hardcover book dropping out of her hand and onto the rope-strewn floor, then collapsed onto Philip's chest.

Philip would have stroked her long soft hair, if not for the fact that he couldn't move his wrists.

Later that night Philip called Eva from a pay phone outside his boarding house and said, "A major breakthrough. She finally admitted it to me."

"That she's a communist?" Eva said.

"Of course, I told her I was too", Philip said. "She promised she's going to take me higher."

"That's just what we've always wanted", Eva said, almost sadly. Then her usual cheeriness returned to her voice. "Why don't you come over here and we can celebrate? I have champagne I've been saving for a special occasion. I'll light those candles you like so much."

At one time that would have been enough to satisfy him. But not anymore. "I'd really like to, but I'm so tired, honey. Let's do it tomorrow night, okay?"

"Of course", she said. "I understand." She sounded disappointed, but Philip didn't know what to say to make her feel better. He couldn't go over there, not in this condition, not with all these cuts and bruises on his body.

"I'll call you tomorrow morning", he said. "I love you, Eva."

"Herb", she said, almost whispering. "I . . . I love you too."

He hung up on her.

116

It wasn't until he was in bed and half-asleep that he realized he'd never uttered those words to her before. He'd planned on saying them under somewhat more romantic circumstances.

He drifted off while thinking about blood and semen and Sophia's long brown hair draped across his bruised, naked thighs and her red mouth wrapped around his cock and the look on Father's face as they dragged him away and the hand of Vladimir Ilyich Ulyanov rising from a grave of useless words words words.

He dreamed that night, but not about Sophia or Eva or his father or Ulyanov.

He dreamed about strange lights darting about the skies above Bunker Hill when he was just a boy.

The next afternoon Philip was surprised when Sophia invited him to a meeting about UFOs.

"A meeting about *what*?" Philip was on the phone at the grocery store and Old Man Ridge was yelling at him to get back to work. He'd heard exactly what she'd said, but asked her to repeat it anyway.

"A UFO meeting", Sophia said. "You don't know what UFOs are?"

"Of course I know what—." He cut himself off, as he found the very mention of the topic to be embarrassing. "I thought we were going to the Solutions Group tonight."

"We are. I'll meet you outside your work at five on the dot. We'll have to drive there."

"Where're we going?"

"Madison."

Even though the old man was still riding him, he immediately hung up and called Eva to tell her where he was going and who he was going with. If Sophia was picking him up at five on the dot (and if she said five on the dot she meant exactly that), he would have no other opportunity to let Eva know his whereabouts.

"What do you make of this whole UFO thing?" Philip said.

Eva said, "That's a quizzer. I'm eager to find out. Call me at the soonest opportunity." Eva told him to be careful again, and Philip told her he would. He told her he would miss her.

Sophia's car rolled up to the front of the store at five. On the way to Madison they discussed nothing even remotely personal. Commie shop talk, that's all. Neither of them mentioned what had happened between them the night before.

They parked outside the University of Wisconsin at around 5:30 p.m., then Sophia led Philip toward a packed lecture hall where someone with the improbable name of Pythagoras Invictus was speaking about "The Coming of the Space Brothers." The lecture had already started, so they had to be quiet as they made their way to a couple of empty seats way in the back of the room. Invictus was a small, very thin Italian man who had the look of an ascetic. He had a soft voice and gentle eyes. A calm temperament, like that of a monk. Philip sat and listened to this man spew the most outrageous drivel he'd ever heard in his life.

"On the planet Orpheum no one has to work for a living", Pythagoras intoned into the microphone. "Everyone is connected mind to mind; therefore, no one on Orpheum would ever allow a fellow man to starve on the streets. If one person feels pain, all feel pain. The collective consciousness of the planet can only maintain balance if every single aspect of the organism is working in harmony with every other aspect."

Someone in the front row, a young college girl, raised her hand enthusiastically. Pythagoras smiled and gestured toward her with his hand outstretched in a slow, deliberate manner. This guy acted like an alien himself.

Pythagoras said, "We have not yet reached the Question and Answer portion of the lecture; however, I can see how eager you are to ask a question of me, and so you shall."

"Yes, Mr. Invictus, it just struck me that what you're describing sounds almost like a communistic system."

Some startled murmurs erupted from the lecture hall. Pythagoras smiled and nodded and calmed down the audience with a mere sweep of his thin, expressive hands. "I myself, of course, do not support any human political system. The only system I personally endorse is the non-human system of Biological Harmony as practiced on Orpheum. This is not a voluntary political system. It is not a democratic system. Nor is it a socialistic system. The Orpheums operate out of pure instinct, like ants. Very enlightened, intelligence ants but ants nonetheless. They could never opt their way out of their system or vote their way out of it. It would be like your arm electing not to be a part of your body. It's impossible. We human beings lack this mind-to-mind facility. We've lacked it for a very long time. Perhaps one day, with help from the Orpheums, we will regain this talent. But to address your point as succinctly as possible, young lady, it is true that the political system that most closely resembles the one on Orpheum would be those practiced in communistic countries such as the Soviet Union." Some offended murmurs erupted from the audience again. Pythagoras didn't seem rattled at all. He just kept talking: "Understand that the political system in the Soviet Union resembles the one on Orpheum like a pigeon resembles a pterodactyl. They might be related, but one is a poor substitute for the other."

"So you don't support communism?" the young lady asked.

Some people behind the girl openly laughed at her question.

Pythagoras smiled kindly and shook his head. "Oh dear me, no. As I said, I support no human political system."

"But, Pythagoras", the girl said with machine gun delivery, almost out of breath, "isn't it true that if we humans are limited to the choices available to us here on Earth—and by what you've said I assume we are, at least for now—then the closest approximation to the perfect, Orpheum-like existence you've described can be found only by adopting a communistic form of government; at least temporarily, until we humans have evolved a little more?"

Pythagoras thought about it for a second, then nodded and said, "I suppose when you put it that way, yes, that's true, but I don't advocate that personally. I advocate nothing except Biological Harmony."

Philip leaned toward Sophia and whispered in her ear, "What the hell is this shit? The educational system has changed a lot since I was in college. How the hell can they let a guy like this talk on a college campus?"

Sophia smiled and said, "The college just rents out the hall to whoever will pay their fees. We still have freedom of speech in this country, or so they tell me. Can't you tell what's going on? Why do you think I brought you here?"

"I have no idea."

Sophia sighed and laughed, one of the few times he'd seen her do so. Even when she laughed, however, she still sounded icy and distant somehow. "Pythagoras is one of us. He's spreading our message through a different medium, one that's so outlandish no one in power has ever bothered to pay attention to him or shut him down. And yet his message gets out to thousands of more people than any pamphlet or broadside you or I have ever written."

Philip glanced back at the unassuming little man. Behind him on the stage was a huge banner that read: WE WELCOME YOU, SPACE BROTHERS! There was also a chalk board on which had been drawn a crude representation of the Orpheums' insignia. If you squinted your eyes and tilted your head to the side and studied it long enough, it actually looked like an abstract hammer and sickle.

Philip laughed slightly. He turned to Sophia and said, "How could this guy be getting away with this?" Real communists had been jailed for making far less radical statements.

Sophia smiled. "People will accept a revolutionary message as long as it's disguised with a little touch of fantasy. We've always recognized the value of fantasy in all its forms. Some of our most popular children's writers are fellow travelers. Perhaps you'll meet them someday."

"Are there other people out there like this Pythagoras fellow?"

"Of course. There are several dozen making the rounds of college campuses even as we speak."

"Was this your idea?"

"I wish I could take credit for it, but no."

"Whose idea was it?"

"Perhaps you'll meet them someday, if you conduct yourself well at the meeting tonight."

Philip had to sit and listen to a bunch of bullshit being tossed around the room by a strange cross-section of people. Some of them were just plain insane. Others were clearly intelligent and articulate, and really should've known better. And yet all of them had something in common: the intense desire to believe in something greater than themselves, something other than the shopworn concepts of the Christian God. As Philip sat and listened to them all asking questions about the paradise-like society of Orpheum, he realized that it should've been no great surprise that the communists would use the flying saucer fad to their advantage. Communists, too, were people who were so socially handicapped that they needed to be a part of something greater to make up for what was lacking in themselves. Philip's father was the perfect example. Philip's father had spent his entire life in a dream world, and he tried as much as possible to drag Philip down into that world. Philip's father explained to him once that his constant promises of an imminent communist utopia were never lies at all, but dreams of a better future. To this day Philip saw little difference between dreams and lies. He was determined to keep his feet planted firmly in reality. He had seen firsthand would could happen when people allowed themselves to confuse dreams and wishes with the real world. And now he was trapped in a room full of such losers.

Philip leaned toward Sophia's ear and whispered, "How many of the people here in the audience are fellow travelers?"

Sophia said, "Very few of them. Some of them are plants who ask the exact right questions at the exact right time, but most of them are just typical bourgeois Americans . . . and as you know, typical bourgeois Americans are only this close to being swayed to our side *if* they can be shown the truth in such a way that they'll believe it. For these people here, well, this is the only way they'll believe it."

Up on the stage Pythagoras ran a scratched 16mm film supposedly taken during his trip to Orpheum. It was clearly hoaxed, shot in some semi-professional film studio, and yet everyone in the room seemed enthralled. The social strata of Orpheum were based on Marxist notions of the perfect civilization. It was a parable, pure and simple.

Philip whispered, "Who wrote the script for this thing?"

"I contributed to it", Sophia said with a sly smile on her face. "In fact, I wrote the initial draft."

Philip couldn't help but be impressed. "Really? How did you do it?"

"I studied literature. A lot of the early science fiction writers used the medium to write socialist parables. *Looking Backward* by Edward Bellamy, *The First Men in the Moon* by H.G. Wells, *The Maracot Deep* by Sir Arthur Conan Doyle, and so on. I just threw a bunch of these ideas together and updated them a little bit.

That's what the writers in Hollywood do these days. It's the same process. Ever seen *The Day the Earth Stood Still?*"

Oddly enough, Philip *had* seen it one night with a bunch of his college friends. "You're not saying you had anything to do with that, are you?"

Sophia laughed and patted his hand. "I wish. It could be that a comrade had his hand in the script. Who knows? It doesn't really matter to us if the screenwriter's a communist or not. Either way, we've drawn upon such films to make Pythagoras's presentation far more convincing."

After the presentation was over, Pythagoras stuck around and shook hands with his admirers and chatted it up. "Let's introduce you", Sophia said. She rose to her feet and motioned for Philip to follow her.

Pythagoras seemed to be engaged in an intense conversation with a wide-eyed sixteen-year-old girl who clutched a copy of his book in her hands. A stack of such books sat on the table behind Pythagoras. An old fat woman with blue hair was selling copies of the book for $3.50 each. As Sophia tried to attract Pythagoras's attention, Philip wandered over to the table and picked up one of the books. It was a hardcover adorned with a crude illustration of gleaming crystalline spires on Orpheum. The title of the book was *How Long Will the Flying Saucer Paradise Be Denied Us?* On the back of the book was a photo of Pythagoras standing beside his adoring wife, a middle-aged Italian woman who was shorter and stouter than Pythagoras. He had a second book as well which was available in paperback. It was called *The Watchers Are Watching.* Philip reached into his pocket, pulled out a ten dollar bill, and bought a copy of each.

Sophia walked over to him and said, "You don't have to do that. I have extra copies."

"It's for the cause", Philip said and handed the fat woman his money.

Sophia nodded in approval. "Very well", she said.

Both of these copies were going straight to Eva—and through her to the FBI—along with his latest report.

"Sophia", Pythagoras said, his smile widening even further. "I didn't see you in the audience. How long have you been here?"

Pythagoras signed a book for the sixteen-year-old girl. Philip casually raised up on his tiptoes to see what he was writing. It looked like a phone number, and a hotel room number underneath it. It had never occurred to Philip that UFO contactees could be chick magnets, but apparently . . . .

The girl ran off, flushed with excitement. Philip wondered if she was going to be having a different and more illegal contactee experience later on this evening.

"We arrived halfway through the lecture", Sophia said, standing up rail-straight and trying to adopt her official demeanor. "You were in fine form as always."

"Thank you, my dear." He lifted her hand upwards and leaned down to kiss it. "There's something different about you today, my dear. Why, you're absolutely glowing. I've never seen you like this. I wonder why . . . ?"

He stroked his smooth chin as his gaze rested upon Philip.

"I'm just pleased to see you again", Sophia said, glancing down at the ground.

"Indeed. Are you sure it has nothing to do with this charming young man you've brought with you? I see you have an excellent taste in books, my friend. Would you like me to sign them?"

"This is Herb O'Leary", Sophia said. "He's done great work for us lately."

"Sure", Philip said and handed the books to Pythagoras who signed both of them with a flourish. Pythagoras even added child-like pictures of flying saucers beneath both signatures. "Thank you very much", Philip said. "I'm honored."

"Oh, you don't have to say that for my sake", Pythagoras said. "Instead tell me what dear Sophia is like in bed. I've always wondered. She seems so rigid and proper all the time, it's hard to imagine her really letting go long enough to be truly intimate with another carbon-based life form."

"Pythagoras, please", Sophia said, "Herb and I have similar political interests but—"

"Is that what they're calling it these days? Please, we needn't speak in euphemisms. On Orpheum everyone speaks plainly. They mean what they say. You could learn from this." For a moment Philip wondered if this man had been playing the role of the contactee so long that he'd begun to believe his own lies.

"Unfortunately, I've never had the pleasure of meeting the Orpheums", Sophia said. "Apparently they haven't found me worthy enough."

"Oh, but they will, they will. Just give them time." Pythagoras put his hand on Sophia's elbow and led her away from Philip. "Please excuse us, Mr. O'Leary", Pythagoras said, "but Sophia and I have to discuss something in private."

Philip remained standing beside the table, leafing through one of the books, while glancing at Pythagoras and Sophia out of the corner of his eye. They stood very close together near the base of the stage, Pythagoras still gripping her elbow. For the most part Pythagoras spoke and Sophia nodded. She finally said a few sentences, then Pythagoras patted her on the arm and walked away as some admirers trailed behind him.

Sophia put on her unaffected face as she walked back over to Philip.

"What was that all about?" Philip said.

"He wanted to know if you were coming to the meeting tonight. So I told him you were."

"And what did he say?"

"He wanted to make sure you were coming to the meeting because you were an asset, and not just because I was fucking you and trying to impress you."

"How the hell does he even know we—?"

"He's awfully perceptive. Sometimes I think the son of a bitch really is from outer space." Sophia was clearly flustered. She wasn't the type of person who liked to take orders.

"Is he your superior?"

"In a way. He's been in this game far longer than I have. He's lived in Wisconsin all his life. He knows everyone here, knows which comrade will have the specific skill we need for a particular operation. Thanks to Pythagoras's efforts, our local cells have grown considerably ever since 1947."

Philip remembered that 1947 was the same year the first FBI agent was sent to Middlesburg, the first one who vanished.

"Is Pythagoras his real name?" Philip said.

"Of course not. That's the name the alien gave him. Come on. We have to get to the meeting place. We don't want to make a further bad impression on our ambassador from the stars." She started walking towards the exit. Philip followed her.

"The name the *alien* gave him?" Philip said, confused.

Sophia glanced at him, her brow furrowed, as if she were confused by his confusion. "Alien?" she repeated. Then she laughed. "Oh. Well, it's the name the alien *supposedly* gave him. Sometimes it's easy to forget that it's all just a story. When you tell yourself something long enough it can become very real at times . . . . You know what I mean?"

Thinking of his father, Philip said, "I know exactly what you mean."

They walked out into the sunlight. Philip caught a glimpse of Pythagoras slipping into the passenger seat of an expensive convertible. His wife was driving.

The poor woman, Philip thought.

But seconds later he thought: Then again, maybe she's not even his wife.

And maybe I'm not Herb O'Leary.

And maybe this isn't Wisconsin.

126

And maybe Sophia isn't really Sophia.

And maybe Eva isn't really Eva.

And maybe my father wasn't a lying traitor after all.

And maybe flying saucers hail from the planet Orpheum in the outer spiral arm of the Milky Way galaxy.

The meeting that night was held at the house of one of the committee members. It was a typical house on a typical block. A white picket fence surrounding the yard, a dog chasing its tail around a tree, etc. It was all a front. The living room hosted an eclectic grab bag of characters. Young and old, hip and straight, loud and silent, all sorts of personalities were mingling in the tastefully decorated home. Upon arriving, Sophia left Philip alone in the living room and went into the kitchen to seek out Pythagoras. Philip found himself standing next to a young Asian man with short hair dressed in a snappy business suit. The man leaned against the mantle smoking a cigarette. Philip didn't think there was anything odd about the man until he got a closer look at him. At that point the gentleman turned to him and started speaking in a woman's voice: "You're new here." A beautiful voice.

"I-I came here with Sophia", Philip said. He had to speak loudly to be heard over the raucous jazz band playing on the stereo. He tried not to seem flustered, but it was clear that this was a woman dressed as a man.

The woman raised one eyebrow. "I didn't realize she *knew* any men."

"What's that supposed to mean?"

"From my experience her interests lay in . . . *other* areas."

Philip had no feelings for Sophia whatsoever, but for some reason he grew rankled over the notion that this dirty circus freak would insult her so blatantly. She wasn't only insulting

Sophia; she was insulting Philip as well. He would never have allowed himself to get this close to Sophia if she'd been some kind of pervert like this thing made her out to be, the Bureau's orders be damned.

But he couldn't cause a stir, not here, not now. "I just met Sophia a few weeks ago", he said.

"Sure works fast. *I* know." The woman blew smoke into Philip's face.

"She's a unique woman." Philip didn't know what else to say.

"Everyone's unique", the woman said. She blew a few smoke rings. "The vast majority of the human race is not aware of that, however. They're born sheeple, live as sheeple, die as sheeple. They believe in patriotism and the Great Eye in the Sky and perpetual guilt. It's all so tiring. I don't understand why they even bother."

"I guess they're weighted down with morals and ethics."

The woman laughed. "Yes, how sad." She waved her cigarette in the air. "How did you end up here? To be quite frank, you look like a Mormon."

Philip glanced around the room. Almost everyone in the room stood out in some small way. There were young beats wearing black berets, older men who looked disheveled, as if they had wandered in off the street after a night-long bender, white men wearing Egyptian-looking robes, and women dressed in provocative, sparkling see-through gowns with esoteric symbols woven into the fabric. One fat man wearing thick glasses was wearing an antennae get-up on his head while twisting dials on some kind of portable metal box, as if he were trying to tune in a broadcast from the heavens.

"I wear my uniqueness on the inside", Philip said.

The woman shrugged. "So do I." She sighed and glanced around the room, as if searching for a better conversationalist. "By the way, my name is Venus de Longpre. What's yours?"

"Herb O'Leary."

Venus smiled slightly. "*Herb*", she repeated, replacing her usual whisper with a John Wayne drawl. "Well, *Herb*, howdy. Have you had contact with the Higher Ones?"

"Not yet. I hope to. I think that's why Sophia brought me here tonight."

"She must really be taken with you then, particularly if you've known each other only for a few weeks. Perhaps I'm one of the Higher Ones in disguise. Did you ever consider that?"

"Perhaps we're all Higher Ones in disguise."

Venus removed the cigarette from her mouth and pointed it at him. "Touché, Mr. O'Leary. I'm going to chat up one of the Plutonian princesses over there and see if she will allow me to rescue her from this dungeon of mediocrity after the meeting is adjourned. Perhaps we'll run into each later. Please give Sophia my best and remind her that she owes me money."

"I'll be sure to do that, ma'am. Before you go, may I have one of your cigarettes?"

Venus handed it to him without a word, then floated away, trailing smoke rings behind her.

Philip spun around and acted as if he were admiring the craftsmanship of the mantel. What he was really doing was pulling out the cigarette lighter the Bureau had given him. He checked to see that everything was in working order, then turned around again and slowly moved from one side of the room to the other as he lit the cigarette, taking photos of every freak in the room. The boys back at the Bureau would have a field day with these photos. He doubted that any of them had ever considered the notion that a bunch of outer space freaks were being used as a front for communist infiltration.

Pythagoras emerged from the kitchen, a striking young woman on each arm. Both women were dressed in the unusual see-through gowns worn by many of the other . . . Plutonians? . . . is that what Venus had called them? Neither could have been over sixteen years old. They looked up at Pythagoras adoringly, as if he were Jesus' son incarnate.

"Oh, it's so good to see all of you again. You're all such lovely people", Pythagoras said with that soft yet resonant voice, "so beautiful. The outside world doesn't understand our motives, but that's to be expected. In a world where it's perfectly accept-able to send an eighteen-year-old boy to die overseas in a use-less and manufactured war while it is unacceptable—indeed, *illegal*—to allow that same young man to smoke marijuana or engage in unorthodox, healthy sexual practices then is it so surprising that highly evolved spiritual beings such as those we find gathered here in this otherwise unassuming abode would be met with derision and hatred and loathing and, let's face it, jealousy?" He spread his double-jointed hands in the air and smiled broadly.

Everyone held up their drinks—champagne, martinis, Scotch, wine, etc.—and toasted their guru. They shouted out slogans in a language Philip did not recognize. He suspected it was supposed to be some kind of alien language.

"Let's get down to . . . well, not business, but *play*", Pythago-ras said. He took a seat in the middle of the sofa, draped both arms across the back with a glass of Scotch splashing around in one hand. The two underage Plutonian attendants slipped into the open spots on either side of Pythagoras and stared up at him adoringly. "Is that not what life is all about?" Pythago-ras added, and played idly with the golden tresses of the lass sitting to his right. "What can we do to bring about the perfect society of the Orpheums?"

A young man (wearing the attire of a very old man) raised his hand and said, "It's obvious that the proletariat will not revolt unless they're forced to."

"That's true", said the golden-haired girl sitting beside Pythagoras. She had a high-pitched voice, like Snow White. "According to Friedrich Engels they identify too closely with the capitalist ideology of their oppressors. They suspect, secretly, that they too will one day reap the benefits of the capitalist system even though they have no hope of ever doing so."

"That's very good, my dear", Pythagoras said as he stroked her cheek. She seemed very pleased with herself.

"The answer", said Venus, "is to instill in the proletariat a fear greater than that instilled in them at birth by the capitalist system."

"Yes", said an old man in the corner of the room, "they live under the constant fear of not being able to make money. That's how they are kept in line like sheep. If we replace that fear with a greater fear . . . ."

Pythagoras stroked his beardless chin. "But how do we *do* this? That's the question . . . . Sophia!"

She snapped to attention. "Yes, Pythagoras?"

"Did you follow that lead I suggested?"

"Absolutely. I'd like to introduce Mr. Hillencott."

A middle-aged man who, strangely, was also dressed in one of the see-through robes of the Plutonian girls, stood up from a bean bag in the corner, and said shyly, "Hi. I work at the Sinsinawa Atomic Power Plant in Hazel Green." That town was located in Grant County, not far from Madison. "I lived a life of total drudgery until I discovered the word of Pythagoras. It was like flipping a switch in my brain. And with the flip of a few switches of my own, I can cause a complete meltdown in that power plant."

Murmurs of awe swept across the room.

"Think about what it would do", Pythagoras said. "To see the capitalists' symbol of hope for the 21st century, atomic energy itself, result in the worst disaster on U.S. soil? All their promises would be revealed as the lies they really are. Even the most brainwashed of the proletariats would be shocked out of their hypnotism. Fear of further disasters in their own little communities would set off a domino effect all across the country. The people would glance around, as if emerging from a dream, and realize for the first time how truly oppressed they've been. The people would demand that something be done about this, and of course nothing could be done. The capitalists have already invested too much in these plants. A mass revolt could be the only outcome."

"Thousands will die", said an old woman dressed like a 1920s flapper. She said it in an odd tone of voice, as if she weren't entirely displeased with the notion.

"Yes", Pythagoras said, "that's very true. And I've had the pleasure of speaking to the Orpheums about that very dilemma. I know what their answer is. The rest of you, unfortunately, do not. Before I inform you of their views, I'd like to hear what you have to say about this. I don't want your personal opinions to be swayed by the Word from the Stars. I need a human perspective. That's why you're all here tonight. Indeed, we all know how the Brothers from Space often like to work through happenstance and coincidence here on Earth. Perhaps that's the reason the universe has seen fit to bring Mr. Herbert O'Leary of nearby Middlesburg here with us tonight." Pythagoras gestured toward Philip. Philip slipped his cigarette lighter into his pocket and smiled nervously. He had not been expecting this.

Standing behind Pythagoras's couch, Sophia looked very proud that her new boyfriend was being singled out by the guru.

"You . . . want *my* opinion?" Philip said.

"Yes", Pythagoras said, "I think the Orpheums want us to hear what you have to say. That's why they influenced Sophia to bring you to us tonight."

Well, Phil, he thought to himself, this is why the Bureau chose you for this gig, right? They said you could think fast on your feet.

For a moment he wondered if the Bureau had made a mistake. It was a moment that seemed to last for a very long time.

And then some primal instinct kicked in, a muscular memory of the words he often heard his father repeating by rote. Fragments bubbled forth from the depths of his brain as he heard himself saying, "Thousands will die . . . . Yes, probably. But think about how many thousands of people die every year because of the capitalists' on-going imperialistic pogroms. How many lynched in the South? How many collapsing from pure exhaustion in back-breaking, non-Unionized industries? How many innocent Koreans mangled and crushed beneath the unrelenting boot of Uncle Sam? If thousands are to die, better they die for the freedom of the future than the continual enslavement of the present. It's not the fear of joblessness that keeps the proletariat in line. It's a far more profound and elemental fear. The reactionary writer H.P. Lovecraft once said, 'The oldest and strongest emotion of mankind is fear, and the oldest and strongest kind of fear is fear of the unknown.' It's the fear of the unknown that keeps them in line. The only way to counteract it is to create an unknown greater and more terrifying than the unknown they're already used to. Atomic energy represents that unknown. It's not just an object of fear, it's an object of *cosmic* fear, the *uber*-fear if you will. Given the fact that the capitalists are continually touting atomic energy as the answer to everyone's problems, a major disaster involving just such an atomic power plant is tailor-made to create the effect we've been dreaming about for so long. How can we pass up this opportunity? The only problem is making sure that the disaster is blamed on the proletariats and not on us."

Pythagoras glanced around at the group and smiled playfully. Then he brought his hands together and applauded. Slowly. For an uncomfortable moment he was the only one applauding in the room. Then he said, "That's almost exactly what the Orpheums said to me earlier this morning. Good show, Mr. O'Leary, good show."

At which point the entire room burst into applause. No one looked more pleased than Sophia.

"The Space Brothers are truly smiling down upon us", Pythagoras said. "Perhaps you and Sophia will be in charge of coordinating this event, to make sure it goes off smoothly."

"I would've requested just such a responsibility if you hadn't suggested it yourself", Sophia said.

"Hey, how come I'm not in charge?" said the young kid dressed as an old man. "I've been here longer than anybody."

"Please", Pythagoras said, "there's no room on Orpheum for jealousy; therefore, there is no room for it here as well. That is, *if* you want there to be room on the space craft for you when it finally arrives." The young man glanced down at the carpet in shame. Pythagoras turned to the rest of the gathering and said, "Don't worry. All of you will have a role to play in this game. And the Space Brothers wish you to think of it that way. As a *game*. The thousands whose lives are lost in this trifling chess match will eventually be reborn in paradise on Orpheum. We're merely speeding their entrance into a place greater than Heaven itself. *Never* forget that."

Everyone nodded.

"Now let's bow our heads in tandem and join together in praise of the eternal wisdom of the Space Brothers."

Everyone in the room bowed their heads and started humming and whistling strangely. Even Sophia began to do this. She glared at Philip from across the room until he bowed his head as well. He didn't hum or whistle, but he folded his hands in front of him and stared at his feet and wondered what the Bureau would say when Eva sent them this next report. The best report of all.

Busting a plot to destroy an atomic power plant would propel Philip to the very top of his field. He'd be able to write his own ticket. And he was determined to take Eva along with him.

The second Sophia was behind bars he could breathe a sigh of relief and know that his personal sacrifices had been necessary to save thousands of American lives. Surely not even Eva could blame him for that.

⚡

The strategy meeting segued into a party. He was disappointed when Sophia disappeared and left him alone with Venus and her passive-aggressive barbs. Eventually he grew impatient and tried to find Sophia so they could leave. He found her in the other room straddling Pythagoras while one of his underage attendants sat naked on the floor watching the whole scene. He didn't know why he felt enraged and jealous, but he did.

"Either join in or leave", Sophia said. "Either way, close the door please. I prefer the dark."

He stood there for a moment, then closed the door quietly and wandered back over to Venus who smiled and said, "Is Sophia at it again with one of the Plutonian spirits?"

"No", Philip said. "Not tonight, I guess."

"Oh", Venus said, "I see. Sophia must be in a very strange mood."

Five hours later, at around midnight, Sophia and Philip drove in silence to an Oasis Motel.

"Why're you stopping here?" Philip said.

"I need to celebrate. Right now. Don't you?" She wrapped her hands around his neck and slipped her tongue into his mouth.

He pulled away.

She said, "You're not angry with me, are you?"

He wasn't allowed to be angry with her. He had to remain on her good side no matter what.

"No", he said.

"I'm not serious about Pythagoras", Sophia said. "I was just excited. I was excited about *you*. He just happened to be there. Through the whole thing I was just thinking about you and what we were going to do in the bed in this motel room."

"Then why didn't you just leave with *me*?"

Sophia laughed. "You *are* jealous, aren't you? No one owns anyone else, you know that."

"Right", Philip said. "There's no room for jealousy on Orpheum."

Sophia waved her hand dismissively. "Herb, that's just a *story*. I'm talking about real life here. If we're to create the perfect society on Earth we have to stop viewing sex as some kind of capitalist commodity that can be bought and sold. Ultimately everyone belongs to each other, if the circumstances are right, if the attraction is mutual. And it *was* between me and Pythagoras, for that particular moment. That's all. There's nothing mysterious or holy about sex. You have to understand that. Otherwise you're going to suffer from the same sexual hang-ups and neuroses as the bourgeois chauvinists. I sincerely hope you don't expect me to be oppressed by an obsolete sense of propriety and ownership."

"No . . . no, I'm sorry", Philip said. He hugged her. "When you grow up in an imperialistic society like this, sometimes its most philistine values get stuck in the back of your head even if you know better. It's hard, sometimes, reversing one's upbringing."

Sophia pulled away from him. "Well, you're going to have to learn. *Everyone's* going to have to if we're to create a perfect society in our lifetime."

Philip nodded. "You're right."

"I'm glad to hear you say that", Sophia said. Then her distant exterior melted once more, she smiled broadly, and said, "Now let's go fuck, shall we?"

She grabbed him by the hand and pulled him out of the car.

Even as he allowed Sophia to handcuff his limbs to all four corners of the poster board he told himself he didn't enjoy any of this, not really. It was all in the line of duty.

Sophia straddled him in the dark and accused him of being a male chauvinist capitalist and even worse things. He agreed to it all with a continual soft whimper that could hardly be understood.

Eva's beloved face crossed his mind once . . .

. . . maybe twice . . . .

After work the next day Philip sat in a booth at Sonny's Bar waiting for Eva. She arrived right on time looking as beautiful as ever. The second she slipped into the booth she kissed him on the cheek then said, "Do you have a lighter? Mine's not working for some reason."

"Take mine", he said, sliding the lighter across the table. "I've got another one back home. That one won't break down on you. It's reliable."

"How reliable?" Eva said, slipping it into her purse.

"More reliable than you could imagine." He said this with a very straight face.

Eva could see the seriousness etched there. "Are you hungry?"

"Not really."

"Let's go back to my apartment."

"Excellent."

The second they climbed into her car Eva said, "Okay, give me the lowdown. What did you get?"

"Everything. Have you ever heard of Pythagoras Invictus?"

Eva shook her head no. "Is that a real name?"

"Of course not. You need to get the boys back at the Bureau to look into this guy's background. He's a UFO guru, or at least he pretends to be. They're using his flying saucer group as a cover organization. Most of his followers are just nuts who're heavy into UFOs and the hollow earth and crap like that. But there's a core membership—the Orpheum Solutions Group—who are commies through and through. And not just your run-of-the-mill 'I've-read-a-couple-of-books-by-Lenin-and-let's-have-a-discussion-group' commie, I'm talkin' about *extreme* revolutionaries. Eva, this is more serious than even *I* thought it was. Are you familiar with the Sinsinawa Atomic Power Plant?"

"Of course, it's in Hazel Green. The story's all over the newspapers. It brought a lot of money into that town."

"Eva, they're planning to blow it up."

"What? How could they possibly—?"

"They've got people on the inside, and they're willing to sacrifice their lives for the cause. They have this cockeyed notion that causing extreme chaos in the country will wake up the proletariat and spark a revolution. It's all in my report." Philip handed her a manila envelope filled with fifteen single-spaced pages. The second he had been able to break away from Sophia he holed up in his little room and typed up an extensive report on his reliable Smith-Corona typewriter, bugging everyone in the boarding house in which he lived. When one of them asked him, clearly annoyed, what he had been writing so early in the god damn morning, he said he was trying to make extra money as a pulp writer and that excuse seemed to be acceptable. He was several hours late to work because of that report. Since Sophia had kept him up with her handcuffs and creative invectives throughout most of the night he was dead tired. He even felt a little faint.

"I can't believe they would do this", he whispered. "Not even my parents—"

"Your parents have nothing to do with this", Eva said. "You should try to focus."

"They have *everything* to do with this!" Philip slammed his fist onto the dashboard and Eva flinched, obviously scared. "The government electrocuted my parents for doing far less than what these people are planning. Can you understand that? Think of the pressure that's weighing down on me. I thought I would be helping to squelch passive types of subversion, like what's been going on in Hollywood lately. I didn't know I'd be the only person between them and mass murder. Think of it. This could result in the deaths of *thousands*. And they don't care. They don't care." Exhausted, Philip slumped down in his seat. He rested his head in his hand and closed his eyes. "Maybe they are like my parents. My parents didn't care what happened to other people because of their little all-important cause. They didn't care what happened to me. They didn't care that their perfect little paradise was a total and complete impossibility."

Eva reached out and stroked his hair. "You've been running yourself ragged. You just need to rest. You've done good work, Agent O'Leary." Coming from her, the formal appellation somehow sounded comforting and sweet. "I'm going to take off your clothes for you and put you in my bed. You can sleep as long as you want. Meanwhile, I'll make sure that copies of your report and this film get to the Bureau overnight. They'll have it by tomorrow morning. Trust me."

"I trust you", Philip said. "You're about the only damn person I've ever trusted in my entire life." The jostling of Eva's car rocked him to sleep before they even reached her apartment.

He woke up to the grating sound of Eva's alarm clock. He almost broke it when he slammed his fist into it. At first he didn't know where the hell he was. He was sweating profusely, but the room wasn't warm at all. He must've been having some kind of nightmare. If so, he couldn't recall what it was about.

He tossed the sheets aside, expecting to see Sophia lying beside him. But this wasn't Sophia's bed. The Monet paintings on the walls tipped him off as to where he was. He reached for his wrists and rubbed the raw pink creases left by Sophia's handcuffs. Staring at them in the bright morning light, he realized how obvious the marks were. How could Eva *not* have seen them? Why didn't she ask him about them?

Where was Eva? He glanced around the room. Beside the alarm clock was a note that read, "Had to go to school, Sleeping Beauty. And you need to go to work. I bought some shaving cream and razors and put them in the medicine cabinet. See you tonight. Oh, and that business we discussed has been taken care of. Relax and go about your day. Love, Eva."

Philip smiled. He wondered now why he had been so worried. Of course Eva would take care of the situation. That's what she was here for. It wouldn't be long now. And then Sophia would be behind bars and he could forget her and that whole part of his life and start a new one with Eva.

He tried to rub the marks off his wrists, but they just wouldn't go away.

He decided to forget about them, just act like they weren't there. He took a shower, shaved, slipped into the clothes he had been wearing the day before, and jogged to work.

The second he stepped through the door Old Man Ridge said, "Weren't you wearing those clothes yesterday?"

Oh, shit, Philip thought. How could he *tell*? The old man was going to rip into him now. "Yes, sir", he said. "I'm sorry, I didn't have time to change. You see, I didn't sleep in my room last night and—."

Old Man Ridge suddenly burst into laughter, shuffled over to him, then punched him in the shoulder. Philip barely felt the blow. "Yes", he said, "I remember when I was your age. That Eva girl, huh? I can smell her all over you. I hope you two are getting married soon."

"That's very possible", Philip said, "but please don't tell her that. I haven't—"

The old man raised his arms in the air. "I understand, I understand. You don't have to explain the birds and the bees to me."

"I was only sleeping there last night", Philip said. "I wouldn't want you to think—"

"You don't have to explain *anything* to me. Eva's a nice girl, I know. I'm glad she finally found someone."

Philip breathed a sigh of relief. He realized it was very important to him, what this man—what *all* the people of Middlesburg—thought about Eva. She *was* a nice girl. The kind of girl you could spend the rest of your life with. Not the kind of girl who needed to debase others in order the make themselves feel superior.

Philip wished he'd worn long sleeves today.

Work, and then sleep. And then nightmares about handcuffs and Sophia and beings from other planets ripping apart the United States in monstrous flying machines.

Philip returned home from work the next day to see Eva and Sophia speaking to each other in the front room of the boarding house. He'd never seen them together before. It was like two alien worlds colliding in his living room. The house was quiet. No one else seemed to be around.

This was unusual as well.

Both women turned at the sound of the door opening, then stopped their conversation the second they saw him.

Philip tried to put on a straight face. "Don't stop on my account."

"Don't be silly", Eva said. "Sophia was just telling me how much you've improved the Youth Council since you joined."

Philip walked up to Eva and gave her a kiss on the lips.

"I don't know how I could get along without him", Sophia said, no hint of emotion in her voice. She held a manila folder underneath her arm. "I just dropped by to give you this." She handed him the envelope. "This contains the speech Donovan wrote for the upcoming anti-segregation rally in Selma. We were wondering if you could look it over and tell us what you think. You know Don. He tends to be long-winded and too precise. You have such a talent for encapsulating a major point into a short, snappy sentence or two." She turned back toward Eva. "Eva, dear, you should convince your boyfriend that he's wasting his time at that little grocery store. It's so beneath him."

Eva took Philip's hand and squeezed. "What do you propose that he do?"

"Oh, he should move on to something more sophisticated. Something that will last a lifetime."

"I'm sure he knows exactly what he's doing", Eva said.

"Perhaps", Sophia said. "And perhaps he needs a little encouragement as well. It would be sad to see his talents . . . wasted." Sophia turned back toward Philip, revealing a tight, restricted smile. "I'll see you at the next meeting." She tapped the envelope with her fingernail. "I look forward to hearing what you have to say about this." She nodded curtly at Eva, then turned on her heel and walked out of the boarding house.

The second the door closed Eva said sarcastically, "She's a very pleasant woman."

"She's very opinionated I suppose."

Eva crossed her arms over her chest and turned her back on him. "Her ambition is showing."

"Don't let it get to you. I think she enjoys getting under people's skins."

Eva raised one eyebrow. "Is that so? Has she gotten under yours?"

Philip laughed. "C'mon, Eva." He reached out for her, wrapped his arms around her waist and held her close. "The second this job is finished neither of us will ever have to see her again."

"I wish I could believe that were true", Eva whispered.

"I *promise* you it's true. I'm going to *make* it happen. And if I don't . . . well, a whole lot of lives are going to be destroyed. I can't fail. If I fail you, I fail everybody. I fail the entire United States."

Eva spun around and caressed his cheeks with her gloved hands. "Let's just leave here. Just get out while we can. We'll leave Middlesburg and communism and democracy and Sophia and everything else behind. We'll go somewhere else, I don't know where, some neutral territory that's not filled with paranoia and suspicion and spies and atomic power plants and . . . oh, Herb, we can be out of the country before anyone even knows we're gone."

"I'd really love to do that", Philip said. "I'd *love* to be able to find a place that's perfect. Where I would never have to worry about any of these things. But that place doesn't exist. My father tried to make it exist and instead he ended up in the electric chair."

"But what if such a place *did* exist? Would you want to live there the rest of your life . . . with me?"

"Of course I would. You don't even have to ask that question. But, Eva, a place like that just is *not* real. So why waste time worrying about it?"

Eva nodded. "I think I'd do anything to make it real."

"My father said the same thing. In the end it wasn't worth it."

"Your father wanted a communist state. I'm not talking about that. I'm talking about a place where the old rules don't apply. An autonomous zone where you can just sit on the porch and watch the sun set and rise and hold each other and make love and walk in the woods and paint and talk and ignore the insanity and the lying and the violence and the needless wars wars wars and watch the whole crazy world go by."

Philip sighed. "You paint a pretty picture. Maybe someday we'll wake up and find ourselves in it. But it's not going to be tomorrow or the next day. Eva?" She looked up at him with those watery, dark, violet doe-eyes of hers. "Why did you drop by? I thought I was going to meet you at the bar."

"Oh, I was feeling restless. I didn't want to wait around in that dingy place. Of course, Sophia showed up a few minutes after I got here."

"What did she say to you?"

Eva walked away from him and stared through the lace curtains at the lawn outside where a couple of neighbor kids were playing with a dog on a leash. They seemed to be tormenting it.

"She was just going on and on about what a talented writer you were. That I should consider myself lucky to have you as a boyfriend."

"Well, that's not bad, is it?"

"Coming from anyone else, no. Coming from her? Yes. It was her tone of voice more than anything else. She couldn't help but mention that you two had become quite 'close' since you'd joined her organization."

"It's not 'her' organization. And yes we've become close. You know that. You told me to get as close to her as possible the first night we met. Those were your express orders."

"It's up to the agent in the field to interpret orders. He can interpret them broadly or very narrowly. How did you choose to interpret them?"

"Maybe we should go upstairs for this conversation", he whispered.

"Nobody's home", Eva said. "I checked when I first came in."

"I'm sleeping with her."

Eva nodded. She bit her lower lip. "Okay." She laughed bitterly. "I knew that."

"You knew?"

"Sure." She shrugged. "Why else would she be giving you so much information so early? It doesn't matter. I understand. I've had to do the same thing, of course."

"You have?"

"Any means necessary, right? I've probably saved dozens of lives by doing it. You think less of me now?"

Philip hesitated before answering. "I . . . when was this?"

"You didn't answer my question."

"I . . . I don't know. I guess . . . yes, I guess I do . . . think less of you."

"I have a job to do. So do you. Why does my job make me less of a person and yours doesn't?"

"I don't know. I just . . . I'm sorry, I'm a little confused now."

"We're not married. You have no obligation to me."

Philip took a deep breath and said, "You don't seem too upset."

She bit her lower lip. She almost started to cry. "It's *killing* me inside. I'm lying in my bed alone while you're off . . . ." She sighed. "Have you told her you love her?"

Philip couldn't help but laugh. "I can't imagine that *ever* happening."

"Okay. As long as you never tell her that, as long as you're not in love with her, it's fine. You still want to be with me?"

He nodded. "I don't want to lose you", he said.

She wrapped her arms around his neck and they kissed. Philip scooped her up in his arms and carried her up the stairway to his room. He kicked the door in, lowered her to his bed, slammed the door shut behind him. They did nothing but kiss and fondle each other playfully for awhile, until at last Philip and Eva began to strip off each other's clothes. Philip covered her body in kisses from her eyelids all the way down to her painted toes and back again. And he was just about to make love to her when Eva suddenly said, "What's it like with her?"

He almost ignored the question, then said, "Please . . . ."

She just stared up at him, waiting.

"Please don't ask me that", he said.

"I see the scratches and bruises." She ran her hands over them. "I've always seen them. Is it different with her?"

"Yes."

"Is it better with her?"

"It's just different."

"Show me what she does."

"No."

"Pretend I'm you. You're her."

"No." He tried to pull away from her.

She wrapped her arms around his neck. She wouldn't let him go. "It's valid psychological information necessary for the operation. I could order you to tell me."

"Fine then. Order me."

"*Show me.* That's an *order.*"

He nodded. "Yes, sir." He pinned her hands to the mattress, tied her wrists to the posts with electrical cords he pulled out from beneath the bed. He straddled her stomach, then did to Eva exactly what Sophia loved doing to him.

He left out the detail about reading from the works of Lenin, however.

That was just too absurd.

"Satisfied?" Philip said.

The sun had set outside. The room was now dark. He could barely see her face. He could only judge by the intense sounds she'd uttered, all of them muffled by the gag stuffed in her pretty mouth.

The second he pulled the gag out Eva gasped, "Untie me." His thumbs had left imprints on her throat.

"That's not how Sophia does it", he said. "I don't think you have enough information for your report." He put the gag back in her mouth. He got dressed, left the room, locked the door behind him, and strolled downstairs. The other tenants had returned home by now. He joined them for dinner.

He took the time to have dessert. Strawberries and milk on angel food cake.

About an hour later he strolled back upstairs. The moment she entered the room she began straining against her bonds, but to no avail of course.

He ungagged her. "Say please", he said.

"You son of a bitch."

"Your report's not done until you say please."

"*Please*, you son of a bitch!"

"Please, master."

"Please. *Master*."

He untied her slowly. He thought Eva might punch him, just like she did on their first date. Part of him was hoping for that reaction.

Instead she just wrapped her arms around her knees, buried her face into her wounded flesh, and said nothing.

"Well?" he said. "Eva?"

He reached out and touched her shoulder. She started to cry. The tears just came pouring out. He hugged her to him tightly . . . but not too tightly.

He would've respected her more if she'd at least tried to push him away, just once.

No sane woman, he thought, would've put up with the things he had done to her.

He woke at four-thirty in the morning from a strange dream he couldn't recall. He was covered in sweat again. He glanced to his left and saw Eva's naked body lying beside him. She would have to leave very early in the morning before anyone else woke up. If the landlady saw her creep out of his room, he'd be out on the street within minutes.

He reached over and lightly shook her. He whispered in her ear, "Eva . . . Eva . . . you need to wake up."

Her eyes fluttered open. "Mm? Yes?"

"Eva, we've got to sneak you out of here now before everyone wakes up. Potter's usually up by five."

"Five? What time is it?"

"Four-thirty."

Eva bolted upright. "Four-thirty? I wasn't planning on . . . ."

"I know. Neither was I."

She ran her fingers through her dark hair. The previous night was coming back now. She laughed slightly. "I almost forgot how I ended up here."

"Eva, I'm sorry about—"

"Let's not talk about it, okay? At least not right now." Eva got up from the bed and began dressing.

"Is . . . is everything okay between us?"

She strapped on her bra. "Why wouldn't it be?"

"I don't know. I'm not sure how you feel about what hap—"

"As far as I'm concerned, you filled me in on some necessary details for my report. Let's just leave it at that."

"Can we just go back to the way we were? You know, I don't want you to be her. That's the last thing I want."

Eva turned toward him with a stoic expression on her face that segued into a bitter laugh. "I never thought you did, Agent O'Leary. You know what Oscar Wilde said. 'Once, curious. Twice, perverse.' I found out what I wanted to know. End of story." She slipped into her dress and high heels, her nylons balled up in her fist. She thrust them into her purse and headed for the door.

"You want me to walk you out?"

"I'll find my own way."

"Eva . . . Jesus, Eva, I love you."

She stopped at the door, turned toward him and whispered, "I love you too. You know that. I'll see you later tonight . . . if you're not busy with Sophia, that is."

"I'm not busy."

She opened the door and crept out into the hallway like a cat. A few minutes later, downstairs, he heard the front door open and close. He peered out the window and saw her walking away down the sidewalk toward her apartment building. The sound of her high heels clicking against cement drifted away into the distance.

The second his head hit the pillow he drifted back to sleep . . .

. . . and returned to his dream in which Eva was whispering something in Sophia's ear in the living room down below . . . all the other boarders stood on the second floor landing, leaning over the railing, trying desperately to hear their secrets . . . Herb came through the door and saw that expression on Eva's face . . .

. . . Philip woke to the sound of a lawn mower outside inter-mixed with a deep voice singing some obscure ditty in a foreign tongue. That old Hungarian was doing chores for Mrs. Potter again. Philip glanced at the clock. 8:30 a.m. He was late for work again. He leaped out of bed, threw on some clothes, yelled out some quick "hellos" to his fellow boarders and dashed out of the house without even eating any breakfast. He ran right past the old Hungarian and jogged down the sidewalk.

He wasn't heading toward the store. He was heading in the opposite direction, toward Eva's apartment.

That look on Eva's face last night when he entered the boarding house was not one of relief. She was not at all thank-ful that he had saved her from a discussion with one of her least favorite people in the world. Though subdued, it could only be described as an expression of guilt.

But what would Eva have to feel guilty about?

Philip whipped out a Swiss Army knife from inside his jacket. He carried it with him always, for within it lay two metal prongs with which he could break almost any lock on the planet.

Eva's apartment was located on the second floor of a small brick building with only five other tenants inside. He knew that all of them, like Eva, would be at work right now.

It didn't take him more than a minute to bypass the primitive lock on Eva's door. Inside the familiar apartment everything was a mess, like usual. Jesus, how could he find something he hoped wouldn't even be here? It would be almost impossible to find, but something told him he had to look, to be sure.

He was careful not to disturb the mess. It looked like chaos, but it wasn't. Eva knew where every pile of disordered clothes was supposed to be. He avoided all the obvious places. Eva wasn't that stupid.

He searched for an hour or two, finding nothing out of the ordinary, hoping this was because she was innocent.

Then he saw the rust . . . small flakes of brown rust coating the edge of her kitchen sink. Anybody else might have overlooked it, including Eva. Philip glanced up and spotted an air vent in the ceiling directly above the sink. The same type of rust lined the metal grating. It was worth a try.

Philip climbed onto the edge of the sink, stood on the kitchen counter, and reached up for the vent. It slid aside easily. Flakes of rust fell from the grating and landed on the edge of the counter. He slipped his hand into the vent and felt something small and rectangular and metallic.

He pulled it out: the cigarette lighter, with all the photos inside.

This was not a different lighter. This was *his*. He could see the telltale scuff marks all over it.

Eva was lying to him. Why? Was she a communist as well? A triple agent? Was she working with Sophia? But *why*? Were the two of them trying to mess up his mind, distract him from the real problem?

He didn't know. At the moment he didn't care. Right now he had to make sure this lighter got into the right hands before a disaster occurred.

He replaced the vent, climbed down off the sink, picked up Eva's phone and called Old Man Ridge at the grocery store. He apologized for being late, but told him that a family emergency had occurred out of state and he'd be back as soon as he possibly could. The old man yelled at him for a few minutes, then told him he hoped everything would be okay and looked forward to seeing him again.

Philip jogged down to the Greyhound station where he had first arrived in Middlesburg and bought a bus ticket for Chicago.

He sat in a bare room with a mirror in it. He wondered if someone was watching him, but he tried not to think about that. He sat in the chair, chain-smoked his Marlboros, and waited for a response. He wondered if it was night or day outside.

Finally two new agents came into the room accompanied by the first one, Agent Oscar Rusch. Rusch, a rugged olive-skinned man with a Bronx accent and a face of craggy stone, said, "OK, we touched base with L.A. Your story checks out."

Philip said, "This deep cover business isn't much of a help when you're in a hurry, is it?"

Rusch shrugged. "The less people who know who you are, the better. Isn't that right?"

Philip mimicked the agent's shrug. "I don't have any opinion about it one way or the other. I just wanted to make sure those photographs made it to the right people before it was too late."

"We've already checked out the photos", Rusch said. "That's what's confusing us."

One of the other agents, Felix Tomney, a tall and thin blond gentleman who appeared to be around Philip's age, asked his questions with a slight British accent. "Why didn't you turn this information over to your handler?"

Philip had gone to the FBI headquarters in Chicago with the intent of telling them about Eva's duplicity. But now that he was here, he just couldn't go through with it. What if he were wrong? He couldn't allow his paranoia to destroy her career, her whole life. He couldn't brand her with the same taint as his parents. She should at least have a chance to explain herself. Perhaps there was a good reason why she had lied to him.

He mentioned nothing about his exact relationship with Sophia either. He wasn't sure how they would react to his debauchery. Perhaps they would be disappointed in him, as disappointed as he was in himself. He didn't want them to make him feel even more ashamed than he already felt. Self-flagellation as intense as his needed no outside help.

"She thought she was under constant surveillance", Philip responded. "They suspect her far more than me. So I decided to deliver it myself. I didn't even ask her permission. I just did it."

"That's not protocol", said a third agent, a fat elderly man with white hair. His name was Schirmer.

"I thought it was an emergency", Philip said. "It was, wasn't it?"

"If you're story's true, I would say so", Rusch said.

"Why would I be lying?" Philip felt like jumping up from the chair and throwing a punch at the man's acne-scarred face. "Do I look like the type of person who lies?"

Tomney patted him on the shoulder. "We don't think you're lying. The people at this party, who did you say they were?"

"Their names are in the notes I gave you." During the bus trip, he had rewritten his extensive notes by memory. Who knew what Eva had done with the original manuscript? Had she destroyed it? Given it to Sophia? Were they both reading it together, laughing at his stupidity?

"Those names don't match any existing persons in our data base", Schirmer said.

"Is that unusual?" Philip said. "Perhaps they've never committed a crime. The whole point of being a spy is to stay under the radar."

"That's what confuses us", Tomney said. "From those photographs we were able to identify every single person in that room."

"Yeah?" Philip said. "Well, that's good. Who are they?"

"They're the twelve FBI agents who disappeared from Middlesburg. They're the exact people you were sent to find."

Philip just stared at them for a second, then burst out laughing. "What the hell? That doesn't make any sense."

"They've altered their appearances, and in some cases dramatically", Tomney said, "but not enough to fool us."

"What are they", Philip said, "brainwashed or something?"

"There's only one explanation", Rusch said. "They've gone over to the other side."

"But . . . that's ridiculous", Philip said. "If they had gone over to other side, why would they disappear? They're all in the perfect position to spy on the U.S. government from the inside. From within the Bureau. To just drop out . . . what would be the point?"

Rusch sighed. "Listen, we don't have all the answers. There's only two possibilities here. Either they're working for the FBI or they're working for the communists. There's no in-between, right?"

"Right", Philip said, "but how do you know they're not deep undercover? I mean, you didn't have any record of who the hell *I* was at first."

"Not at first", Tomney said, "but it only took us a few hours to find out. If they were deep undercover there would be some record of it. You, Philip, never would've been sent in to find them. They *vanished*, presumed dead for years. It's obvious that they did this of their own accord."

"Could it be . . . hypnotism?" Philip said. "Brainwashing?" It sounded so outrageous, Philip was almost reluctant to say the words.

Schirmer nodded. "It could be. We want you to go back to Wisconsin and find out everything you can. You're in the perfect position to do it."

"But . . . aren't you boys going to go in there and break up this ring before they can cause major damage?"

"They can't be arrested until they actually try something", Tomney said.

"*What*?" Philip said. "We have to wait around until they actually *try* to blow up the power plant before we go in there and slap handcuffs on them? You guys are getting sloppy. What do you have to do in this country to get arrested? My parents did less than they're doing and they got the chair."

"That was a different time", Schirmer said. "Different standards. We have more to prove now. Some people in this country, liberal politicians in Congress for example, are convinced the communists aren't a threat at all. They're trying to convince the public of this myth. We have to create a counter-myth."

"A *counter*-myth? Wouldn't that be . . . the truth?"

"Exactly", Tomney said, "we have to get the American public to see the truth of the danger that's facing them. If that means catching these sons-of-bitches in the act, then that's what we're going to have to do."

"But . . . what if something goes wrong?" Philip said. "What if we don't stop them in time?"

"You're going to be there to make damn *sure* we stop them in time. That's your job."

"My job was to keep you informed of their plans. I just did that."

"And you're gonna *keep* doin' it", Rusch said. "Right until the last possible second. And if you fuck up, then guess what? Thousands of innocent lives will be on *your* head, not the damn commies'."

"That's too much responsibility", Philip said. "I'm just one man."

"You knew what you were gettin' into when you signed onto this job", Rusch said. "Don't try to pretend you didn't."

"I'm not pretending anything", Philip said. "I'm being more realistic than any of you. I'm just saying it's dangerous to play so fast and loose with something like this."

"We're not playing", Tomney said. "And neither are you. We all want to get to the bottom of this mystery. You're the only person in the position to do it. You need to take it from the top and tell us everything you know."

Philip sighed. "Okay", he said, "once more from the top . . . . "

The next day he found himself once again standing outside the Greyhound Bus Station in downtown Chicago. He had remained at the FBI headquarters all throughout the night and into the morning and early afternoon. It was around two o'clock by the time he arrived at the station. He thought it would be wise to call Eva and let her know where he was. He hoped she hadn't noticed that her cigarette lighter was missing.

He knew she'd probably still be at work at this time of day, so he called the Middlesburg Elementary School and asked for Eva. The secretary, an aging obese women with an incessant cough, recognized his voice from all the other times he had called. "Hey, Herb", she said, "how's it going? She just walked right by my desk. Hey, Eva!"

He heard the receiver switching hands. "Herb?" Eva said. "Where are you? I've been so worried."

"I'm in Chicago."

"Why're you there?"

"I don't know." Philip felt tears brimming in his eyes. He did not want to think that this woman was betraying him. "I just needed to clear my head, Eva. I feel real guilty. I just got on a bus and went away, I didn't care where." I'm lying to her, he thought, I'm lying to her again. "I'm so sorry about what happened", he said, "so sorry I lied to you." I'm apologizing for lying while lying. That doesn't make any sense.

"I understand", Eva whispered, "just come back to me. I couldn't stand not knowing where you were. Do you want me to come get you?"

"No, that's okay." He brushed at his eyes with the back of his sleeve. "I'm at the bus station. The bus leaves in . . . . " In truth, the bus left in an hour. He would be back home by five. But some internal instinct told him to hold his tongue. His instinct told him to lie again. "The bus will be leaving in a couple of hours. I should be home by seven or eight."

"Will you promise to come straight to my apartment?"

"Yes. Will you be waiting for me?"

"I just remembered I have a PTA meeting I have to attend here at school at around five o'clock. It's sort of a special meeting and only happens once a year, so it's kind of mandatory. But the second the meeting is finished I'll be at my apartment and we'll be able to spend the whole evening together. Okay?"

"I'll see you soon then."

"I'll see you soon. I love you, Herb."

"Eva . . . I love you. I'm so sorry."

It didn't seem as if she knew what to say. "We'll talk about it when you get here."

He hung up and sat on a bench and he waited for the train to take him back to the only woman he'd ever really loved.

While on the train various erotic fantasies unreeled in his mind. Oh, the things he would do to her tonight . . . and yet Sophia's lashes, her unrelenting grip around his neck, her cruel insults, somehow always managed to push past his veneer of gentle lovemaking and distort the illusion into something twisted and perverse.

He couldn't get Sophia out of his body, no matter how hard he tried. In fact, the harder he tried the more he thought about her.

Focus, Herb, Philip thought. You're Special Agent Herbert O'Leary and you've been sent to Middlesburg to complete a very specific task. You're the only thing standing between the communists and disaster. You can't afford to be distracted by nonsense. The second Eva returns from her PTA meeting you'll sweep her up in your arms and you'll kiss her all over and you'll try to get to the bottom of the real Eva . . . you'll dig deep inside her, deeper than you or anyone else has ever gone before . . . you'll tie her wrists to her bed posts and you'll force the information out of her . . . and if she doesn't choose to cooperate at first, well, then that just means you'll be justified in taking whatever action you have to in order to get at the real truth beneath the façade . . . .

Special Agent Herbert O'Leary felt himself getting an erection. He put a magazine over his lap to hide it from the others on the train. No one else could know. No one else could know what he was thinking. Were they watching him? Did they know who he was? Were they all communists?

At one point he got up and locked himself in the bathroom and masturbated furiously into the sink as he imagined tying Eva to a chair and forcing the truth out of her with Sophia's toys . . . that would end the fantasy, he hoped, but it didn't . . . the fantasy just came back twenty minutes later, stronger and more vivid than ever . . . .

While coming into the sink, his brain retrieved a passage from a famous book on the communist conspiracy that he had read in college in order to understand the minds of his dead parents . . . .

The title of that book was *Communist-Socialist Propaganda in American Schools* by Verne P. Kaub. In that book it stated quite clearly that the PTA was one of the organizations the communists preferred to use in order to infiltrate and sabotage basic American values. What did Eva mean when she said the meeting was "mandatory", that it was "special?" Philip decided that Special Agent Herbert O'Leary would have to get to the bottom of this grand mystery.

Middlesburg Elementary was almost entirely dark except for the auditorium where all the little tykes usually ate lunch. Outside the auditorium was a huge banner that read "PTA Meeting Tonite—Come One, Come All!" Herb peeked over a window sill and saw what was happening behind the foggy pane of glass. Harry Mason, the writer from the boarding house, stood behind a podium addressing the crowd. There was Eva sitting in the front row. A few rows behind her sat Officer Chuck. And there was Venus and the other interplanetary whores from the UFO party. They were dressed less outlandishly, but it was them. Everyone from the party, including Pythagoras Invictus. Everyone, that is, except Sophia.

"We have to deal with this Philip Trowbridge issue once and for all", Mason was saying.

They knew his name. They knew Herb's other name . . . .

"I assure you we can bring him in on it", Eva said. "He's sympathetic to our beliefs. I've had conversations about this. He'll understand. You have to *trust* me. I know him better than anyone here."

"We know you do", Mason said, "which is why we can't trust what you're saying."

Herb felt something cold and hard press against his spine.

"I see you've taken a special interest in education", Sophia said. He started to turn around until she said, "Just keep your eyes forward or I'll pull the trigger. Raise your hands into the air." He did as she asked. "It's a good thing I was late. Seems you're a little early. You weren't supposed to get here until seven or eight."

"Did Eva tell you that?"

"Who else? Now get inside, lover. I have a brand new bullet point to bring up at the meeting."

They circled the building and entered through the double doors.

The heated discussion devolved into silence when the two of them entered.

"What the hell is *this*?" Mason said.

Eva shot to her feet. "Herb!" She had an expression of genuine concern on her face.

"Looks like the subject of this meeting was just made moot", Sophia said. "Now we don't have a choice."

Eva ran up toward the podium. "He won't give us away, I promise he won't."

"We can't take that chance", Pythagoras said.

"Pythagoras's right for once", Venus said calmly, almost seeming bored as she blew smoke rings through her nostrils. "Do you want to destroy everything we've worked so hard to build here?"

"Stop the debate", Herb said. "Just get this over with. No matter how long I live I'll never work for you people."

Mason shrugged as he looked at Eva with a genuine expression of pity. "See? I'm sorry, Eva. Sophia, you take him out to the car and we'll drive him somewhere far away. Up into the hills, perhaps."

Sophia began to tug at his collar when Eva shouted, "No! He doesn't even know what we're about yet. Let's at least give him a chance. Let's *explain* it to him. Then he'll understand."

"I never want to understand you people", Herb said. He felt dizzy. He felt as if his body were being jostled somewhere back on the train, as if he were still asleep between Chicago and Middlesburg . . . asleep and dreaming . . . .

"No, no . . . you don't understand", Eva said as she walked over to him. She reached out and caressed his scruffy face. "We're not communists. None of us are."

Herb laughed. "Right. You're going to kill me because you all work for the Federal Communications Commission."

"Remember that conversation we had about creating a utopia", Eva said, "a place where the old rules don't apply? That's what we've created here in Middlesburg. Mason was the first FBI agent to be sent here. His purpose was to track down communists. But Almos Biriescu was the only communist in the entire town at that time. When Mason arrived he realized he had a prime opportunity. He hated World War II and all the lives it

159

had destroyed. He didn't want to be a part of another senseless war, even a cold one. So he settled down here. He helped Biriescu grow the communist party. He sent out word through the grapevine of dissatisfied Special Agents. Agents who were on the verge of being fired anyway for insubordination dropped out of their current assignments and came here, altered their names and identities, took root where they could be protected by other agents who sympathized with their newfound idealism. Their pacifism. And the more the communist party grew, the more agents the Bureau sent in to investigate Middlesburg. Some of us could afford to cut off all contact with the Bureau, and those are the twelve who vanished completely. Others of us need that Bureau paycheck coming in every month, otherwise we'd starve or have to go out and get a real job and why bother? You know how much evil the Bureau has committed during its existence. It's about time they started giving back. And so they have."

"We've created our own little retirement fund here", Mason said.

Eva said, "This is a place where a Special Agent who no longer wants to play this stupid Cold War game can just relax and drop out of the nonsense entirely. We can just sit on the sidelines and watch this whole insane world go by. And as long as the 'communist' influence keeps growing, Herb, we can keep this little hidden paradise forever. Keep it an autonomous zone. Just like we talked about, Herb. Remember?"

He glanced around. He was dreaming. That's exactly what he was doing. "Is this some kind of joke?" Herb said. "Some kind of brainwashing technique?"

"We're not communists", Venus said. "Why don't you listen to what your lady's telling you?"

"We're a Search and Avoid Tactical Team", Pythagoras said. "Curiously clever, isn't it?"

Herb looked at all of them. None of them were laughing. They were serious. "This is impossible", he said.

"It's not impossible", Eva said. She tried to caress him again, but he pulled away from her. "Utopia *is* possible. You just have to *want* it, Herb."

Herb laughed. "You people are all sick. You can't just drop out and avoid all of your responsibilities to the Bureau." Pythagoras and Venus both sighed in tandem and raised their eyebrows. "This country isn't perfect, I know that, but that doesn't mean you turn your back on it. You fight to make it better. You fight from the *inside*."

"We're tired of fighting from the inside", Mason said. "There's too much stacked against us to enact any real change. We'd rather live out the rest of our lives in relative peace. Right here, in Communist Town, U.S.A."

"You lazy fuckers!" Herb shouted and took a step forward, but the click of Sophia's gun prevented him from moving too far. "You're all delusional. There's a real war going on out there. You have to take a *side*."

"Why?" Mason said. "What if *both* sides are evil?"

"Both sides?" Herb said. "Evil? That's impossible."

"Oh, please put a stop to your bifurcated thinking", Venus said. "I don't have time to get this guy up to speed on the inadequacy of the Hegelian dialectic. Let's just get rid of him."

"Yes", Pythagoras said, "the world isn't as black and white as you want to believe it is, Herb, my dear. I think you'll need another lifetime to figure that out, though."

Tears streamed from Eva's eyes. "Please, let's just give him some time before we . . . ."

"There's no time", Mason said, "his attitudes are clear. He won't change."

"Is this your utopia?" Herb said to Eva. "Where you have to kill everyone who doesn't agree with you?"

"Herb", Eva said, "we've never *had* to kill anybody before. Every single FBI agent who's come through Middlesburg has immediately understood what it was we were trying to do here.

They all stay here voluntarily. They understand. They *get* it.
Why can't you just get it, Herb? We could stay here together,
just the two of us. We could be happy."

"What about the power plant?" Herb said. "How many people will die if you follow through on the plan?"

"Jesus", Venus said, "you're incapable of listening, are
you? We don't want to kill anybody. That's not the purpose of
all this. But we have to keep upping the ante in order for the
Bureau to continue funding our little operation here. That's
why we conjured up that power plant scheme. That was entirely
for *your* benefit, love."

"We needed you to write a report about the plan", Pythagoras said. "I'm sorry to disappoint you, Agent Trowbridge, but
Eva here kept all your photos. They never made it to L.A. But
your report *did*."

Herb glanced at Eva. A expression of guilt washed over her
face. She didn't know about the missing film. None of them did.

"This dreamland can't last forever", Herb said.

"It *can*", Eva said. "As long as there are bloodthirsty bureau-
crats running this government willing to spy and kill for money
and power, we'll always be safe here. That's the ironic beauty of
the situation. Can't you *see* that?"

Mason sighed and shook his head. "I knew you were unlikely
to sympathize with us and our mission", he said, "once we
studied your psychological background."

"The shit with your parents", Sophia whispered in his ear.
"It fucked you up permanently."

"Jesus, I wish my parents were here", Herb said. "I respect
them more than I respect any of you. At least they took a side
and stuck to it. At least they believed in something."

"We all believe in something too", Eva said. "We believe in
peace."

"That's a lie", Herb said. "You're all lying to yourselves.
You think you're just fake communists? Have you ever consid-

ered the possibility that the *real* communists might have used your fake front as a cover?"

"Oh, God", Pythagoras said, pretending to yawn, "this boy is over the deep end."

"Please, let's just get this over with", Venus said.

Philip thought of Sophia. "You're all in denial", he said. "There's at least one real communist standing right behind me." Lenin's insomnia-inducing prose would never be capable of inducing an orgasm into a fake communist, Herb thought. But he was too much of a . . . too much of a *gentleman* to say it out loud. Sophia was the real deal, red through and through. It was the only thing that explained her love of deep perversity.

"And what makes you say that?" Venus said. "Do you have any *proof*?"

Herb opened his mouth to give them the evidence, but Philip couldn't form the words. He wanted to reveal everything about her, but that would require admitting exactly what he had done with Sophia in front of a whole auditorium full of other FBI agents. No, he couldn't do that. Not even in front of these traitors. *Especially* not in front of them.

He spun around and snatched the gun out of Sophia's hands. He clocked her in the jaw and sent her sprawling to the floor. He could've killed her in that moment, but didn't. He was angrier at Eva. She had lied to him. Just like his parents, she had lied to him over and over and over again.

He spun on his heel and tried to fire the gun at Eva but before he could pull the trigger Officer Chuck leaped up from the audience, shouted "NO YOU DON'T, YOU SON OF A BITCH!" and pumped six bullets into his chest.

Eva shrieked.

Herb slumped to the shiny auditorium floor. Right beside his head lay a piece of macaroni that must have fallen there from some kid's lunch earlier that afternoon.

Herb thought, The janitor must have missed a spot. Bad, bad janitor.

He still had the gun in his hand. He tried to squeeze the trigger, but nothing happened. He couldn't move his fingers.

Must've missed a spot. Bad, bad janitor.

Herb saw Eva drop to her knees in front of him, saw the pool of blood seeping out of his chest and staining her nylons and pristine white dress. Someone, maybe Sophia, took the gun from his hand. Eva cradled him to her chest and cried real tears. These . . .

These were not the tears of a liar, of a traitor, were they?

As the room grew dark he remembered taking the stand at his parents' trial. He remembered the way the jury reacted to his tearful testimony. He remembered putting on his sad face more than necessary, to gain the sympathy of those twelve random men and women gathered in that room to judge his mother and father. He had wanted to kill his parents so much that he made up whole conversations to which he had never even been privy. The prosecutor had hinted so many times that these damning lines of dialogue *might* have been overheard by him that he began to remember them exactly as they had been described to him.

He had never realized, not until this moment, how much he'd hated his parents simply because they had refused to pay attention to him when he craved *their* attention the most above all others, above his teachers and friends at school. No, Mother and Father were too busy with their all-important meetings, too busy trying to make a better world, to pay attention to their only son.

Never realized, until this moment, that he had lied on the stand just because they had not measured up to his ten-year-old standards.

They were communists, that was never in dispute, and the prosecutor assured Herb over and over again that he was a true hero. And Herb was certain this was true. Even now, as his entire world grew dim, he was certain he had been a hero at least in that one instant.

Memories of his parents were replaced with Sophia's face staring down at him with a typically uncaring expression. She was studying him with nothing more than curiosity, as if he were an experiment that had gone slightly awry. He recalled everything they had done together and held Eva's pale hand tightly and gasped, "Please . . . forgive me."

"I do", Eva whispered. "I already forgave you. I *love* you. You know that."

But Herb wasn't talking to Eva. He was talking to God. He listened closely, but God was not responding.

Not yet.

He could only hope that what little Philip Trowbridge had done to his parents would make up for the wickedness Special Agent Herbert O'Leary had committed here in Middlesburg with that damn woman, a woman he wished he had never touched.

At last the special agent closed his eyes and went to sleep.

Philip Trowbridge followed soon afterwards

3

SPIES AND SAUCERS

LATE ONE JANUARY EVENING IN 1952, Curt Adamson sat at his desk in his cramped West Hollywood apartment composing the most important speech of his life . . . or at least trying to. His girlfriend Tina grabbed a sculpture the size of a fist, an abstract rip-off of Picasso Curt had picked up at an artist's fair downtown, and hurled it across the room. It flew past Curt's head and slammed into a Willem de Kooning painting leaning against the wall. It ripped right through the canvas.

"I could've sold that sculpture for the rent!" Curt said.

Tina picked up yet another sculpture, this one even larger, and said, "You know damn well you wouldn't get a dime for that piece of shit. Every painting you own is a forgery!"

"It's an original de Kooning, I'm *tellin'* you!" Actually, he'd bought it on the cheap from a friend of his who could replicate the style of almost any painter alive. He thought it might impress people, the studio types who sometimes came over for his raucous parties. Though he hadn't thrown a party in months . . . .

"You know what", Tina said, "I think you believe that. You've been lying so long you don't even know what the truth is anymore."

"I've never lied to you", Curt said, reaching out to snatch the sculpture from her hands. She pitched it towards him like a speedball. He barely ducked out of the way.

"How *dare* you!" she screamed. "What about all the times you told me you were going to stop drinking?"

"I didn't say how *long* I was gonna stop!"

"Everything's a comedy to you, isn't it? Just another movie." Tina's pretty round face, her babyish chubby cheeks, turned red with rage. Some women looked beautiful when they were upset. Tina didn't. Tina was a fragile little doll, 5'5 with unblemished pale skin and sandy blonde hair, who appeared to fracture like china whenever she was in pain. She'd been trying to be an actress forever, but her emotions were not controllable enough to be used to her advantage in that way. She was well-meaning and ambitious, but had limited range. She'd landed only a few commercials, always playing a young mother. She just had that look about her, one of perpetual innocence. And yet at the same time she had a body that could have earned her money on a runway if only she'd been a tad taller; most of the time, when she tried to dress sexy, she looked like a teenager playing dress-up. It was this unique dichotomy that first attracted Curt to her. All he wanted was to make her happy. Before the allegations, they *had* been happy.

But now . . . now Tina's intense rage transformed into grief.

"Everything's a piece of fiction to you. But the one time I *want* you to lie, you just won't do it."

"I don't know, babe . . . I don't know what to tell you", Curt said. "You and I have very different definitions of the word 'lying.' Just because I write a story about you and change some of the details, that's not lying."

"You know I'm not talking about that fucking story anymore. What about the gambling?"

"Babe, I haven't gambled in *months*." He'd visited Dino's Poker Palace in Wilmington just two days ago, but since he'd used money loaned to him by a friend, he didn't consider that to be gambling, at least not by his personal definition.

Tina sank to her knees on the hard wood floor and began sobbing into her palms. "God, I can't do this anymore", she said, "I just *can't*."

"Hey, babe", Curt whispered and kneeled down beside her. "Please don't cry. Everything's going to be all right." He tried to hug her, but she pushed him away.

"That's what you said when they first started accusing you of being a god damn commie. You said it didn't mean anything. You said you never even *went* to any of those meetings."

Curt sighed. "I didn't want to worry you. Besides, I didn't consider those meetings to be *communist* meetings. Hell, I've never been a communist. I just went to those things a few times . . . you know, for research purposes." Actually, he'd gone because a friend of his—the art forger—had told him there were a lot of cute socialist chicks who hung out at the meetings. According to his friend these chicks had some deeply-held progressive notions about "free love" and were willing to spread their legs for almost anyone fortunate enough to have memorized the correct rhetoric. Alas, Curt hadn't memorized the rhetoric very well at all. So he couldn't even say he'd gotten a good lay out of the experience. It was all just wasted time.

"Just give them a few names, one or two", Tina said. "The names of people you don't even know, or people you're not friends with anymore. Can't you do *that* at least?"

Curt shook his head, rose to his feet, and wandered over to the closed window. Dried white bird shit stained the wooden sill. "I'm just going to tell them the truth. I don't have anything to hide. These bullies can't push me around. That's what these people are, schoolyard bullies. Jesus, can't you see that?"

"Can't you see you're slitting your own throat?"

"Not if I tell them the truth. That's why I have to finish this speech tonight. I need to know exactly what I'm going to say. That's why you've got to stop harassing me. I need time to write."

Tina gestured toward the pages next to his typewriter with a disgusted sweep of her hand. "If you say even a *word* of what's in that speech they're going to hang you."

"I'd rather hang for telling the truth than hang for the opposite."

Tina just shook her head. She tore the ring off her finger and tossed it on the ground. "You'll lie for yourself every day but you won't lie for *me* even once, will you?"

"Tina, please, it's not like that at all—"

She swung open the door. "By the way, I know all about Dino's Poker Palace. A friend of mind saw you there. Two nights ago."

"Babe, it must've been someone who *looked* like me."

Tina laughed bitterly. "Did you make enough money for the rent?"

She just stared at him with contempt, then slammed the door behind her. He listened to her high heels clicking away from him quickly . . . too quickly.

"No", he whispered at the floor. He left the ring where it had landed. It wasn't the first time she'd stormed out of his apartment. He'd learned not to go after her. That only made things worse.

He sighed, sat in front of his typewriter and stared out his third story window. Despite the thin curtain of rain, he could see through the windows of the apartment buildings across the way. Some of his neighbors were watching TV, some vacuuming, some heavy petting, some arguing as loudly as him and Tina. None of them were typing. He envied them.

The big clock was winding down, the devil hordes closing in on him. He could feel them out there, invisible presences as tangible as grief. From a safe distance he'd watched many of his colleagues go down: Everett Sloane, Dalton Trumbo, Burt Gordon, Ring Lardner, so many others. Some of them weren't even communists.

Everett Sloane wasn't a communist. Quite the opposite. Unfortunately, he shared the same name with a man who *was* a communist and had attended far too many leftist meetings, signed too many subversive petitions. The Congressmen serving on the House Un-American Activities Committee thought their signatures looked a hell of a lot alike. They didn't, not really, but that didn't matter. They needed to fulfill their quota of scapegoats that month and Sloane fit the bill. After all, he used to associate with that pinko Orson Welles, right? That alone was suspicious. It didn't matter that Sloane was a hardcore Conservative. The Committee badmouthed him and the word went out in Hollywood and a great actor was blackballed into increasingly obscure roles. Unlike Burt Gordon and the other writers Curt knew, an actor couldn't hide behind a fake name. They were stuck with their face and identity. Curt wondered how much more painful the blacklist would feel for someone who, politically, held the same exact views as the Congressmen who were lynching him. That would be too much of an identity crisis for Curt to handle.

But that wasn't Curt's problem.

Curt's problem was that he *was* a leftist. He *had* attended communist meetings. He'd signed petitions for Russian War Relief and desegregation. He'd even helped write the speeches of a third party socialist candidate for President . . . in between cranking out cheap science fiction movies for small independent production companies that hung on like leeches to the torso of mainstream Hollywood. But he wasn't a commie. Never had been. Sure, he had friends who leaned that way, and that was fine, but Curt had always found the communists to be far too authoritarian for his tastes. He didn't want to trade in one authoritarian structure for another. He considered himself to be a loyal American. The only change he wanted to bring to this country was through the democratic process, not riots and revolution.

He'd written several short stories in obscure literary journals in which certain characters mouthed socialist rhetoric, but he had simply been basing those characters on his friends.

They weren't *his* views. Since when could *fiction* be used against you? The Committee had to know it was all bogus. He didn't even understand where they had dug up those journals. He'd written the stories years ago, when he was still in his teens. Did someone he know send them the stories? Who? Why? Oh, he didn't want to be thinking about any of this. Tomorrow the Committee would try their best to use his juvenilia against him. Somehow, he always knew his early fiction would rise from the grave to bite him in the ass. But he never thought it would be used to question his patriotism . . . .

All his friends, even some lawyers he'd contacted, told him to do the same thing: Say as little as possible. Plead the Fifth and ignore their questions and get the hell out of there. But Curt had seen what that strategy had done to his friends. Avoiding the inquisitors' questions by pleading the Fifth didn't help. It just made them even angrier. Of course, this was better than going to jail for contempt of Congress. Better than becoming a snitch. But in the end you still lost your career . . . forever. It was the easiest solution, but hardly the best.

No, they only left you alone if you insisted you weren't a communist. Look at Bertolt Brecht. Curt had met Brecht a couple of times. He knew people who were close to the playwright. Everyone in the world knew he was a socialist. His politics hovered somewhere to the left of Julius Rosenberg, and yet he sat there in front of all those neckties and cameras and insisted he had never been a communist. Everyone who knew him rolled their eyes and laughed. When it came down to the bottom line the staunchest communist of them all laid down and played dead. Perhaps, in his mind, Brecht saw the whole thing as a performance, a mere adjunct to one of his many existentialist plays. The Theatre of Alienation. Perhaps. After all, what could be more alienating than a hot seat planted smack dab in front of the craggy, hate-filled faces of Robert Stripling and Richard Nixon?

174

Curt had thought about lying, but he just couldn't bring himself to do it. And he refused to plead the Fifth. It didn't seem right. If he pleaded the Fifth, the world would think he was hiding something. He would show the Committee he had *nothing* to hide. Nothing.

So he decided to tell them the truth. He would tell them he was a socialist . . . but, of course, that didn't make him a communist or a subversive. It just made him a normal joe who wanted to see the world remade into a better place without racism and rampant homelessness and starvation. He'd written about utopias in his science fiction movies. These notions weren't silly to him, despite the cheesy special effects employed to bring them to life. These notions were very serious. A better world *was* possible . . . through reform and the ballot box. Not through violence.

He would say all of this, and he would be so eloquent that the American people watching the hearings at home would be able to do little else but sympathize with his sincere beliefs. If they asked him to rat out his communist friends, he would simply tell it like it is: that he had attended the meetings many years ago, and the political beliefs of his friends had changed and evolved by now. So there was no point in mentioning their names. And that was all true.

The truth. That's what would save him this time.

He wrote for over an hour, his calloused fingers banging away on his Smith-Corona typewriter, when there came a knock at the door. He was in the flow of things, almost near the point where he would wrap up his stirring speech and address the people at home as if they were sitting right there beside him. But the knocking continued, and there was no way he could pretend he wasn't home. This small one-room apartment had walls so thin they couldn't keep the clackety-clack sound of his typewriter keys from drifting into the halls.

He once had a beautiful apartment just off Melrose before being tainted with the red brush, before the work started to fade . . . slowly . . . slowly. Now he was in a little studio apartment on Virgil Boulevard. He had been on the brink of selling a play to be produced on The Great White Way. His intent had been to direct it himself. No more low budget sci-fi flicks for him. He was on the verge of the Big Time.

Then HUAC came a-callin', and interest in his play suddenly dried up just as his agent was about to seal the deal.

And now . . . someone *else* had come a-callin'. Who would it be this time? The storm troopers, ready to smash his face in with their leather jackboots just as they did to his relatives in Germany fifteen years before, when Curt was still a boy?

He wouldn't be surprised if it were. What else could go wrong in the United States of Amurrrica?

Curt sighed and rose from the desk. He stopped writing in the middle of a sentence. (He found this enabled him to get right back into the flow of things when he was interrupted, like now.)

He swung open the door, knowing it wouldn't be Tina, and said, "Yeah?"

The man who stood in the hallway looked like an aging tennis pro, or an actor just on the verge of going to seed. If Richard Carlson had had an older brother, it would've been this guy. He wasn't wearing a suit and tie, just casual clothes, as if he were ready to go to a family picnic. At eleven o'clock at night.

"Mr. Adamson?" the man said.

Curt hesitated. His instinct told him to tell the guy that he was just house-sitting for Mr. Adamson. The rumors of his pro-communism had been floating around for some time now. There were a lot of rightwing nuts out there, American Legion drones from Dairyland, who wouldn't hesitate to shoot a suspected communist dead in the street. Or the hallway of an apartment building gone to pot. That's what patriotism meant in 20th century America.

But Curt hesitated too long, and the man said, "Listen, I know you're Mr. Adamson. I was just being polite in asking. Can you just invite me in?"

"Invite you—? Why the hell would I do that?" He glanced over his shoulder at his speech. Jesus, he had important work to get back to. All these interruptions . . .

"You're gonna want to invite me in. I can't say what I need to say to you in the hallway."

"Why?"

The man pulled a cigarillo out of his jeans pocket and slipped it into his mouth. "I've got the only possible way for you to survive the inquisition you're gonna go through two days from now. Unless you want to end up ruined forever, teaching high school English in Littleton, Colorado like your father, you better listen to what I have to say. If you choose not to listen . . . well, that's your choice. I'm just gonna say my piece and then leave. It shouldn't take more than five minutes, if I don't have to repeat myself."

This man with the slate-gray eyes didn't seem threatening at all. There was no tone of annoyance or malevolence in his voice. Everything he said was stated matter-of-factly, as if he were ordering a new sofa over the phone.

Curt said nothing and opened the door wide. He stepped aside, allowing the man passage into his cold little grotto.

"You're one of the few people who's been inside this place the past couple of months", Curt said.

"You been too busy writing to have guests over?"

"I wish. I haven't been writing much lately. This thing . . . this grilling in D.C . . . .it's got me anxious as all get out. I can barely concentrate on eating, much less writing." He pointed at the sheet in the typewriter. "That's the first thing I've written in weeks. No, the real reason I haven't had anyone over is become I've been depressed. This type of thing can make you a little paranoid. Tell you the truth, you're not helping matters any with the whole mystery routine. Who the hell are you?" Curt was already beginning to regret letting the man inside his apartment. If the man pulled a knife on him, would he be able to scream loud enough to bring the neighbors? He thought he could, if he really had to.

The man glanced over at the typewriter. "Mind if I look?"

"Why not? It's only my words . . . my typewriter . . . my apartment . . . ."

The man puffed smoke rings into the air while reading the page. He shook his head, as if in pity. "This isn't going to do anything except get your neck caught permanently in a noose."

"Thanks for the vote of confidence. That'll help the writer's block. Did Tina put you up to this?"

"Oh, listen, don't take it as a disparaging remark about your writing. The speech is very well-written, as far as I can tell. You're a good writer. I've seen some of your movies and TV shows. I liked 'em. I'm no judge. I don't know much about literature. It was never my strong suit."

"Which movies did you see?"

"*Night of the Saucers, The Venus Cube, Hell Is a Planet.*"

"Oh." Curt sighed. "The science fiction stuff." The crap he had to write to pay the bills while he worked on his "serious fiction", fiction that almost no one had ever seen.

"That 'science fiction' stuff is the reason I'm here."

"Okay. Forgive my complete and utter confusion, I don't understand what you're talking about. Didn't you say this would take less than five minutes?"

"Bottom line." The man pulled a wallet out of his back pocket and flipped it open. The badge clearly read OSI: Office of Scientific Intelligence.

"Jesus Christ, is this real?" Curt said. "First I've got the FBI followin' me around, now I've gotta worry about the OSI too? What's next? The IRS about to pound on my door?"

"I wouldn't know", the man said. He slipped the wallet back into his pocket and extended his hand. "But they definitely won't be if you come work for us."

"Work for you? What do you mean, as some sort of double agent or something, like Herb Philbrick? Look, I'm not a communist, I never have been. How can I spy on the Russians if I've never met one?"

"Just calm down. I know you're not a double agent. We're hardly as stupid as the FBI. The FBI's run by J. Edgar Hoover, the biggest moron this side of McCarthy himself. Everything they're doing is just making the commies take root even deeper in this country. They don't care about their country. They care about making a name for themselves and holding onto power for as long as inhumanly possible. The OSI doesn't care about petty shit like that. While they're busy in the spotlight having press conferences, we're busy behind the scenes trying to save the world. And you can help us out, if you want to."

"How could I possibly help you guys?"

"Unfortunately, it's Top Secret. In fact, it's so Top Secret I can't tell you anything about it until after you've agreed to join us. And once you agree . . . once you're aboard, you see . . . there's no getting off. You have to see it all the way through to the end."

"How the hell can I accept your offer if I don't even know what it is you're asking me to do?"

The man smiled a reptilian smile. "That may seem like a paradox, but those are the facts. It's the reality of how intelligence work is performed these days. We can't risk any leaks. If we told you the nature of the project and you subsequently refused, well . . . then you might tell someone. And we can't have that. All you need to know now is that your country sincerely needs your help. Some of the brightest minds in the OSI decided you're one of the few people on Earth who can help with this particular project. You can trust us or not trust us. It's up to you."

"But what would I be doing . . . I mean, in general?"

"You'd be writing. Exactly what you do now."

"Writing what?"

"I can't tell you that. But you'll be rewarded handsomely. You'll make ten times as much as the average amount you'd get for a screenplay, or even that stage play you were hoping to sell."

"So you know about that." Curt lit a cigarette. "You really do your homework, don't you? What does all this have to do with the hearing?"

"It solves your immediate problem. The day after tomorrow you're going to plead the Fifth and stroll out of those chambers as calmly as if you were heading off to a picnic with your grandma. Within the hour you'll be working for us and under our protection. You'll fade away from the headlines while the Committee goes after someone else. You'll pretty much disappear from your old life, at least for a little while. Believe me, once you see the proposal, you won't care too much about what you're leaving behind." The man glanced around the cheap surroundings with an amused sneer.

"This is crazy. I need more verification than a damn badge. I need proof you actually are who you say you are."

"Sounds wise. So you're interested?"

"How could I not be interested?"

"Want to take a brief ride with me to headquarters?"

"Right now?"

"Sure."

"What about the five minute time limit?"

"I just said five minutes because I thought you were going to tell me to get lost. Turns out you've got more balls than I thought you had, Mr. Adamson. If you want to meet my superior, you can."

"But . . . wait a minute." He was beginning to feel certain this wasn't a hoax. "What if I decide not to take your offer? I'll still need time to finish my speech. How far do we have to go?"

"The L.A. branch of the OSI is downtown, right across from the Los Angeles National Cemetery. I can have you back in an hour."

It was one of the most important hours in his life. Curt came back to his tiny studio apartment, marveling at how much tinier it seemed now. He plopped down on his ratty mattress, trying to ignore the metal spring in his back. He had a decision to make. He'd met the Director of the L.A. branch. Face-to-face. The proposal was real. He still had no idea what this writing project was all about, just that they'd pay him a heap to do it. Isn't that what he'd wanted, ever since he was a kid living in the rundown tenements of Bunker Hill? To be paid for all the crap floating around in his imagination? To sustain himself through nothing more than thoughts inscribed on paper? Why not accept their cash? It was as good as anything the New York publishers or the Hollywood studios could throw at him. Almost certainly better, in fact.

But this whole secrecy business, that's what bugged him the most. Every writer wants acknowledgement for his work. But the Director had made it clear that he could not talk about these projects to anyone. The only people who would ever know were the members of a very small cell of agents who would be working with him closely.

That's when he spotted the eviction notice the landlord had no doubt slipped under the door while he was out.

Curt rose from the bed, leaned down and read it without touching it. He didn't want to acknowledge its existence by actually putting his flesh on it. Sixty days to quit.

Curt sighed and sat in the chair in front of the typewriter. Despite his fatigue, he lit a cigarette and returned to the speech. He finished it around 5:00 a.m. while the first crimson patches of dawn rose over L.A. It was one of the most eloquent pieces of oratory he'd ever written. He knew it was persuasive.

Too bad, he thought, that no one would ever hear it.

It went into the rusty file cabinet. Another one for the archives.

Just before dropping him off at his apartment, the OSI agent whose name Curt still did not know gave him a card with nothing written on it except a phone number. Curt was told he should call the number within forty-eight hours if he wanted to accept the assignment. If he waited even a minute after the deadline, the offer would be withdrawn forever.

With no sleep he hopped on a plane at 8:00 a.m. At 9:15 the next morning, on January 10th, he testified in front of HUAC in room 330 of the Old House Office Building in Washington, D.C. The head of the committee, Representative Marshall Hull, was an amorphous mass of flesh who rather resembled the Arthur Rackham illustrations in Kenneth Grahame's *The Wind in the Willows* (one of Curt's favorite novels). Curt wanted to reach out and strangle the arrogant beast, but didn't think he could find its throat buried under all that desiccated flesh. His only wish was to never share the same breathing space with this fat toad of a man.

It took him only a few minutes to plead the Fifth. The whole process might have lasted only a short while, but the neckties up there had to keep barraging him with a slew of questions to which his only response continued to be, "I plead the Fifth . . . I plead the Fifth . . . I plead the Fifth." This took over an hour.

The second he left the chambers he pushed through the horde of yellow journalists and sprinted down the street to a drug store. A pay phone stood in the back. He got inside, closed the doors behind him, and dialed the number. It was exactly 11:11 a.m. He would never forget that.

The OSI man answered the phone. He didn't even bother saying hello. "I guess this means you accept."

"Guess so."

"We need to rendezvous ASAP."

"You probably know I'm dying of curiosity. I don't know if I can wait until I get back to L.A. Can't you give me any information over the phone?"

"No. But I can give it to you in person. How about an hour from now?"

"Sorry, I haven't mastered the powers of teleportation yet. I won't be able to get back to L.A. until later tonight."

"I'm not in L.A."

"You're not?"

"I'm here, in D.C."

"Because of me?"

"I just finished watching the coverage on the TV here in my hotel room. You seemed very calm."

"It's my nature to seem calm, even when I'm withering up and dying inside. Did you follow me all the way out here?"

"No. I was on the plane with you."

"I never saw you."

"You wouldn't."

"Why're you guys spying on me?"

"I was *protecting* you. That's my job now, among other things. You're priority number one for me. From now until the foreseeable future."

"What if I hadn't called? Wouldn't that have been a lot of . . . wasted effort?"

"We knew you'd call."

"How?" Everyone likes to think they're unique and unpredictable, Carl thought. "How could you possibly *know* that?"

"You're a writer. You're naturally curious. You've been fishing around for new subject matter to write about. How could you pass this up, particularly after the Director stroked your ego so much? All writers have huge egos. That's their Achilles Heel. C'mon, you know that. Don't you?"

Curt hated smugness. He wondered if he'd made a bad decision. Of course, there was still time to back out. But then he'd wonder forever what would've happened if he'd taken the other path . . . and there were too many lost opportunities in his past already . . . .

As much as he hated to admit it, the agent was right. "Do I at least get to know your name now that I'm on board?"

"You can call me Ray."

"That was my brother's name."

"I know. A coincidence. Life's full of 'em. Where are you?"

"At the drug store on Independence Avenue, just down the street from the Cannon House Office Building."

"Grab yourself a seat at the counter. Buy a cup of coffee. I'll be there to pick you up as soon as I get dressed."

Ray pulled up outside the drugstore and honked his horn three times. Curt spun around, having just started his second cup of coffee, and waved at his new best friend. Ray. He wondered what the man's real name was.

Curt slipped into the passenger seat of the white Cadillac convertible and said, "Okay, where do we go from here?"

"You're used to working to tight deadlines, right?"

"Yeah, so?"

"Well, this deadline might be a little tighter than most."

Curt laughed. "I once wrote an entire screenplay in two days. I didn't sleep for forty-eight hours. What's worse than that?"

Ray pulled away from the curb. "You'll have considerably more than forty-eight hours. Unfortunately, you have to do a lot more than just write a screenplay. You have to build a world."

At first Curt had no idea how to respond to such a statement. It was clear from the tone of Ray's voice, the look on his face, that he was quite serious. So there was no need to ask him if he was or not. Curt took the statement at face value and said, "Would you care to be more specific?"

"No . . . but the Director will."

He wasn't seeing the Director of the L.A. branch this time. He was seeing R. H. Ashwill, the Director of the *entire* OSI organization. Curt was feeling very important all of a sudden.

This worried him. If an organization as vast as the OSI needed *him*, then what the hell did that say about the people who ran the OSI?

Ray drove all the way to the East Coast headquarters of the OSI in Fairfax County, Virginia. The compound was located in the middle of the country, surrounded by woods and farmlands. A small town had built itself around the compound. The town was almost self-contained. Once you entered it, according to Ray, you never really needed to leave if you didn't have to. Some of the OSI agents, the scientist types, apparently hadn't left the compound in years.

"Wow, looks fun", Curt said. "Listen, I've got a life to live. I don't want to end up stuck in a basement somewhere. A writer can't produce a masterpiece if he can't interact with the outside world."

Ray smiled. "Believe me, these eggheads I'm talking about aren't here against their will. They *like* it. We give them everything they need and they tinker with their little machines twenty-four hours a day. They're in Heaven. They could leave whenever they want to, but they never will. No, your job is going to be a little more complicated than theirs. Not only will you be writing for us, but your job will no doubt take you all around the country. Your contact with human beings might be slightly limited, of course. Or so I've been told. Don't judge by me. Anything I say is just rumor. Nothing is real until the Director says it."

"I've heard a lot of horror stories about the Director", Curt said. It was true. Curt had followed the gradual expansion of the OSI for the past few years, ever since its inception in 1947. "Is he as bad as I've heard?" Curt asked.

"Yes . . . but if you shoot straight with him, he'll shoot straight with you. You don't want to get on his bad side. If he ever catches you in a lie . . . oh, man, watch out. The kindly exterior vanishes. Like *that*." Ray snapped his fingers.

Curt nodded to himself and said nothing. He couldn't help but worry. Five girlfriends had left him because they couldn't tell where his fiction ended and his real life began. Sometimes even *Curt* couldn't tell. He told himself his habitual lying only helped him construct his fiction. Maybe that was true. But if his ex-girlfriends could see through his façade after awhile, how long would it take for the Director of the OSI to do the same?

Ray parked the car in an underground structure, then led Curt to an elevator that rose nine stories to the very top floor of the labyrinthine building. The elevator doors opened into a long corridor lined with plush carpet and walls decorated with the finest works of modern art. Curt recognized several original Jackson Pollocks hanging not more than five feet away from him. This surprised Curt. The Director didn't seem like the kind of man who would be sympathetic to Pollock . . . or any modern artist, for that matter.

Curt had read about this hallway in the press. Whenever an agent was called in on the carpet, he had to walk this corridor to the Director's sanctum sanctorum. For that reason this corridor was called "The Bridge of Sighs" by those inside the OSI.

Ray guided Curt down The Bridge of Sighs, past the Director's wizened old secretary who said not a single word to either of them but simply continued typing away on her Underwood typewriter as if Ray and Curt had walked this path a thousand times before. The Director was on the phone when they entered the office. He was in his early fifties, had curly white hair and wide blue eyes, and was about eighty pounds overweight. Despite his age, his eyes made him look young. And innocent.

This man who could kill with a single word looked innocent.

Curt knew full well that those fatherly features could turn savage at a moment's notice. Perhaps less than a moment.

Without a word Ray gestured toward a cushioned chair that sat in front of the Director's desk. "I'll be waiting outside to escort you back to your hotel when you're finished", Ray said, and left the room. This made Curt feel uncomfortable. He had already come to depend on Ray's company. He felt abandoned in the middle of the Minotaur's maze.

Curt heard the double mahogany doors close shut behind him.

Ashwill finished his conversation, something about arranging a public appearance in Miami, locked eyes with Curt, folded his chubby hands on the desk in front of him, and said, "Were you satisfactorily briefed on the reason I arranged for you to be brought here today?"

Curt shifted around in his seat. "Um . . . no. Not really, sir."

"What have you been told?"

Curt stuck his thumb over his shoulder and said, "Ray . . . Ray mentioned something about . . . ." Curt laughed. It seemed so silly now. "About building a world."

The Director didn't share in the laughter. "Is that all he said?"

"Well . . . pretty much. Except that I would be writing for you. Working to some tight deadlines."

"That's right." The Director pointed at several film reels that sat on a shelf behind him. Curt recognized the titles on some of them. Many of them were movies he himself had written. He now noticed a film projector sitting on the other side of the room, and the blank white screen hanging on the opposite wall. "I've been watching your films", the Director said. "I'm a big fan. And I want your autograph on a five-year contract with the OSI."

"Five . . . five *years*?"

"After five years we can reassess the operation and your part in it. At which point we can renegotiate the contract."

"Should . . . my agent be informed of this deal?"

"She can arrange the details, but she won't be dealing with us. She'll be dealing with a fictitious corporation created solely as an OSI front. Let me tell you something, Curt . . . ." The Director rose from his chair and placed his meaty, sweaty palm on Curt's left shoulder. "I love movies. *King Kong's* one of my favorites. I've got a print of that film and watch it whenever things get too stressful around here, which is most of the time these days, what with the pinkos and the commie sympathizers moving in from every corner." He began pacing back and forth in front of Curt, his hands clasped behind his back. "A good movie can change the opinion of the entire world, or at least it has the potential to do so. Your movies I don't like so much, but that's not your fault. The special effects, the acting, the sets . . . pure cheese. I'm sure you know that."

Curt nodded.

The Director leaned forward and planted his hands on Curt's arm rests. Curt could smell a trace of peppermint on his breath. He whispered, "We can give you a budget you never dreamed of, if you play square with us." The Director just continued staring at him, not saying a word.

At last Curt said, "Yeah, sure, I'm willing to play. Square."

The Director chuckled and patted Curt on the shoulder. "Good, my boy, good." He went back to pacing. "I'm sure, in the past, you've been forced to reign in your imagination due to budget constraints. Don't do that this time. Let your imagination run wild. Allow the technical boys to iron out the details."

"I don't understand, sir", Curt said. "What is it exactly that I'm writing? A screenplay?"

"No . . . think of it more as a *play*. But don't think in terms of traditional dramatic structure. Think of a play that has several hundred acts rather than just three or four . . . think of a play consisting of loosely-connected vignettes . . . a play that will continue over the course of several years . . . even decades, perhaps. Can you imagine something like that?"

Curt frowned. "No. But it sounds fascinating." After all, he'd missed out on his one chance at Broadway. He had wanted to change the world with his revolutionary approach to the stage. Perhaps the Director, the U.S. government of all people, would give him a second chance to do just that.

The Director chuckled again. His laughter was deep; it came from somewhere within the pit of his bulging gut. "I knew a guy like you couldn't resist the temptation to take part in the . . . what do they call it? The *avant-garde*? No one's ever attempted a play like this. You'll be the first."

"And where will it be performed?"

"You don't need to know that. This is Top Secret, tantamount to the Manhattan Project. You'll only know what you need to know, you understand? If you don't ask too many questions, you'll get everything you ever wanted and more."

"But . . . understand, sir, a writer has to ask certain questions in order to get the job done. That's the job of a writer: to ask questions."

The Director craned his blubbery neck toward him. He didn't seem like a man who was used to being contradicted. His tight smile seemed more like a spastic muscular disorder than any genuine sign of merriment. "You'll be provided with all the information you need. Ray will take care of all the details. He will be your . . . main liaison in this project. He can answer any question that you have."

"He's been a bit vague up to this point."

"That was necessary. Until you decided to accept the assignment, we couldn't let you know too much."

"I still feel like I'm in the dark."

"All that will change within the next few moments. The entire purpose of this meeting was simply to instill in you the seriousness of this matter. There's no room for fuck-ups. This will not be a normal play in which a minor flub will result in a brief suspension of disbelief in an unarmed audience. With this project, a minor flub could result in the death of a man with a family waiting for him at home. Think about that while you're writing your script."

That was a sobering thought . . . but strangely invigorating at the same time. "This script . . . you mentioned unlimited special effects . . . what kind of play is this? What's the genre?"

"The genre?" the Director said. He sat back down in his chair, pressed a button on his desk, then began jotting something down in a little black book. "I thought I had made that clear already. It's science fiction."

Curt nodded. His least favorite genre, the one he had been attempting to escape for so long now.

He heard the double doors opening behind him. He turned and saw Ray's silhouette standing there, beckoning him away from that massive desk and the intimidating presence that sat behind it still scribbling in his notebook. Curt had the feeling the scribbling was about him.

Curt and Ray flew back to L.A. together on the same plane. Ray rarely let Curt out of his sight. Even when Ray wasn't around, Curt felt like he was. Somewhere. Just out of sight.

Back in Los Angeles Ray took him to a series of bungalows located on Sunset Boulevard, a new movie company called Empire Studios. Actually, the studio had never made a movie before. They were, Ray explained, an elaborate OSI front. One day, of course, they would have to release a movie just to keep up the front, but their main purpose was research and development in what Ray called "the colonization of idea-space."

Ray first mentioned this phrase to Curt while they grabbed a bite to eat in the cafeteria at Empire Studios. Curt was taken by surprise, as he didn't understand the phrase at all.

"The colonization of *what*?"

"Listen, I don't know all the details", Ray said, "I'm just a field man. The guy who came up with the phrase is Dr. Kenneth W. Dolbraith. In fact, he's the one who came up with the idea of hiring *you*. He came up with this whole operation. He told me the purpose of this job was 'the colonization of idea-space.' Apparently, he has this theory that the imagination is this physical place, see, like Africa or the dark side of the moon (which we'll be colonizing soon as well, you can bet your bottom dollar on that). And this doctor, he thinks we can plant our flag in this space where all possible ideas are located. He figures there's only a limited amount of ideas available to mankind, so he figures the U.S. should lay claim to all the ideas that haven't been invented yet. That's where you come in."

These days Curt felt like he was trapped perpetually on candid camera. "The guy sounds looney-toons. Are you serious?"

"The man has five PhDs. You think that's looney-toons? Listen, the guy's a genius, you'll know that when you meet him. Maybe I'm not explaining myself right. I've never been very good with words. Not a lot of operatives are. That's why we have people like you, my friend." Ray reached out and gave Curt a gentle punch to the shoulder, then went back to eating his ham and cheese on rye.

"Well, when do I get to meet this guy?" Curt said.

Ray glanced at his watch. "In exactly twenty-two minutes."

Dr. Kenneth W. Dolbraith was an overweight gentleman who wore a beard with no moustache, a style that had always disturbed Curt for some reason. He was a relatively young man, no doubt in his early thirties, and yet Ray introduced him as if he had racked up a list of accomplishments possible only for a senior citizen. A black briefcase dangled from his gloved hand. Curt couldn't help but notice there was a combination lock on the briefcase.

The three of them stood outside the corner office of a bungalow on the lot of Empire Studios. The office had Curt's name on the door. This was the first time Curt had worked for a studio affluent enough to provide him his own office. Unfortunately, it didn't come with any sense of satisfaction, since Curt knew this wasn't a studio at all, but a false front, like the prop buildings in a Republic western serial.

Ray handed Curt a key and said, "Go ahead, open it. It's all yours."

Dr. Dolbraith nodded and gestured toward the door with his thick hands. Curt slipped the key in the lock and opened the door. What lay on the other side was a modest room that contained all the essentials: a desk, a chair, a manual typewriter. Sitting beside the desk: a box full of ribbon, typing paper, and yellowish second-sheets sprinkled with tiny flakes of wood pulp that Curt would need in order to make multiple copies of his manuscripts. Hanging on the walls were posters of his low budget films. One of the films, *Dr. De Muerte Contra Los Vampiros del Espacio*, had only been released in Mexico. It was the only poster printed in Spanish. Curt had never even bothered to see the finished film.

Ray gestured toward the framed posters. "We thought they might put you in the right mood. We figured you could decorate the rest of the office however you like." He walked over to a door in the back of the office and nudged it open. A small bathroom stood inside. "All the comforts of home. You don't even need to leave."

"Well, I doubt I could sleep here." Curt strolled over to the couch and ran his hand over the cushions. "It's comfy, but I like a bed."

"We have a fully furnished apartment here on the lot", Ray said. "It's only a block away."

"Really? It's like I'm back in college again", Curt said. "Dorm room living."

"We took the liberty of moving all your furniture from your previous apartment and placing it in the new apartment in almost the same exact configuration. The furniture that was too far gone, we replaced. We also had someone talk to your ex-landlord. The matter of your delinquent rent was taken care of."

"You guys think of everything."

Dolbraith strolled around the room, examining the contents of the cardboard boxes beside the typewriter. "You're a lucky man", Dolbraith said. "I fancied myself a writer when I was a young man and—well, let me explain. I *have* written books, but only about matters of psychology and sociology. You, on the other hand, deal in dreams. In fiction. Idea-space. I'm envious. I'd love to be able to dream dreams like that. I tried to write a novel when I was eighteen. I thought you had to do it like Hemingway, so I hitchhiked around the country and lived in flophouses and discovered it was very difficult to write when you didn't have any typewriter ribbon or paper with you. But I did manage to scribble down a thousand-page novel on yellow legal pads."

"Really?" Curt said, lowering himself into his padded swivel chair. "You still have it?"

"No", Dolbraith said, smiling sadly. "I just tossed it." He mimicked throwing away a piece of trash.

"Why?"

"It was a rotten pile of excrement. There were no human beings in it. The characters were all inanimate objects. I realized I didn't know anything about human beings. So I decided to become a psychologist in order to overcome that particular defect."

"Yeah? Did it work?"

Dolbraith grinned. "I'd like to think so. But I've never tried my hand at fiction again. Perhaps the urge has been fulfilled in other ways." He leaned down and picked up one of the typewriter ribbons. "I remember how frustrating it was to be interrupted in one's work due to a lack of the appropriate office supplies. This stuff looks like it should last you quite awhile. You needn't worry about any such impediments to your imagination."

"Yeah, that's a relief. I sure wish I knew what I was writing, though."

"Well, that's why *I'm* here."

"I'll leave you two alone", Ray said. "I have some business to tend to. I'll come back a little while later and escort you to your apartment, okay?"

Curt nodded and waved politely. Dolbraith did the same. "Please close the door on your way out", Dolbraith said.

Ray did as Dolbraith asked. The second the door closed Dolbraith set his briefcase down on Curt's desk, unlocked it, and removed a black metal box with an antenna on it. It looked heavy. Dolbraith lifted it into the air and moved it slowly around the room. A crackling sound emerged from the box, as if he were checking the office for signs of radioactivity.

Curt said, "What're you—?"

Dolbraith motioned for him to shush. He followed the crackling sound all the way to a radio sitting on a desk beside the bathroom. It had been on, but the volume was low, the sounds of muted Bing Crosby music rising quietly from the speakers. The box began crackling the second Dolbraith neared the radio. Dolbraith kneeled down on the carpet and unplugged the radio from the wall. The crackling lowered now quite a bit. It resumed a steady level, like the sleep-inducing noise that accompanies the snow on a TV set at four in the morning.

Dolbraith did two full walks around the room, including the bathroom, then returned the metal box back inside his briefcase. He took a seat in the swivel chair that faced Curt's desk. As Curt stared at Dolbraith, he suddenly felt as if *he* were the Director of the OSI conducting his own interrogation. "So? What the hell was *that*?" Curt said.

"Just a precaution", Dolbraith said. "I know Ray and his men probably already checked the entire bungalow, but it never hurts to double check."

"Double check? You mean for listening devices? Bugs?"

Dolbraith nodded. "The room's clear, though. Nothing could fool this machine."

Curt leaned across the desk and whispered, "Who would have planted bugs in here?"

"The Russians, of course. Other interested parties."

"But no one even knows what we're doing here."

"Exactly. You've worked in this town long enough to know there are men in Hollywood who consider themselves to be tantamount to kings. If a new studio lays down stakes in this town, there are people who are going to want to know what projects they're developing. If they're good projects, well . . . who knows? They might want to steal the ideas and beat the fledgling studio to the punch. It's happened before."

Curt nodded. Yes, he was aware of industrial espionage among the studios. Fellow writers had told him outrageous stories about such shenanigans . . . .

Dolbraith added, "It would be a shame if, while attempting to listen in on a simple pitch meeting, they instead came across what we're *really* doing. There are men in Hollywood who wouldn't hesitate to sell such secrets to the Russians."

Curt leaned back in his chair. "Well, I have met some pretty cold-hearted bastards here. Patriotism certainly wasn't their strong suit."

"You're talking about the communists you used to hang around with." Dolbraith removed a cigarette from a pack in his inside coat pocket. He offered Curt a cigarette as well.

Curt waved him away. "Listen, I just want to make it clear, I was never a communist. Those people were just friends of mine. We parted ways a long time ago."

"I understand. We all did strange things when we were younger. That's the prerogative of youth. In my case I wasted about four years writing a 1,000-page novel about inanimate objects. You hung out with communists. Fortunately, my form of stupidity didn't land me in trouble with Representative Marshall Hull and his friends. *Yours* did. And now you're here."

"So maybe it all worked out in the end after all. They say things happen for a reason."

"Do you believe in God, Mr. Adamson?"

Curt seemed taken aback by the question. "God? I-I'm not sure. I couldn't say one way or the other."

"You're an agnostic?"

"I suppose so, yeah."

"Perfect for a science fiction writer. All possibilities are on the table, eh? That's the sort of attitude you're going to need for this particular writing project. I believe the Director already gave you some hints as to the nature of the project?"

"Only a few. You could barely call them hints."

Dolbraith crossed his right leg over his left, as a lady might do. "You'll be constructing a planet. You're going to be writing the entire history of this planet. You'll categorize every detail about this distant star, right down to the type of flora and fauna that exist in its Northern and Southern hemispheres. This is a planet suitable for life; therefore, there needs to be fully realized, sentient beings to make the picture complete. We would like you to come up with distinct types of metaphysical and theological cosmologies for each of the various races on this planet. We want a definite location for the planet. We want to be able to locate it on a star map. We want, Mr. Adamson, for this planet to be completely *real* by the time you're finished with it."

Curt just stared at Dolbraith for a few moments before saying, "So . . . you're not joking, are you?"

"Not at all. That's your project in broad strokes; of course, there are still more instructions to come. It's a tad bit more complex than your previous forays into the science fiction genre I'd say, but we deemed the imaginative touches you showed in your previous scripts to be more than up to the task. What do you think?"

"You're kinda crazy."

Dolbraith laughed. "Well, you know what they say about psychologists . . . ."

"What the hell's the purpose of all this?"

"I'm sure the Director already told you about the cell-like structure of this operation? Answering your question, you see, might not only jeopardize your life but the integrity of this entire project. We're spending too much money on all of this to jeopardize it in such a casual manner."

"Is this all *your* idea?"

"Not just mine. Me and a committee of . . . other experts, you might say. Fellow psychologists. Sociologists. Philosophers. Nuclear physicists. We'll all be reviewing your work to make sure it all coheres, you see."

"A planet by committee."

"No, not quite. If that's what we wanted we could've done it ourselves. But we all decided that such an approach would lack . . . what do you call it? Inspiration? A touch of . . . authenticity? Something only a singular author can bring to a piece of fiction, any piece of fiction. A committee would reduce it all down to a conglomeration of meaningless factoids. We don't want that. We want this planet to have a *soul*. That's where you come in. We're simply going to be . . . well, technical advisors, I guess you could say."

"I wonder if God had technical advisors." Curt wasn't smiling when he said this.

Dolbraith was. "I've often wondered the same thing. You've worked on TV shows in the past, haven't you?"

"Briefly. I don't work well with others, though."

"That's another reason we chose you. Do you recall what the manual for the writing of an average TV show is called?"

Curt nodded. "A Bible."

"That's what you'll be constructing for us. But instead of a Bible for a TV series about cops or renegade doctors or whatnot, it'll be a Bible for a whole world. Doesn't it make you feel just a little bit heady?"

"Just a little. I feel like someone just wrapped the Titanic around my neck and ordered me to swim ashore."

Dolbraith chuckled. "Oh, it's not as bad as all that. I think a creative guy like you won't have any problem rising to the challenges. You like challenges. That's why you get involved with the type of women you do, right?"

"Yeah? And what would you know about that?"

"Don't be naïve, Mr. Adamson. We ran a complete background check on you before we approached you. Some of your choices have been . . . well, *interesting* to say the least. If you survived Tina, you should be able to survive this."

Curt planted his cheek in his right palm and chuckled derisively. "You got that right."

Dolbraith reached into his briefcase and pulled out a thick pile of papers. "Here are further instructions regarding the project. Make sure these papers never leave this room."

Curt nodded.

"I think it's time for me to leave. I'll check back on you in a week or two to see how you're coming along."

"Wait. That's it? Where the hell do I even begin with something like this?"

"Well, what do you usually do before you begin writing?"

Curt thought about that for a moment, then said, "Research?"

Dolbraith spread his hands in the air. "You have a nearly unlimited research budget at your disposal. Take advantage of it."

"But . . . how do I research something that doesn't even exist?"

Dolbraith rose from the chair and headed for the door. He shrugged. "You're the writer, not me. Have fun."

Then he was gone.

And Curt Adamson was alone in an office at a fictitious studio, wondering how to build a world.

Curt remained in the office reading over the instructions that Dolbraith had left him and soon sank into a deep depression. They were the most complicated instructions he'd ever seen. He'd never done well with instructions. Machines of any kind vexed him. He'd broken every phonograph he'd ever owned.

And that's what they wanted from him: to build a planet that operated like a machine. Planets weren't machines. If alien life existed, surely they wouldn't cow tow to the preconceptions of a bunch of anonymous PhDs. What the fuck had he gotten himself into?

He thought about Tina.

Curt grabbed his hat and coat and stormed out of the office. He'd take a walk around the block, try to clear his head. He strolled up the main pathway that led to the front gate. A burly security guard in his early thirties stood guard. He looked like an ex-Marine. Curt tipped his hat at the guard and tried to walk through the gate.

The guard halted him. "Wait, sir. May I see your pass?"

"Are you kidding? I'm not trying to *enter* the studio, I'm trying to *leave* it."

"I know. That's why I need to see an I.D."

"Who told you you needed an I.D. to leave? I'm coming right back."

"Sorry. I'm just following orders."

"Obviously. From *who*?"

Curt heard the sound of one of those little rickety golf carts behind him. Ray sat behind the wheel. "Sorry about this", Ray said as he pulled up beside him, "I should've told you about this before. It's just a precaution."

"A precaution against *what*?" Curt said.

Ray glanced at the security guard, then said, "Why don't we talk about it on the way to your apartment?"

"Why don't we talk about it here? Or in the bar across the street? That's where I was heading."

"That may or may not be true. The fact is, there's a bar here on the lot. There's even a mini-bar in your apartment. I think you'll like it. Why not go there?"

"Because I don't *want* to go there! I want to go to the one across the street!"

The security guard placed his hand on the revolver strapped to his hip and said, "You should just do what the boss says."

Curt glanced at the mean glare in his beady black eyes and said, "My apartment it is." He climbed into the golf cart beside Ray, and Ray wheeled away.

"I'm sorry", Ray said. "I don't like it any better than you do. But consider it from their perspective. They're investing a lot of money and time and trust in you, and they can't risk you suddenly getting cold feet and hopping on a Greyhound to nowhere."

"I honestly hadn't considered it until just now."

"Please don't feel like a prisoner—" Curt guffawed. "—because you're not. You can leave the lot anytime you wish . . . as long as I'm there with you."

"So we're Siamese twins?"

"Sort of. But only for five years. Or if they reassign me to a different project."

"Are you *happy* with this assignment?"

Ray shrugged. "I do what I'm told."

Curt smiled and leaned back in the seat. "Jesus, I wish I could be like you. Just do what you're told. I've heard that from everyone starting with Mom and Dad and then my teachers in school and then all the little tyrants who *thought* they were my boss and every single girlfriend I ever had. Just do what you're told. You know, I really try, or at least pretend to try, but I can't quite seem to pull it off. So when the façade begins to break down I just start drinking. That seems to solve the problem temporarily. You know, some of my best screenplays were written when I completely ignored what I was told to do?"

"If that works for you, then fine. It depends on what's most important to you. Are *you* what's most important to you? For me, my country comes first. First and last. Nothing else matters."

"Really? You know, I think you're serious. I've never met anybody like you."

"You were never in the military."

"4-F, thank God."

"I doubt we see many things eye to eye, Mr. Adamson . . . but there is at least one thing we can agree on."

"Yeah? What's that?"

Ray parked the golf cart in front of a quaint, two-story Spanish-style building located smack dab in the middle of the lot. "That drinking can solve most problems, at least temporarily. Your apartment is the one in the corner there. There's a nice cross breeze inside. I think you'll find it very spacious and comfortable." He handed Curt the key.

Curt stared at it for a second, then swiped it out of Ray's hand. He sighed and climbed off the cart. He started walking toward the building, then paused, turned around and said, "You say there's a mini-bar in my apartment?"

"Yep."

"You want to come up and have a drink?"

"I'm afraid I'm on duty."

"Don't you get a lunch break or something?"

"Yes." Ray thought about it. "Well, one martini won't hurt, I guess." Ray climbed out of the cart and followed Curt up the stairs. Like a shadow.

Or a conjoined twin.

"—and then she picks up this huge chair and throws it right at my head", Curt said, already slurring his words. "Almost cut my fuckin' head off! She calls the police and guess what?"

"What?" Ray said, starting in on his second martini. Curt was already on his third Scotch.

"They arrested *me*! Can you believe that? *Me*! *I* was the victim!"

The two of them sat on Curt's expensive sofa. The OSI had gone all out for him. It was the best apartment he'd ever lived in.

Ray shook his head. "That's the way it always is, isn't it? Jesus. Have you ever been married?"

Curt nodded. When Curt got drunk, he tended to lie even more than usual. This was one of those times. He'd never been married, but he could never resist improving the story of his life when afforded the opportunity and a receptive audience. "When I was eighteen", Curt said. "It was the worst time of my life. But it was the best time too. You understand?"

Ray nodded. "Absolutely."

"I was in love for the first time. You know how that is?"

"Of course. What was her name?"

"Nina Auerbacher. Beautiful! Red head. Green eyes. Tits out to here. My dream girl. Hell, she was *your* dream girl! We were in love." Curt had harbored an intense crush on Nina Auerbacher all throughout high school. He'd never even spoken to her.

"What happened to ruin it?"

"She turned out to be a fuckin' *whore*! She tossed me aside for every meathead on the football team. Fuckin' bitch. She told me she loved me. But every time she cheated on me I just accepted her back."

"You can't do that."

"I know, but she was my first. We had sex for the first time on the front lawn of the high school, around midnight. We'd been drinking all night. You know, one thing led to another, blah blah blah. For me it was this . . . Jesus, *incredible* experience. I told her I loved her. She barely even remembered it the next morning she was so smashed. But for some stupid reason I thought it was destiny that we end up together. We got married in Vegas, secretly, behind her mother's back. I was still living at home and she was still living at her parent's house. Can you believe that? We were married for a whole year before they found out."

Curt didn't lose his virginity until he was twenty-two. He didn't have his first drink until he was twenty-three. He'd never been to Vegas.

"How'd they find out?"

"Nina broke down and told them. I told her not to. They were Seventh Day Adventists, so . . . if you've ever met one, you'll know why I was scared . . . I knew they were real disciplinarians, if you know what I mean. Four of her brothers came over to my house while my parents were gone and beat the crap out of me. We never even really got divorced. I had to leave town. This is when I was living up north. I came to L.A. after that. But we've managed to stay in touch, me and Nina. She sends me little postcards from time to time. Despite all our problems, I still think of her as The One. If she walked through that door right now I'd take her back. Let me tell you, if I'm ever in any trouble I'm going to run right to her." He took another swig off the Scotch. It amazed Curt that he could keep the lie going even while drunk. Wasn't alcohol supposed to be some kind of low-level truth serum? It never worked that way for him. In fact, it always seemed to have the opposite effect.

"Where does she live now?"

Curt waved his hand in the air. "She moves around a lot. I've gotten her postcards from all over. Let me tell you, leaving aside the fact that she was a whore, Nina treated me better than any other woman I've ever known."

Ray took another sip from his martini, then said, "I don't have a story quite as dramatic as that. I lost my virginity on my eighteenth birthday. My dad paid for a prostitute."

Curt's eyes widened. "*Really*? Holy shit. Your dad was . . . some kind of a guy. I wish he'd been *my* dad."

"No, you don't. He was a sadistic wife beater, a hypocrite, a philanderer. He was stationed in the Philippines at the time. The whole family was living there with him. Dad was a military man."

"Just like you."

"Not like me!" Ray snapped. "I'm not in the military anymore. He used to visit the whore houses there pretty regularly, behind my mother's back. That's why he took me there.

It's not a pleasant memory for me at all. I wish it had been more . . . well, romantic." One more sip turned into several. "Does that . . . sound silly to you?"

"No", Curt said quietly.

"I would be more than happy to switch experiences with you. You should be satisfied with the memories that you have. At least you felt a real connection with someone, even if it was just for a short period of time. That's not true for a lot of people. It's nothing to be depressed about. So don't be." Ray downed the rest of the martini.

"I . . . I won't be", Curt promised, meditating on the late afternoon sunlight reflecting off the amber liquid sloshing about within his glass.

"I stayed too long", Ray said, standing up rail straight, "and drank too much. I have to get back to my duties."

"I thought your duty was shadowing me."

"That's my main priority. But I have other duties that need tending to as well. I suppose you'll begin writing soon?"

Curt laughed. "Yeah, after I polish off this glass."

"Don't drink too much. You need to concentrate."

"I do my best writing when I *don't* concentrate."

Ray seemed to tense up. "It's not my place to tell you how to do your job. But it is my duty to make damn sure the job gets done. If you need to . . . disregard your specific instructions in order to get the job done, then I suggest you do so. Whatever it takes. I don't pretend to understand . . . artists. Writers. Whatever. I'll see you later, Curt. I actually enjoyed the conversation. I . . . don't have a lot of simple human interaction these days, ever since I joined the OSI."

"Why *did* you join?" Curt said.

Ray smiled a tight smile and said, "I didn't want to be a military man. Good day." Ray turned on his heels and marched out of the room, leaving Curt wrapped in a pocketful of deadening silence.

Curt remembered the pile of perfunctory instructions sitting on the table in his office, and wished he'd brought them home with him so he could—with a spontaneous, dramatic flourish—dump them into the trash. Instead, he performed the action in his imagination. Which was good enough for him.

He downed the Scotch and walked toward the Smith-Corona waiting for him in the bedroom.

He'd always liked writing in his bedroom.

Sleeping and writing were so similar to him.

By the next morning he had produced little more than a few vague notes on the project. Eventually, he decided to test the limits of their "unlimited budget." As a kid he had been a voracious reader. He'd read any pulp magazine he could get his hands on, genre be damned: westerns, blood and thunder action stories, Oriental adventures, even true confessions. Though his tastes were diverse, he had always enjoyed the science fiction magazines the most. Oddly enough, however, it was his least favorite genre to *write*. He wasn't quite sure why that was—perhaps because it paid so very little. His favorite among all the magazines had been *Astounding Science Fiction*. He had fond memories of being sick in bed and waiting breathlessly for his mom to bring home the next installment of "At the Mountains of Madness" by H.P. Lovecraft. Unfortunately, his mother had thrown out all his copies when he was sixteen and away at summer camp. He'd always wanted a complete set of the magazine, if only to replace what he'd lost.

He got on the phone and dialed the special number that would connect him to Ray. When Ray answered, Curt said, "Uh, listen, I need some research material. Could you arrange to have it sent here?"

"Sure. What is it?"

"I need the latest, cutting edge books on astronomy, I don't care what it is. Also, I need a set of *Astounding* going back to 1930."

"*Astounding*? What's that, some pulp magazine?"

"One of the most famous."

"Well, where the hell am I supposed to find a complete set?"

"You're the OSI agent, you figure it out."

Ray sighed. "Does it have to be a *complete* set?"

"Well, as complete as possible. This is crucial to the project."

Ray sighed again. "I'm on it."

Indeed he was. The astronomy books came first: about three dozen of them from Universities all around the globe. Some of them were far too technical for him, so Curt focused on those intended for popular consumption. He'd blown through four of them by the time the weekend rolled around; along with the weekend came several extremely large cardboard boxes.

He opened the boxes with trembling hands. Inside lay an almost-complete set of *Astounding* going all the way back to 1933. Curt spent the better part of the day simply looking at the illustrations. Why reinvent the wheel? If better minds before him had already done the work, then why not use it to his advantage?

He began to categorize the types of aliens depicted in the illustrations. He segregated the various aliens into separate piles. He gave each species a different name. There was the "insectoid" pile, the "reptoid" pile, the "angelic human" pile, the "midget-with-oversized-cranium" pile, the "hairy giant" pile, the "hairy dwarf" pile, the "tentacled blob" pile, the "robot on rampage" pile, etc.

He began to notice, also, trends in varying spacecraft designs. So he categorized those as well. There was the "rocket ship" pile, the "flying saucer" pile, the "cigar-shaped craft" pile, the "crescent moon" pile, the "oblate spheroid" pile, the "perfect sphere" pile, the "triangular" pile, the "diamond-shaped" pile, etc.

He then tabulated the results of this limited survey. The most common form of alien depicted in the magazine appeared to be the "midget-with-oversized-cranium" type, the most popular type of craft the "rocket ship." But Curt knew that a highly advanced civilization wouldn't be using a design similar to what human beings were now contemplating. The design had to seem *alien*, at odds with the known laws of physics. The "flying saucer" design was already popular, so why not go with that?

He began to assign each of the races their own type of spacecraft. He postulated that all of these creatures were coming from the same planet. Why not? The Earth was populated with diverse races, multitudinous species, so why couldn't an alien planet be blessed with a similar variety? He began to map out the planet, the type of atmosphere it would require, the varying landscapes this world could contain. Constantly he referred back to the magazines. There were numerous illustrations of possible extraterrestrial landscapes. Again he categorized them: the "ice planet", the "desert planet", the "crystalline planet", the "hollow planet", the "jungle planet", etc. But why couldn't all these environment exist on the same planet? He described the various environments by mimicking what he saw in the pictures, then adding his own twist here and there.

He needed a name for the star around which the planet revolved. Of course, the aliens themselves might call it something else, but Earth scientists might have christened the star already. And indeed they had. Curt needed a star that was plausible—perhaps a star that scientists had already identified as being conducive to sentient life. Curt found it in the August 1944 issue of *The Astronomical Journal* in an article called "The Star of Lowest Known Luminosity" by G. van Biesbroeck. Wolf 359 in the constellation Leo, near the ecliptic. He located it on a star map. He pressed his finger against the microscopic dot and whispered, "You're my ticket out of this mess."

Over the course of a single weekend, Wolf 359 had gained a stellar companion inhabited by over a billion different living beings.

Curt Adamson had to transform himself into an astronomer, a biologist, an engineer, a metaphysician, a poet, a chemist, a mathematician, a moralist, a painter, a geometer . . . and a god. And he had to do so on deadline. Yahweh, of course, hadn't had any help. Or had he?

Just as he segregated the varying extraterrestrial categories, Curt now segregated his writing material in terms of categories as well. He created a different file for each race that existed on the planet. Within those categories were sub-categories: their various religions, the types of jokes they would tell, how they regarded the nature of time, etc. He created a separate file for each geographical environment on the planet. Within those categories were further sub-categories: the unusual flora and fauna of each environment, the average ranges of humidity as it correlated with the time of year, the depths of its oceans and the even stranger secrets they contained.

He categorized the dreams of the people with large craniums. These people didn't consider dreams to be mere fantasy. For them dreams merged in one continuous stream with the rest of their daily lives.

The reptoids didn't dream at all.

The tentacled blobs didn't recognize the past or the future, only the present.

The hairy dwarves had never heard of the concept of time.

For the insectoids, time was worshipped like a god.

For the robots, time *was* a dream.

Some of these beings traveled to Earth in physical space craft. Others were capable of slipping through rifts in space and teleporting to other planets; they were born with this ability. Others visited the Earth only in the form of astral bodies released from their physical shells during prolonged ceremonies involving deep meditation.

He didn't bother to generate these facts in any structured or chronological manner. When an idea popped into his mind he simply jotted it down and placed it in the proper file. He could sort through it all later. One moment a notion regarding the connection between the electromagnetic field of the planet and the life cycle of insects would occur to him, and the next a thought about the unusual effect of sunspots on the psychology of the angelic humanoids who lived at the planet's Northern Pole, followed by . . . .

And on and on and on.

These facts poured out of Curt's head. He worked like this for a month-straight with little surcease. He began to immerse himself so deeply in this fantastical world that he began to believe he wasn't dreaming up the planet, but rather recreating a place that actually existed . . . or at least existed at one time. He ignored the fact that some of the concepts were being pilfered from prior sources. Nonetheless, what if all human beings were capable of tapping into this knowledge, but no one had ever tried? What if little bits of the truth had emerged from time to time in the form of cheap pulp illustrations and penny-a-word melodramas? Perhaps . . . .

One Saturday evening (Was it a Saturday? Perhaps it was a Wednesday. He'd lost all track of time since engaging in this weird endeavor.), he became so excited by this sense of discovery that he picked up the phone and dialed Tina's number. It felt like he hadn't spoken to her in years. Perhaps she had forgiven him by now . . . .

The second he heard her voice he said, "Tina? God, I love you."

A moment of silence. "Curt?"

"I need to tell someone", Curt said, pacing back and forth in his living room, "I'm now engaged in my greatest masterpiece ever."

"Again?" Tina said. "What is it this time, *The Beast That Ate Pasadena*? When do I get that money you owe me? You know, everything you *didn't* lose at Dino's Poker Palace?"

"Right now. I have access to all the money in the world. The new studio I'm working for is paying me a truck load of cash for the new . . . whatever it is. A play. A novel. An atlas. I don't know what the fuck it is. If you come over we can discuss it. I have a mini-bar here in my new apartment. I know you can't resist a bottle of Jack."

"Well . . . I have to admit that is tempting. I'm shocked any studio would hire you after your little performance in front of the Committee."

"You saw that?"

A moment of silence. "I happened to see it on the news."

"You never watch the news. You were monitoring it. So you *do* care."

"I . . . I just wanted to see if you would take my advice or not. I thought you'd call me right afterwards. You never did. So I figured you'd moved on."

"I *couldn't* call you. I've been writing twenty-four hours a day. This new studio hired me right after the hearing."

"But . . . why would they *do* that? It doesn't make any sense. I thought you said you'd have to move to Europe to get away from the taint of those hearings."

"Listen, don't worry about that right now. The studio set up an apartment for me on Sunset. How soon can you get over here?"

"Can't you pick me up?"

Curt sighed. "I can't leave."

"Why not?"

"The studio doesn't *want* me to leave."

"The studio doesn't want you to leave your own apartment?"

"No, no. I'm living on the studio lot, you see. They don't want me to leave the lot."

"But why?"

"It's complicated. Do you want to come over or not?" He could tell he had her hooked. He been through this routine enough to know she would give in. It'd been so long since he'd caressed her sandy blonde hair, since he'd felt her bare hips beneath him, since he'd . . . .

"Okay, okay, I'll drop by. But just for a minute." Even through the phone he could hear her smiling, just slightly. For a *minute*? They both knew she was lying. "What's the address?"

Curt could feel the erection forming in his pants. "Do you have a pen, a piece of paper?"

"Don't I always?"

"Okay, listen, it's—"

The line cut off. A dial tone hummed angrily out of the receiver. "What the *fuck*?" Curt said. He slammed the receiver down, picked it up again and began to redial the number. But then he noticed there was no longer any dial tone at all. He checked the cord. Yes, it was plugged into the wall. Everything seemed to be in working order. Nothing was wrong with the phone.

That's when it dawned on him. It was no accident. Of course it wasn't. What had he been thinking?

He lowered the receiver gently into the cradle, sat down in

212

his wooden straight-back rocking chair, and just stared at the phone. About a minute later it rang. He waited three rings, then picked up. "Yes?" he whispered.

"I apologize for ending your call prematurely", Ray said, "but you understand we can't have you talking about this project to anyone."

"I wasn't going to tell her anything", Curt said. He stared at the blank white wall opposite him, and realized that Tina would insist on hanging something pretty up there. A forged de Kooning, perhaps?

"You weren't going to show her your writing?"

Curt thought about that. "Yes, I suppose I was. I was just excited. I forgot. I'm sorry, I'm not used to this . . . whole situation . . . ."

"I understand. Just make certain it doesn't happen again."

"Listen . . . Ray . . . Tina used to be my girlfriend. She might *still* be again. I didn't realize how much I missed her until I heard her voice. I'd like to see her. I promise not to say anything about the project. Other . . . *people* working for you . . . other agents . . . they must have wives, right? They manage to lead two lives without revealing anything about their work. Why can't I do the same?"

"The difference is that these men are pre-screened. We know they're the type of individual who can keep a secret before we even consider hiring them. They're trained agents. You're not. You're a writer with an ego and a tendency to shoot your mouth off. If you were married or engaged we never would've approached you in the first place. I'm afraid it has to be like this."

Curt reached out, grabbed the underside of the glass coffee table in front of him, and flipped it over onto its side. As the glass cracked against the edge of an expensive wooden desk he yelled into the phone, "I can't even be with a fucking woman for five *fucking* years, is that what you're telling me? You never mentioned *any* stipulation like that before I agreed to this god damn situation!"

"I told you your contact with human beings would be limited. You didn't object to that at all."

Curt sighed. Well, yes, Ray had said that. "I . . . I know . . . but I didn't know what that really meant at the time."

"Listen, I'm not the villain here. I understand how you feel. Maybe I can do something about it. Let me contact my superiors. I'll call you within the hour."

"You think they'll let Tina visit?"

Ray paused. "I can't say for sure. Maybe. I'll call you back. Just grab a drink and stay put." Ray hung up.

Curt lowered the receiver into the cradle, glanced at the mess of glass shards on the carpet, walked over to the mini-bar and poured himself a Scotch. He downed two glasses while standing in the middle of the room staring at the front door. He considered making a run for it, but knew he wouldn't even get as far as the front gate. How did this happen? He always prided himself on being independent. No ties to anyone. Even when he was working for a studio, he never considered himself to be *their* employee. He was his own boss. They were paying him for his time and words, but not his mind. He was Zorro and Winston Smith and Batman all rolled into one. And now . . . now he was waiting for a call from Big Brother allowing him to play with one of his little friends down the street.

He had been reduced to a child.

After awhile (he wasn't quite sure how long), Curt grabbed a dust pan and a small broom, kneeled down on the carpet, and began cleaning up the broken glass. He had only picked up a few long shards when there came a knock at the door.

He thought it might be Ray. He didn't want to answer. He didn't want to see anybody associated with "The Project." But what the hell. It's not like he could pretend he wasn't at home.

He sighed, rose to his feet, and swung open the door. He was surprised to see a young woman standing on his front door step. She was blonde and thin, but not *too* thin, just like Tina. In fact, she was exactly his type.

Curt thought she looked to be about five years younger than Tina, probably about twenty-two.

The young woman lit a cigarette and slipped it between her painted red lips. She was wearing a lot of make-up, but this wasn't unbecoming.

"I understand you're in need of some . . . companionship for the evening", the woman said with a low, throaty voice like Lauren Bacall, and smiled an inviting white smile.

She was beautiful. He desperately wanted her to be Tina . . . but she was beautiful, and she was there, and all he had to look forward to that evening were shards of broken glass and a damn broom.

"Yes", he whispered, "I am."

He opened the door for her. And as he did so, he knew he was only sinking himself deeper into their trap.

But that didn't stop him from offering the young woman a drink, and shutting the door behind her.

A personal assistant to Kenneth W. Dolbraith, an agitated young graduate student at UCLA where Dolbraith taught classes in behavioral psychology, dropped by Curt's apartment to pick up the first bundle of information regarding the planet of Qutius (the closest English approximation of the name by which the inhabitants referred to their home planet). The assistant name's was Gordon Something-or-other. He seemed to realize that the information was important, and yet claimed not to be privy to the envelope's contents. His job, he explained, was simply to deliver the envelope to Dr. Dolbraith as soon as possible. Gordon then passed along the message that Dolbraith would get back to Curt about the manuscript as quickly as feasible.

Before Gordon left he paused on the front patio and said, "Is this some kind of screenplay you're working on?" He lifted it up in the air with one hand, as if testing the weight. It was clearly heavier than any screenplay in existence. The manuscript was already five hundred pages long. "I know Dr. Dolbraith has been a consultant on several movies during the past few years", Gordon added, "so I just figured . . . ."

"Well, not exactly a screenplay", Curt said, leaning against the doorframe, proud of the fact that he was wearing a bathrobe at two in the afternoon. "It's more like an encyclopedia, I guess you could say."

Gordon stared at the package with some curiosity.

"I wouldn't try to open that if I were you", Curt said. "Believe me, kid, it's not worth it."

"Oh no, I would never even *think* about that", Gordon said. "I've delivered plenty of packages to Dr. Dolbraith's office. I've never peeked at any of them. Dolbraith is a very strict man. If he even *thought* I was breaking the rules, he could blackball me out of the entire medical community for the rest of my life."

"Really?" Curt said. "Sounds like a tough man. Why would you want to work for a guy like that?"

"Why *wouldn't* I? He's one of the most influential psychologists working today. A single word of praise from him could set me up in my own private practice for life."

"I see. He can make or break careers, then?"

"Absolutely. He doesn't pick just *anyone* to be his personal assistant."

"I'm sure that's true. But . . . if you ever insulted or crossed him, even by accident, what do you think would happen to you?"

"Well, he's not a forgiving man. He's got friends everywhere. Once Dolbraith is through with you, the whole *world's* through with you too. He'll ride you until you surrender or die. Take my word for it. I've heard horror stories."

"Horror stories", Curt said, nodding. He smiled. "That happens to be one of my specialties."

"Oh? You're a horror writer?"

"Well, I've *written* horror movies. Horror and science fiction."

"Then you probably know that Dolbraith is a science fiction fan. He's got a lot of paperback books in his office. Some real weird stuff. He once told me he'd love to be a science fiction writer, but he just doesn't have the imagination for it. He says his specialty is the real world. He can't afford to let his head drift off into the clouds. You understand. He needs an anchor."

"Well, my specialty's the opposite", Curt said. "Perhaps that's why we make such a good team. I can't wait to hear what he has to say about the manuscript."

"I'm sure he'll get back to you soon." Gordon turned his back on Curt and proceeded to stroll down the narrow, bush-lined path that would take the graduate student back onto the main road leading to the front gate of Empire Studios.

Just as Curt was about to close the door, he stuck his head out and shouted, "Hey, Gordon!"

The student turned. "Yes?"

"Did Dolbraith ever mention to you who his favorite science fiction writer was?"

The student thought about it for a moment, then grinned and said, "Oh, yes. I couldn't forget that. Some guy with a funny name. Carmichael C. Forrest."

Curt nodded. "Thanks", he said, "I was just curious."

The student waved and walked on.

"Carmichael . . . ", Curt mumbled to himself. It would be difficult to forget that. The name sounded vaguely familiar.

Curt closed the door behind him, pulled a pile of magazines out of his closet, and began digging through them . . . .

After a week had passed, during which time Curt continued to obsessively write (or perhaps "research" would be a better word) new information about Qutius, Dr. Dolbraith appeared unannounced on Curt's doorstep. Curt happened to be wearing the same tattered bathrobe he'd worn when Gordon had shown up at his doorstep the week before.

Dolbraith glanced over his disheveled state and said, "Yes, I'd been told you keep unusual hours."

"Been up since eight", Curt said, "I just haven't gotten dressed. I've been scribbling. Or building. However you want to put it. Let's get down to brass tacks, Doc. What do you and the boys think of my baby?"

A very serious expression washed over Dolbraith's face. "Let's talk inside." His wide girth pushed past Curt's arm. Curt closed the door behind him.

Without sitting down Dolbraith took his hat off and said, "The material's excellent. Almost the entire board agreed it was more than satisfactory. In fact, you exceeded my expectations."

"That's good to hear." Curt strolled over to the mini-bar and began making a martini. "Want a drink?" Though Curt had always been somewhat anti-social, these days he liked it when people came over. It gave him an excuse to drink. His father had always told him that an alcoholic was someone who drank alone.

Dolbraith shrugged and nodded.

"Now wait a minute", Curt said, "what do you mean *almost* the entire board. Who didn't like it?"

"Well, obviously, Mr. Adamson, if I can't tell you who's on the board I can't very well tell you who objected to your material. Rest assured they were in a minority. Just a couple of left-leaning scholars who object to the entire concept of The

Project. But The Project will move forward, with or without their approval."

"What are their objections?" Curt slipped an olive into the martini, then handed it to the doctor.

Dolbraith smiled. "You're a sly one, Mr. Adamson. If I told you their objections, it might reveal the exact nature of The Project. Trust me, at this point you're safer if you didn't know."

"I don't disbelieve you there", Curt said and sat down in the comfy new sofa provided by the OSI. Dolbraith remained standing.

"If we feel you need to learn more about The Project in order to continue your work", Dolbraith said, "believe me we'll inform you immediately. The only thing that matters to us now is the success of The Project. Many, many lives are depending on this."

Curt raised his eyebrows. "Not too much pressure, is there?"

Dolbraith smiled again. "I'm sure you're enough of a professional to disregard such pressures and focus on the task at hand."

"It hasn't been a problem so far."

"Then you feel comfortable here? All your needs have been met?"

Curt thought about the regular visits of his new companion, as well as her various colleagues, and nodded. "The situation is . . . more than satisfactory. In fact, it's even exceeded my expectations."

"That's good to hear. Yes, *very* good." Dolbraith downed his drink, then set the empty glass on a napkin sitting on the coffee table. "I think you'll find that the negatives of being involved in this project are far outweighed by the positives. Fairly soon, after the board has reviewed your material in greater detail, we'll be asking you to move on to the second level of your assignment."

"Which is?"

"You're going to be writing an actual scenario, a *scene* involving some of these beings you've invented. Let's call it a one-act play? It'll involve several distinct characters, and these characters will be required to understand their roles to the smallest detail if the operation is going to occur without a hitch. We'll hand you a brief, um . . . what do they call it in Hollywood? A 'treatment'?"

Curt nodded.

"We'll be handing you a brief *treatment* within the next few days. With that in hand, you should have no trouble constructing the first act. *Au revoir.*"

Gordon delivered the treatment five days later while Curt was sitting on his front patio drinking a beer. He offered a beer to Gordon, but the student declined. So Curt offered the kid a cup of coffee instead. He looked like he needed it. "As long as it doesn't take too long", the kid said and took a seat in a plastic lawn chair on the other end of the patio. Curt walked into the kitchen and began making the coffee. While it was brewing, he opened the package from Dolbraith and glanced over the treatment. He was surprised to see that the instructions appeared to be clear and precise, perhaps the most clear and precise document he'd received since this whole affair had begun. The overall purpose of this entire project, however . . . well, that was still as opaque as mud.

After downing half the coffee and exchanging the barest of pleasantries, Gordon insisted he had to get back to Dolbraith's office at UCLA asap. He thanked Curt for the coffee and began walking down the path. Before he could get far, however, Curt said, "Um, before you go . . . I have a question about Carmichael Forrest."

Gordon turned. "Forrest?"

Curt stepped away from the patio. He doubted the OSI's little microphones could pick up what was being said *outside* the house. "Did the good doctor ever mention *why* Forrest was his favorite writer?"

Gordon took off his glasses and began wiping them with a handkerchief—a nervous tic he'd exhibited before. "Well, I don't know if Forrest is his favorite writer of all *time*. Dolbraith's a pretty voracious reader. Almost anything interests him, everything from epic Russian tragedies to pulp westerns. He always has his nose in something. All I know is that Forrest is his favorite *science fiction* writer."

Like all scientists, Gordon seemed to be a stickler for details. "Okay, sorry I wasn't specific enough in my question. Do you know why Forrest is his favorite *science fiction* writer? Is there anything about his style, his themes . . . sense of humor? Whatever?"

"Well, it's probably because he knows him."

"Dolbraith knows Forrest?"

Gordon nodded. "They served in the Office of Strategic Services together during World War II. I believe they worked in the propaganda division together. Forrest was a master at using propaganda to solve strategic problems in a peaceful way."

"Yeah? How so?"

"Well, for example . . . a couple of years ago, while serving as an advisor in Korea, Forrest realized that the English words for 'I Surrender' sound exactly like the words 'love,' 'virtue,' and 'humanity' in Chinese. So he and his team dropped flyers all over Korea telling Chinese soldiers to come forward and wave their guns in the air while saying those exact words to the American soldiers in the event that they were captured, or about to be captured. The psychology of the Chinese preclude any sort of 'official' surrender, but as long as they could say *those* words instead of actually surrendering, they seemed more willing to give up their arms. Forrest probably saved thousands of lives that way."

"Pretty impressive."

"Forrest wrote the book on psychological warfare . . . I mean *literally*. It's called *Psychological Warfare*, the first full-length book to ever be published on the subject, at least for public consumption. I've seen it on Dolbraith's bookshelf. Of course, Forrest wrote that book under his real name."

"*Real* name?"

"Yeah, Carmichael Forrest isn't the name he was born with. He has several different names for every type of writing that he does. Forrest is just his science fiction name. He writes all his technical papers under his birth name."

"What's that?"

"Anslinger, I think. Phil Anslinger? Felix Anslinger? Something like that."

"What's he do now? I mean, do Dolbraith and him still work together?"

"No, I don't think so. Forrest works for the U.S. Embassy in China, doing what I don't know. I don't think he's been in the United States for years. According to Dolbraith, they haven't seen each other in awhile. I got the impression they had some kind of falling out. I remember Dolbraith saying, just in passing, that they stopped working together about . . . five years ago? At the end of the summer of '48, I think he said. But don't quote me on that. In fact . . . don't mention any of this to Dr. Dolbraith, okay? He doesn't like it when people . . . well, when they talk about him behind his back."

"Would you call this 'sensitive information'?"

"Oh, no. I doubt it. It's just . . . you know, you can never be too careful."

"I'm learning that more and more every day, friend. Anyway, thanks for the conversation. I'll see you around."

Gordon nodded and smiled again, then hurried down the path—perhaps to make up for the time that had been lost during the conversation. The good doctor must've been a hell of a taskmaster.

Curt opened the front door, shut it behind him and locked it. He walked toward the closet door once more and opened it. Though it had taken him a few hours the week before, he had managed to rout through all the magazines the OSI had provided him and pull out every issue that included a story by Carmichael Forrest. There were only about a half-dozen. Forrest wasn't a very prolific writer . . . though apparently his creator, Anslinger, *was*.

The six stories all had intriguing titles: "Adrift in the Supersargasso Sea", "The Dead Harlequins of Har Meggido", "The Trollops Who Fell from the Moon", "The Cryptoterrestrial Manifesto", and "The Ship of Devanagari." Curt decided to put the new treatment on the back burner for the moment while he settled down in his sofa and read all six stories in a row. The sun was setting by the time he reached the final tale.

All the tales were well-told and unique. They had a rather baroque, complex story structure. Though all of them were set in the future, they read like fairy tales translated from an unknown language. All six stories seemed to take place in the same world, only a few years after a limited nuclear war had turned the present geopolitical situation upside down. And yet these were not necessarily dystopian stories. Indeed, they all possessed a subtle, lighthearted tone, as if the author didn't think a complete upheaval of the present geopolitical situation would be a *bad* thing. Most of the stories dealt with an alien race of telepaths who had infiltrated the governments of various planets in the solar system in an apparent attempt to covertly guide these worlds into a single, utopian future. All of the governments in question, no matter the race or planet, seemed to resist this path. So the aliens were forced to resort to psychological trickery in order to manipulate said planet into accepting what was best for both them and the entire solar system.

The last story, "The Ship of Devanagari", impressed Curt the most. It was about two planets at war with one another. One planet was in a state of decline and fading fast. The planet's government no longer possessed the riches or the man power to resist the other planet's invading fleet. So instead they poured all their resources into a last ditch effort. They began spreading a rumor throughout the solar system that they had discovered a fully functional mother ship that had once belonged to a powerful alien army now extinct for millennia. The empire had complete control of this ship; its destructive power was awesome. The dying empire manufactured a shell of a ship that matched the mythological magnificence of the legend and arranged for various enemy fleets to catch a glimpse of this ship and the apocalyptic destruction of which it was capable. Before long the rumor was more powerful than the reality, and the invading army decided to play it safe, bypass the planet, head instead for a world not protected by such an omnipotent guardian.

Upon finishing the story Curt double checked the publication date of the magazine: September 1949. Only three years ago. About thirteen months after Dolbraith and Forrest had ceased their wartime collaboration. Curt tossed the magazine aside and just stared up at the bare white ceiling for several minutes, not moving.

Then he picked up the treatment and re-read it, looking for the hints that lay hidden between the lines.

Late one night Curt dreamed about strange lights darting about the skies above Los Angeles when he was just a boy.

The lights danced above the rooftops like fireflies with no sense of direction, exhibiting nothing more than an inherent love for the dance. These fireflies almost seemed to be performing, loving the attention from the passersby below. Loving the sense of mystery they instilled in those few who witnessed them.

Curt and Tina were two of those passersby fortunate enough to see the lights. But why, as a mere child, was he out on the streets at night with a full-grown Tina? Maybe it didn't matter. This was dream logic, after all. It *felt* real, and so it was.

The fireflies fused together suddenly to form an immense saucer made of pure light. It hovered about an immense brownstone in the distant Hollywood Hills, then spun away . . . up, up, up into the clear night sky.

He turned to say something to Tina, but she was gone too. Had she gotten into the saucer?

A hollow sensation penetrated Curt's stomach, a lingering sense of loss and regret.

"We're having a bit of a problem."

The baritone voice on the other line was that of Dr. Kenneth W. Dolbraith. It was one o'clock in the morning. Curt had just fallen asleep.

"What the fuck?" Curt said. "Can't this wait until morning?"

"Watch your language!" Dolbraith screamed. This outburst woke Curt right the hell up.

"Uh . . . sure", Curt said, "whatever."

Curt had finished writing the first act about a week earlier at exactly midnight. The millisecond he wrote the last word of the little play he felt like he was on fire. He felt so much more focused now that a part of the puzzle had been revealed to him.

He felt good about what he had written. In fact, for the first time in a very long time he even felt good about himself. Was it possible . . . was it just *possible* . . . that he might actually be playing a small role in building a positive future for the world?

He hadn't heard back from Dolbraith on what he or anybody else had thought of the play. But now here he was waking him up out of a dream about Tina to tell him there was a problem. What the hell kind of a problem could there be?

"I'm eternally at your service", Curt mumbled sarcastically.

"I'm glad to hear that", Dolbraith said. "We'll be needing your presence asap at Lot 13. The rehearsals aren't going well."

"Rehearsals?" Curt said. "I didn't even know you'd cast the fucking thing!"

"Language, Mr. Adamson", Dolbraith said, "language."

"All right, all right. Who knew you were so fucking sensitive?"

"There's a way to conduct oneself and a way not to conduct oneself. I'll send someone to pick you up. Please do not come down here in your bathrobe. I've seen you lounging around the cafeteria in that dirty old thing. It's embarrassing."

"To who? You want my words, don't you? I have to feel comfortable in order to write."

"I'm sure you were not writing in the cafeteria."

"I was takin' a break. What business is it of yours?"

Curt's only answer was a dial tone. The son of a bitch had hung up on him. Curt sighed and forced himself to climb out of bed. He slipped on his tattered bathrobe and slippers, lit a cigarette, and strolled out into the night. A golf cart came by to pick him up about five minutes later. Ray was behind the wheel.

Curt slid in beside him. "I see they dragged you out of bed too", Curt said, crossing his arms over his chest in a futile attempt to keep warm.

"I was already up", Ray said.

"Oh, yeah? Who was it? One of those chicks you send over to cheer me up?"

Ray remained silent for a moment. "I'm afraid not", he whispered. He almost sounded offended by the suggestion. "I don't sleep much."

Curt slumped down in the seat. "I wish I were more like you. If I never slept I could get more writing done. Me, my problem is I sleep too much."

"I'd switch lives with you any day of the week", Ray said. "I haven't had a good night's sleep since I was a kid."

"Why is that?"

"Migraines."

"Yeah? Bad ones?"

"As bad as they come. You know, Dolbraith's not going to be happy about your attire."

"Fuck him."

Ray halted the golf cart in the middle of the lot. He leaned toward Curt and whispered, "Listen, you don't want to push this man too far. He's a ruthless son of a bitch who always gets what he wants. *Always*. I've seen him operate. I know what I'm talking about."

"He's not going to do shit to me", Curt said. "He needs me. Me and my words."

"For now he does. How long is that situation going to last?"

"Well, at least five years, according to my contract."

"If you want to outlive the contract you'll play nice with the doctor."

"So why didn't you warn me? Don't pretend to be my friend now. If these people are so damn ruthless, why didn't you just tell me to hit the wind, get out of the country or something?"

"Listen, I'm just doing my job. I'm as monitored as you are. Maybe even more so. I would never get away with wearing what you're wearing. You have far more freedom than I do, at least for the time being."

"Why do they work this way? What's it all for? Have you ever wondered that?"

"It's all for the good of the country."

"Are you sure?"

Ray paused for a moment. "If I ever stopped believing that, I'd go crazy."

"Well, I hope you're right. I hope you're not crazy. I hope this whole thing pays off in the end. I hope the world's a better place because of the nutty scheme they're brewin' here." Curt paused a moment to study the impassive expression on Ray's face. "You really don't know what it's all about, do you?"

"I told you. My job is to be your handler. You're writing some kind of science fiction film about another planet. That's all I know."

"And you never wonder about it? You never ask questions."

"I'm not paid to ask questions. That's your job. I do know certain things about Dr. Dolbraith, however. I know he has several powerful politicians in his back pocket. Blackmail. This man doesn't fool around. Neither should you."

"Politicians?" Curt said. "Senators?"

"Several of them."

"Which ones?"

"I shouldn't tell you that."

The picture was beginning to grow clearer. "Any of the Senators involved with the House Un-American Activities Committee?"

Ray stared at him. Curt remembered how brutally the Chairman had grilled him that morning in D.C., just before he gave himself over to Ray. "Senator Hull?"

Ray laughed and said, "Dolbraith wishes." Then started the golf cart up again.

In his mind Curt began retracing all the events that led to this moment. HUAC on his ass. The studios dropping him one by one. The loss of the gig on Broadway. The landlord evicting him. Tina leaving him. Had the OSI taken advantage of the situation? Or had they caused it from the beginning?

His brief, positive attitude toward The Project began to wither. What kind of utopia could possibly arise from such Machiavellian tactics? Certainly nothing more than a false one.

A utopia for the people on top.

The golf cart stopped outside Lot 13. Curt tipped his nonexistent hat toward Ray, then entered the gaping dark maw that lay beyond a pair of massive double doors big enough to drive a truck through.

The sound stage was in chaos. The scenery was that of the interior of the massive mother ship Curt himself had designed. It was a circular metal room in the center of which stood a glowing, crystalline structure shaped like a rose. Something inside the rose kept swirling around and around, creating a disorientating, strobe-like effect. This was the power center of the ship. This would be the room to which the aliens teleported their first abductee in Curt's script. In the middle of the chamber, lying on a metal slab, was a naked man in his early twenties. Judging from his build and haircut, he seemed like a real military-type. Perhaps some kind of mercenary.

The figures huddled around the metal slab gave Curt quite a shock. He'd never seen such realistic costumes. In the previous films he'd worked on the special effects for the monsters amounted to little more than an old rug thrown over a stuntman. This was something quite different indeed. These creatures looked exactly like the descriptions he'd cobbled up for the elfin aliens with the oversized craniums. The special effects guys had added their own touches, however, giving them bulging eyes the size of cue balls and long, thin willowy arms that moved in an inhuman fashion, like something out of a nightmare. They were painted a bluish-gray color, like that of a living corpse.

The man on the slab was screaming.

Yes, if such things visited Curt in the dead of night, *he'd* be screaming too.

"We've come a very long way to meet you", one of the aliens said in a very unconvincing manner. "We mean you no harm. Please, what is your time-cycle?"

"God *damn* it! Are you all *total incompetents*?" A deep, booming voice echoed through the sound stage. "What's *wrong* with you people?" The voice of Kenneth Dolbraith. Dolbraith pushed a metal cart filled with donuts onto the floor and said, "My lab animals can act better than this!" Dolbraith caught a glimpse of Curt out of the corner of his eye. His eyes widened. "Curt!" For the first time, Curt saw the man smile.

Dolbraith moved toward him as fast as his stubby legs would allow, wrapped his arms around Curt's shoulders, and led him toward the blazing lights.

"Listen, we need your expertise." Dolbraith was trying his best to sound pleasant. "You've worked on movie sets, and I haven't, so I thought . . . ."

"Hey, doctor", one of the aliens interrupted, "can I take this head off for a little while? I'm burning up in here."

"You son of a bitch!" Dolbraith screamed. "You'll stay in there as long as I tell you to. What are we paying you for, you god damn jackass?" He turned back toward Curt and said, "You see what I'm dealing with? Total unprofessionals."

"I'm not the unprofessional around here", the alien said. "I've been on more military operations than you can possibly count. How many years did *you* serve in the military?" The alien waited half a second, during which total silence dominated the set, then said, "That's what I thought." The man pulled off his alien head and tossed it on the ground. The other aliens mimicked his actions, grumbling in dissatisfaction.

Dolbraith's face turned bright red. "You're not in the military now, you stupid little faggots! You'll do as I say when I say it or I'll—"

Curt gripped Dolbraith's shoulders and whispered calmly, "Where's the director?"

"*Director?*" Dolbraith said. "We don't need a director! *I'm* in charge around here!"

"But have you ever directed actors before?"

"*Actors?* These sons of bitches aren't actors! They're jarheads! I just need this fucking scene to be convincing is all. How hard can it be? You just say the lines the way they're written! Suddenly these mannequins think they're Laurence Olivier!"

Curt patted Dolbraith on his bulky shoulders and said, "You're right, doctor, I've had some experience in these matters. So just let me talk to them."

"Better talk sense into them quick. We can get anyone else to replace those assholes." The doctor wandered off into the corner to sulk.

Though Curt had never directed a movie himself, he'd seen it done over and over again on productions with far less resources than this one. He'd known some directors very well. And he himself had directed numerous stage plays back in college. And, needless to say, there was that chimerical Broadway show that had been wrested from his grasp at the very last moment . . . .

The four actors were now huddled together to one side of the mother ship set, gulping down Coca-Cola and wiping sweat from their brows. Curt approached them and said, "Hi, I'm Curt Adamson, the writer of this . . . screenplay." Is that what it was? Curt still wasn't sure quite what to call it. "I can see you're having some problems with the doctor over there. What's the problem?"

The first protestor spoke up. "The problem is he's a grade-A son of a bitch, that's the problem! He's not a director. He doesn't know what the hell he's doing."

"Listen, how did he cast you guys? I mean, do you have any experience acting?"

"We're all former military", one of the aliens said. "I killed more Japs with my bare hands than anyone else in the South Pacific."

"Next to *me*, that is", another alien said, laughing.

Then the two of them started telling jokes about dead Japs.

"I was in *Arsenic and Old Lace*", the first protestor said. "Off-off-Broadway. I was Jonathan Brewster. That was before I got drafted."

"*Really*?" Curt said, impressed.

"And I was in *A Midsummer's Night Dream* in high school", the fourth alien said. "I was Puck."

"Okaaay", Curt said. "Look, I'm a little puzzled. How did you all drift into this? I mean, why aren't you still in the military?"

"Well", one of the aliens said, "we've exchanged notes and it seems that each of us ran into a little bit of trouble in the military. We were sort of . . . well, drummed out. We did our jobs too well, I guess."

"I see", Curt said. Just like *he* was drummed out of Hollywood. Accidentally. On purpose.

He turned toward Jonathan Brewster and said, "What do you need to do this scene?"

"Better suits, for one. These things are killing us. We can't even see out of them."

"Maybe we can do something about that, but not today. Okay, what else?"

"We haven't had a lunch break yet, and we've been working all morning. Also, it's hard to memorize these lines. They're kind of awkward. We want to be able to ad lib a little bit."

Curt bristled at this comment. He felt like punching the jarhead in the nose, but he doubted he could hold his own against someone who had probably strangled Nazis in his sleep.

"Okay, well, we can work on the lines together. Anything else?"

"Yeah", said Puck, "what's our *motivation*?"

"What?" Curt said.

"The 'director'"—he put air quotes around the word—"isn't directing us. We're not machines. It's very hard to get into the heads of these aliens. What's my *motivation* during the scene? Where are we emotionally?"

"Okay. Listen carefully. All of you are part of an insectoid-minded race. In other words, your brains are linked together at all times. So you communicate to each other through telepathy. So you're sort of like ants. It would be nice if you could synchronize your movements a bit as you move through the scene, almost like a dance number—but we want it to be subtle, not overt. So why don't you guys break for lunch, then we'll take about twenty minutes to block out the scene, okay?"

"Gee, that sounds great", said Puck. "You're the kind of guy who needs to be directing this farce."

"Yeah", said Brewster, "we need to make sure this goes smoothly now so there aren't any fuck-ups when we finally go live."

"Live?" Curt said.

"Sure", said Puck, "that's the whole point of this operation. To go live. You must know that, right?"

"Of course", Curt said, "of course."

"That's why we're so damn nervous", Puck said.

"Well, I wouldn't say I'm *nervous*", said Brewster, "just annoyed."

"Well, *I'm* nervous", Puck said. "Just a single mistake might mean blowing the whole operation. That's a lot of pressure. All the other operations I was involved in were real simple, just in and out." He used his hand to mimic the firing of a revolver. "Bang, and you're gone. Collect the money and go on vacation until the next assignment. Those were the days."

The three other aliens nodded in agreement.

Curt placed his hand on Puck's muscular shoulder and patted it gently. "Think of this as an exciting new adventure. For all of us. I promise you we'll get this whole operation running smoothly. Now you guys go grab something to eat."

"Thanks, Curt", Puck said.

One alien said to the other, "Hey, that joe's all right."

Curt walked over to where Dolbraith sat in the director's chair with his bloated head resting in his hands. He realized the doctor's head could easily be mistaken for that of the alien. Curt tapped him on the shoulder and the doctor jumped slightly.

"I think I've got these men under control now", Curt said.

"They're ready to do the scene?"

"I sent them off to lunch."

"*What*?"

"Listen, you need to finesse these people in order to coax a good performance out of them. You have to play to their egos. Treat them like children. Give 'em a carrot on a stick, just like you would with a child. All actors are the same."

"They're not *actors*! They're trained *killers*!"

"I know, I know", Curt said, "but now they're actors, so you have to treat them that way. It's the only way they're going to get the job done the way you want it."

"I don't know", Dolbraith said, "I don't have time to finesse overgrown *children*."

"Perhaps I should take over then", Curt said. "I do have experience in this type of thing."

Dolbraith thought about it for a moment or two, then said, "All right. As long as you keep everything on schedule you can run this ship however you want. But we need this whole show ready in two weeks. That's when we go live."

"So this is some kind of . . . elaborate rehearsal then?"

"You might say that."

"Why the secrecy? Why not let me in on it? I did write this whole thing."

"Yes, based on *our* directions. You don't have a need to know yet. You just need to shoot the scenes the way we want them shot." Dolbraith relinquished the director's chair, rose to his feet and stormed off the sound stage.

234

There goes Herr Director, Curt thought. This wouldn't be the first time a director failed at his job because he knew nothing about human psychology.

But he wondered if it was the first time a world-famous *psychologist* failed at his job because he knew nothing about human psychology.

Probably not, Curt thought.

Curt glanced around the elaborate saucer from space, surveying his new world.

The first scene Curt directed went over well with the actors and the crew. So did the second and third and so on. That old feeling, the one he used to experience while writing the stage plays he'd scribbled in college, came back to him as he and his players brought his words to life. The second Dolbraith left the soundstage, the whole operation moved along much more smoothly.

It felt odd not knowing the exact purpose of what they were doing. Was this film meant to be shown somewhere? Or was this all really just an elaborate rehearsal for some far more crucial event? He didn't want to let on to his players that his superiors had kept him in the dark, so he fished for details from his actors during breaks between scenes.

It soon became clear to him that they didn't know what it was all about either. All they knew is that they had to memorize their movements and lines for a later performance, one that would be live and, as Dolbraith put it, "interactive." Neither Curt nor the actors knew what that meant.

It took them a week to film the thirty-page script. Curt was certain he could have done it even quicker if only he had been prepared and had been working with professional actors. Nonetheless, he was happy with the end product.

He met with Dolbraith at the end of the final day and asked to be included in the editing sessions, but the good doctor told him that would be unnecessary. The Committee had their own vision for how the final product should look.

Curt asked if he could at least see the film when they were done.

Dolbraith tipped his fedora in a mockingly polite gesture and assured him that Curt would be indeed be privy to the final product and furthermore would reap lifelong benefits for his vital participation in this project, per their written contract. Good day to you, sir.

And that was that.

Curt was shut out of the rest of the project and knew nothing about what was being done to his film in the editing room. He felt like Orson Welles, post-*Magnificent-Ambersons*.

Without any further writing assignments, Curt retreated into his cave on the lot and requested a projector and a screen and prints of various films for his "research." Indeed, all he really wanted to do was get lost in his favorite films. He watched them in the random order they sent them to him: *Jane Eyre, Dracula, Citizen Kane, Duck Soup, Lady from Shanghai, The Mummy, Monkey Business, The Stranger, White Zombie, Horse Feathers, The Magnificent Ambersons, Island of Lost Souls, Animal Crackers, Macbeth, Black Magic, Son of Frankenstein, A Day at the Races, The Third Man, Bride of Frankenstein, Cocoanuts, Journey into Fear, Mad Love, A Night at the Opera, The Black Cat, Go West . . . .*

By the time he was done with this marathon he had a four-day-beard and hadn't moved from the sofa in his living room except to go to the bathroom or make something to eat. By the time he was done he had come to the same conclusions he had already reached many years before: 1) All the great movies had already been made, and 2) All you really needed to know about the art of filmmaking could be found, compressed conveniently for the casual viewer, in the films of Orson Welles, the Marx Brothers, and the pre-code horror films of the 1930s.

Even the most serious student of cinema needn't venture too far beyond those parameters in order to understand the esoteric language of celluloid.

The ghosts of these old movies haunted him in his sleep. He'd always wanted to write something as immortal as those films, and he wondered if this project had pointed him in the right direction. After all, people weren't afraid of vampires or monsters conjured up in laboratories. Now they were afraid of *themselves*, of the communist next door and the egghead scientist who had conjured up the atom bomb and the politician in human form lurking just outside the door ready to attack at the barest provocation. Now they were afraid of the demons that might possibly lay beyond the farthest star, ready to arrive in metal crafts shaped like halos to upset the cosmological view instilled in them by decades of intractable religion. They were no longer afraid of God's punishment, but the notion that God might not exist at all. Instead, perhaps nothing lay beyond the stars but creatures of pure Darwinian instinct . . . .

It was these fears that Curt had now tapped into. It was these fears Curt had just finished immortalizing on the silver screen. But Curt suspected these almost surreal images would not be presented to the public as fiction. This wasn't a revolutionary idea. After all, Orson Welles had already beaten The Committee to the punch with his *War of the Worlds* radio broadcast back in 1938. Hell, it was possible Orson had given The Committee the idea in the first place, but perhaps all that panic had served some sort of higher purpose. Perhaps fear could be used to bring about peace. What else would prevent a full-scale nuclear war from devastating the entire planet with the push of a few buttons? As easy as it was for Curt to flick on this film projector and invoke twenty-year-old images of Bela Lugosi cloaked in shadow, it was even easier for some faceless automaton to give the signal that would rain atomic death down on the heads of every single person living on Earth.

Did fear itself serve a Darwinian purpose?

Could fear bring people closer together rather than pull them apart?

Curt settled back into his sofa and reached into the latest package sent to him by The Committee. There were three movies in this one: *The Invisible Ray, The Seventh Victim,* and *At the Circus.* Perhaps, Curt thought, the absurdity of the third film would offset the utter grimness of the others . . . .

He spooled *The Invisible Ray* into the projector and settled in for an education about the dangers of mixing cosmic rays with a dash of hubris . . . .

Nothing beats watching a beloved movie with someone who's never seen it before.

His first instinct was to call Tina, but of course he knew he couldn't do that.

And he was getting tired of all the girls, no matter how beautiful they were. Besides, he couldn't imagine any of them sitting still long enough to watch *The Invisible Ray*.

So he picked up the phone and called his shadow.

"Listen, I'm feeling in a rare sociable mood and thought it'd be nice to have . . . well . . . a companion."

"I see", said Ray. "Who will it be this time? Genevieve? Veronica? Rita?"

"No, no. You don't understand. By 'companion' I mean . . . I mean a *friend*. You want to come over and have a drink?"

Ray laughed. "Sure, what the hell. Why not?"

When Ray arrived Curt offered him a drink. Ray accepted a martini, then picked his way across the cluttered floor to find a clear spot on the sofa. Curt's months of research materials lay scattered about the carpet.

"Are all writers as messy as you?" Ray said.

"Yes", Curt said, "at least the ones I know. What kind of movies do you like?"

"Westerns."

Curt started searching through the boxes and boxes of prints. "I think the closest I have to that is *Go West*. Will you settle for *Son of Kong*? It arrived just the other day . . . ."

"I don't really have time to watch a movie. You see, I was going to contact you in the morning anyway to give you the news, but since you called I figure I might as well do it now."

"News? What news?"

"You have a new assignment."

"Really?" Curt grew elated. None of this marking time anymore. Now he could move on to the next act. "Do you have the treatment? How come Gordon's not delivering it to me like he usually does?"

"This isn't a writing assignment."

"Am I . . . am I directing something that someone else has written?"

"Your expertise is required in a completely different arena. It involves acting skills more than anything else. You've had some acting experience, haven't you?"

"Well, back in college, yes."

"Excellent. Tomorrow afternoon you and I are hopping on a plane and heading to Wisconsin."

"Wisconsin? Listen, I'm a California boy, born and bred." Actually, he was born in Washington state. "I can't handle the cold weather. I do my best writing in the sunlight."

"I told you, this isn't a writing assignment. And you don't have a choice. This assignment comes from Dolbraith himself. Straight from The Committee."

Curt sighed. "Where is Dolbraith? I haven't heard from him in a week."

"He's out on assignment. Deep undercover. You probably won't be hearing back from him for awhile."

"Well, at least that's good news. Okay . . . how long are we going to be in Wisconsin?"

"Only a couple of days. Just long enough to snap a few photographs, then leave."

"Am I going to be the one snapping the photos?" Curt said.

Ray reached into his inside jacket pocket and withdrew a silver cigarette lighter. He tossed it toward Curt, who just barely managed to catch the lighter without fumbling it.

Ray sat three rows back and to the right. For some reason he preferred not being seen with Curt during the plane ride. Curt didn't care. He could use the time to catch up on some reading. He felt as if he'd been cut off from current events for the past few months. He wasn't even sure what was going on in the real world these days. At 30,000 feet he snapped open the Saturday edition of the *Los Angeles Mirror*, which he'd picked up for seven cents at an airport newsstand. Blazoned on the front page, as was the case lately, was yet another UFO story. A sighting had occurred over San Pedro by a couple of airline pilots. Curt read the article with some interest. It continued onto page A-29. Beside the final column of that article was yet another UFO story. It was small, only a few paragraphs. Space-filler. State Representative Anton McPhillips of Wisconsin had been found by local police on the side of a lonely country road babbling to himself about aliens. McPhillips was a rising name on the political scene. He was well-known for his controversial, leftwing politics (a rarity these days) and his vocal opposition to the House Un-American Activities Committee. In the hospital he told news reporters that alien beings had abducted him out of his own car during a midnight drive in Heathville. His description of the aliens sounded eerily familiar. He claimed not to remember very much about the encounter, except that at one point one of the beings asked him, "What is your time cycle?"

Curt tossed the paper onto the floor. When the stewardess tried to give it back to him, he refused to accept it.

Curt and Ray checked into separate rooms at a modest hotel in Middlesburg, Wisconsin—one of the smallest towns in the entire state. Ray directed Curt to sign in under the name "Maxwell Ryder." It was in this obscure village that Curt was to begin his second mission for the OSI.

After unpacking, Curt met Ray in his room down the hall. Curt paced the carpet. "I don't know if I have the constitution for all this spy stuff."

"Too late now", Ray said as he pulled a bundle of complex looking equipment from a small suitcase sitting on his mattress. "Your job is simple. You're going to be wearing a wire tonight. I'll be listening to the entire meeting in real time."

"What am I supposed to be doing?"

Ray sighed. "It's very simple. You just have to attend the meeting. Just sit and listen. Take some photos with that cigarette lighter I gave you. And most important of all, try to get *as many names as possible*. We want to know who's at this meeting."

"But why *me*? Why can't *you* do it? Why can't *anyone else* do it?"

Ray rolled his eyes. "We've already been over this. This meeting's ostensibly a gathering for UFO enthusiasts, but we think it's really being used as a communist front to disseminate propaganda in the heartland. This is your area of expertise. You're the only agent who's qualified. We need someone who speaks their language. Anyone else would stand out like a sore thumb."

"Listen, I've written a *few* science fiction stories. A *few*. And always for *money*! That doesn't mean I'm an expert in UFOs, for Christ's sake! It's hardly the same thing!"

"It's close enough for folk music, as far as the OSI is concerned. So just get used to it. All you have to do is sit there, take some photos, talk to a few people, and keep your ears open. How hard is that?"

"What if they discover I'm wearing a wire?"

"They won't, unless you tell them."

"When's this meeting begin?"

"At six." Ray glanced at his watch. "Three hours from now. You've got time to relax. You want to take a shower before I put this stuff on you?"

Curt sighed and nodded. He considered mentioning to Ray the article in the newspaper, the one about Representative McPhillips. At the last second he decided against it. After all, why bother? Perhaps Ray already knew, perhaps he didn't. Either way the man could do nothing about the situation at all. He had a job to do and he would do it no matter what his personal feelings were. Did the man even *have* any personal feelings? Perhaps Ray was right that evening when he said *he* was more of a prisoner than Curt ever could be.

"You want to say anything else?" Ray said. "For the record?"

Curt shook his head. "Not that I can think of."

"Then be back here in an hour."

"Wait a minute. Yeah, I do have another question. What'd you say this guy's name was? The leader of this group?"

PYTHAGORAS INVICTUS, OF THE ORPHEUM SOLUTIONS GROUP!

That's what the large banner read outside the Masonic Hall on North Orange Grove Lane. The group must have rented the hall for the night. At the door stood a little old lady, hunched over, a mess of blue hair growing wildly out of her scalp. She held a wicker basket in her frail hands. A tangle of ones and fives peeked over the rim. A "suggested" dollar donation (or more) was required in order to gain access to this special meeting about the imminent arrival of the Space Brothers.

The hall was fairly large, and contained enough folded metal chairs to accommodate sixty or more people. But there were only about thirty people in the room, if even that. It seemed to Curt that the OSI was going to a hell of a lot of trouble for a whole lot of nothing.

The room was made up of a varied cross-section of humanity: acne-scarred teenagers, hip looking college students too cool for the room, overweight middle-aged blue collar workers who looked like they might be mechanics or telephone linemen or something similar, even senior citizens. Though there seemed to be far more men than women, the few women weren't exactly hard on the eyes. In the front row sat about half a dozen lithe young beauties dressed in outlandish silver robes. They all had long straight hair, pale skin, wide glassy eyes; they appeared to have been poured from the same esoteric mold, perhaps the one used to manufacture Bolshoi ballerinas. They were chattering amongst themselves in a language unknown to Curt. Curt wouldn't have minded getting to know any of them a little more intimately.

Curt didn't want to seem conspicuous. He didn't want to sit in the front, nor did he want to sit in the back. So he stuffed a dollar into the old woman's basket, then planted himself down as close to the middle of the group as possible. He sat beside a harmless looking woman in her late fifties with snow white hair. Curt glanced at his watch. Five minutes to six.

The woman glanced up at him and smiled. "Is this your first meeting?"

Curt nodded. "Yes. I've always been interested in this subject, but I never really . . . you know . . . ."

"Oh, I do." The woman patted Curt on the back of his hand. "Some people scoff, but rest assured *we* know the truth about you."

"You do?"

"You're among friends now. What's your name?"

Curt hesitated for a moment. "Maxwell Ryder." Curt wondered who came up with that alias. He thought the pun in the last name was a little over-the-top.

"My name is Madeline."

"Hello, Madeline", Curt said and shook her thin, bony hand.

"Are you a contactee?" Madeline said.

"No. No, not yet. I mean, I've never . . . I've never actually *seen* anything out of the ordinary. But I'm very interested in the subject."

Madeline patted him on the back of the hand again. "Don't you worry. It'll happen to you if it's *meant* to happen. The Space Brothers know what they're doing."

"That's very reassuring. Uh, is everyone here a . . . you know, a contactee?"

"Oh, no, not all of them. You don't have to feel out of place. We're all fellow travelers here. Did you notice the cookies in the front?" She then launched into a long coughing jag.

At first he thought she was talking about the girls. It was a euphemism he had never heard before. Then he glanced over at the corner of the room and spotted one of the silver-robed beauties standing in the corner serving coffee and cookies.

Curt reached into his inside jacket pocket. "Do you, uh, mind if I smoke?"

Madeline laughed. "I was about to ask you the same question. Light?" She reached into her oversized purse and pulled out a long, slender cigarette. She continued to cough even as Curt lit it for her.

"Excuse me while I grab a cup of coffee", he said.

"Go right ahead", Madeline said. "That's what it's there for." The last word segued into another coughing jag.

Curt stood up, strolled over to the young woman behind the table, and said, "Hello, this is my first time."

"We hope you enjoy your stay here", she said in a very clipped, precise manner. "Once you have melded with the group-mind, you will find that all worries vanish into the void."

"That so?" Curt leaned against the wall beside her and lit his cigarette. As he did so, he turned the lighter in a slow half-circle, trying to get photos of everyone in the room in one sweep. "And how long have you been coming here?"

"Since I was six and ten years of age."

"Oh? How old are you now?"

"Nine and ten years of age."

"Mm. Those are formative years." Curt couldn't help but glance over her body. Until now he didn't realize how young she really was. "Where are your parents?"

"We in the Orpheum Solutions Group have no need of parents or family of any kind. Pythagoras is our only father, our only priest, our only son, our only husband."

"Did you say husband?" Curt said.

"Pythagoras is husband to us all", the girl said and gestured toward the other silver-robed beauties in the front row.

Curt gave them all the once-over and nodded. "Pythagoras is doing very well for himself I see."

"As we *all* will be once the ways of Orpheum are brought to Sol-III for all to enjoy."

"That doesn't sound like a bad plan to me. What the heck is Sol-III?"

"I am sorry. It is most likely known to you as Earth. Would you like some coffee?"

"Sure." Curt slipped the lighter back into his jacket pocket and accepted the steaming cup. It was as black as midnight, just the way Curt liked it.

At that moment the six beauties in the front row stood up and started singing a bizarre song that sounded like nothing

Curt had ever heard before. It sounded to him like a hostile alien choir lobbing in hymns from another dimension like grenades . . . and yet somehow it wasn't unpleasant.

Curt took his seat next to Madeline. "What's this?" he whispered.

Madeline smiled and nodded to the music as if it were a favorite Al Jolson tune remembered from her youth. "This is the planetary anthem of Orpheum."

"*Really*", Curt said. He glanced around the room and saw that everyone else was tapping their feet to the unharmonious music as well. He realized that he was way out of his depth. The OSI had absolutely no idea what they were dealing with here. Just because he knew a little something about science fiction didn't mean he could communicate with these nutjobs on any level. The OSI assumed UFO buffs and science fiction fans were the same. In his experience, the few science fiction fans he'd ever met were hardcore rationalists, very logical people, hostile to even the vaguest hint of the metaphysical. These people were the total opposite. He had walked into nothing less than a religious cult.

At that moment a pair of red velvet curtains parted and from between them emerged the man of the hour, Pythagoras Invictus himself. He was a small, dark-skinned man, unimpressive physically. His head had been shaved. He too wore the distinctive silver robes of Orpheum, though his were far more ornate, decorated with esoteric sigils and such. He crossed his arms over his chest, then raised them high toward the ceiling. He intoned some sort of prayer in a language Curt didn't understand. This went on for quite some time while the beauties continued singing. At last the song and the prayer reached a crescendo, then everything ended abruptly. The sirens resumed their seats and Invictus faced the crowd from behind his wooden podium and said, "The Space Brothers from Orpheum require the constructive thoughts of seekers

such as yourselves in order to manifest on this plane of existence. The more positive thoughts you project into this fallen
world, the more sightings will occur around the globe. This is
truth. We are all connected. We are all one. This planet, like
Orpheum, is destined to be transformed into a virtual paradise in which all will act and think and move in harmony with
one another. No negative thoughts will exist. What we think
and dream will become manifest in three-dimensional reality
instantaneously. We must trust each other if we are ever going
to convince outsiders to trust us.

"In order to bring about this paradise we must step up
our attempts to educate the profane. We encourage you to
interact with one another outside the confining walls of this
drab meeting hall. Talk to one another. Call one another on
the phone. Meet at each other's houses. Discuss what you have
learned here in the past few months. To that end, my lovely
Venusian princesses will now distribute vital information that
all of you should hold onto. Please make use of it."

As he spoke, the silver-robed sirens fluttered about
the crowd handing out mimeographed sheets of papers
on official Orpheum Solutions Group letterhead. A redhead with otherworldly green eyes handed Curt one of the
sheets. Cartoony flying saucers decorated each corner of
the page. It seemed to be a complete list of everyone in the
room including their addresses and phone numbers. Curt
couldn't believe it. His job was done. All he had to do now
was copy this stuff down onto a separate sheet of paper and
hand it to Ray. Mission accomplished. (Ray: "Wow, Curt,
you're a better spy than I thought you'd be. Congratula-
tions! Here's a bonus.")

Curt smiled at Madeline, folded the sheet into fourths,
and slipped it into his pocket.

"Excuse me", Madeline said, "could you . . . ?" She handed
her sheet to Curt along with a pen.

"Oh, of course", Curt said and jotted down the name MAX-WELL RYDER along with a random address and phone number.

She smiled happily, then turned her attention back on Invictus.

The leader had removed a model of the planet Orpheum from beneath his podium and was explaining how most of the population lived in the interior of the planet. "Inside the earth people lean *toward* each other, thus creating psychic harmony. On our planet the situation is sadly reversed. You see, we live on the outer surface of our planet; thus, we lean *away* from each other, creating *dis*harmony . . . ."

Curt settled back in his seat to watch the show.

When Curt returned to his hotel room he was surprised to find Dolbraith waiting for him. The doctor was lounging on his bed like a whale that had chosen to wash up on a mattress instead of a beach.

Dolbraith was reading a book called *The Mind String and How To Pull It* by Dr. Bart Keppel.

"Is that a good book?" Curt said.

Dolbraith tossed it aside. "It's by a colleague. I'm supposed to write a review of it by Friday. You know, as a favor. It's a festering piece of camel dung, to be honest with you. We in the OSI have gone far beyond his techniques. But, of course, we can't let anybody know that. So I'll write a positive review of it for the *L.A. Times* and assure everybody how cutting-edge it is. Any success tonight?"

"I'd say so." Curt reached into his jacket pocket and pulled out a piece of notebook paper on which he had copied all the names of the people who had attended the meeting. He left out most of the phone numbers and addresses, however (he figured that would look a little *too* good).

"My oh my", Dolbraith said when Curt handed him the list. He glanced over it quickly, then said, "You make a *far* better spy than I thought you ever would. I'm pleased."

"Thank you. Now may I ask why you're in my room?" Curt began taking off his tie.

"You certainly may. I'm here to show you a movie." Dolbraith gestured toward a film projector sitting in the corner. Curt hadn't even noticed it.

"Did you bring popcorn?"

"Rum will have to do." Dolbraith removed a silver flask from within his coat pocket, then tossed it toward Curt.

Curt sniffed it first. What the hell, why not? He took a few swigs. Captain Morgan. More than a few swallows would kill him, but nonetheless he felt compelled. It had been a long night.

"Thanks", Curt said. "I needed that." He gestured toward the projector with his thumb. "So is this *our* movie?"

"No, it's even better", Dolbraith said. "It's a sequel."

"You guys work fast."

"We do indeed." Dolbraith rose from the bed with a groan, then waddled over to the projector and flipped a switch. He pointed it at the blank wall across the room. The images that appeared were far from clear; however, within seconds Curt understood that he was staring at a live performance. A man being dragged into a dark room by a pair of familiar-looking aliens. Curt could tell this was no normal performance just from the sounds of the man screaming. Not even the finest method actor in the world ever screamed like that.

The man was naked, overweight. The cameraman drew in for a close-up. Curt recognized that face from the photo in the newspaper. Anton McPhillips. Two other aliens entered the scene from stage-left. Each alien grabbed a different limb and lifted him onto a surgical table. A blindfold was strapped around his eyes. At that point an overweight man in a surgical mask, clearly Dolbraith, entered the scene and injected

McPhillips in the arm with a very long needle. He then exited the scene, the blindfold was removed, and McPhillips calmed down considerably.

McPhillips's hysteria segued into a laughing fit that lasted for several minutes while the aliens continued to stare down at him impassively. At last he calmed down enough to say, "Who . . . who are you?"

"We've come a very long way to meet you", one of the aliens said, this time—thanks to Curt's prior direction—in a very convincing manner. "We mean you no harm. Please, what is your time cycle?"

"What . . . what're you talking about?"

The alien then wheeled McPhillips over to a large screen, a star map, and pointed at a tiny area on the map—the planet Curt had christened Qutius.

"Is that where you come from?"

The alien nodded. "We hail from Wolf 359."

"And what do you want from me?"

"We want to learn more about you."

"About the human race . . . or about *me* in particular?" The alien pointed at him. "But why . . . why me?"

"You are *special*."

Whatever Dolbraith had given the man now kicked in full-force. His speech started growing more and more slurred as he whispered, "Where is this place? I'm seeing . . . seeing all these colors . . . ."

"You are entering hyperspace", the alien said. "You are one of the very few humans to have been so privileged."

McPhillips started laughing again. "I-I *like* hyperspace . . . ." Now he was staring past the aliens at something that wasn't even there. Whatever it was, however, was causing him great joy.

From off-screen Curt could hear Dolbraith scream, "God damn it, ask him the questions before he floats away entirely!"

One of the aliens leaned close toward his face and said, "Tell us about communism. What do you think of it? Would you prefer to see this planet ruled by communism?"

McPhillips just couldn't stop giggling. The alien sighed and threw his willowy arms in the air.

"Don't give up now!" Dolbraith yelled. "You asked him too many god damn questions. Just ask him *one!*"

The alien leaned in again and said, "What do you think of communism?"

McPhillips cried, "*Wheeeeeeeeee!*" like a child on a see-saw.

"I guess that means he likes communism", one of the aliens said sarcastically.

"God damn it!" Dolbraith entered the scene again, his face still covered by the surgical mask, and pushed the tallest alien out of the way. He grabbed McPhillips by the shoulders and shook him. "Name your fellow communists in the House of Representatives! Do it!"

"*Wheeeeeeeeeeee!*" McPhillips said.

"Too bad I don't have a degree in psychology", the sarcastic alien said.

Dolbraith balled his hand into a fist and said, "If you don't shut up I'm going to . . . ."

The head alien decided to have another go at it. He put his hand on Dolbraith's shoulder and said, "Let's try to take a different approach."

The alien leaned down toward McPhillips's face and whispered, "We have great powers, the power to grant you any wish you desire. Tell us what you want most in the world."

McPhillips was crying tears of joy. "I want . . . I want . . . ."

"Yes?" the alien said.

"Yes, *yes*?" Dolbraith said.

"I want . . . I want peace."

"Piece?" Dolbraith said. "A piece of what?"

"I think he said *peace*", said the head alien.

251

"*Peace?*" Dolbraith said. "You think communism can bring peace to the world, is that what you're saying?"

McPhillips said, "Peace . . . peace of . . . peace of mind." Then he started giggling again. This laughing jag was bad. He wasn't going to break out of this one easily.

Curt glanced at Dolbraith while the murky images continued to flicker on the wall. "*The Keystone Kops Meet the Martians*", Curt said. "Why didn't Hal Roach ever think of that one?"

Dolbraith didn't even crack a smile. "You haven't seen the entire film yet. He gave us good information, enough to call our first outing a success . . . but not enough of a success. We're going to need more results to keep the funding coming in. So we need your advice."

Curt had known Dolbraith long enough to understand he wasn't joking, not even in the slightest. "This is what this has all been about? An Inquisition for the Atomic Age? The Atomic Fucking Inquisition?"

"I don't have time for moral platitudes. We need results, and we need it *now.*"

"What information could you possibly have gotten out of him?" On the screen McPhillips was saying something about beautiful trails of light.

"Names. A mistress with communist ties. Enough to establish a link. Enough to destroy the son of a bitch."

"So that's what you're going to do? Destroy an innocent man?"

"Innocent? I'd hardly call sabotage and espionage 'innocent.' We can't let these Reds just take over our country. Our entire American way of life will be decimated in no time at all if we just let these pinkos march in here and turn the United States into *1984.*"

"Don't you see that that's what *you're* doing? By trying to stop them you're bringing about exactly what you're afraid of. Jesus, you really can't see that?"

252

"We hired a writer, not a political scientist. You signed a contract, mister. We need to improve your hack scenario before we try this in the field again. I want suggestions."

"Why do you want to *improve* it? You said it worked just fine. Besides, if the whole point is simply to torture people for fun and profit, why go through this whole rigmarole at all? Just kidnap them, shoot them up with your little truth serum—whatever the fuck it is—and go to town on 'em exactly like you did here."

"Don't you see? The details have to match from incident to incident. The OSI doesn't bother to initiate any long-range operation like this unless it's going to scratch a lot of itches at the same time. Bringing you to Wisconsin, for example. Yes, we wanted you to infiltrate the Orpheum Solutions Group, but we also wanted you here because of the McPhillips operation. The point of all this isn't just interrogation. That's an aspect of it, yes, but not the main goal. Over time, as more and more people like McPhillips have experiences like this and leak the information to the press and to friends and family members, people will begin to notice similarities between the various stories and therefore will be more likely to believe that *all* of them are true. Lies and disinformation and propaganda can only work if they have some basis of *truth* behind them. You're looking at the truth on the screen. A legend in the making."

"But why? Just to fuck with people's minds?"

"The benefits are numerous. Not only is this a convenient cover for our on-going experiments in mind control and behavioral modification, but once we've planted a few more tall tales in the media about crashed saucers and recovered alien technology we'll have the Soviets shitting their pants wondering what kind of horrible new weapons we have in store for them. The Russians are a very superstitious people. They'll believe the stories, no doubt. We've consulted with a number of prominent Russian psychologists on this matter. Bargaining chips are always useful. They're even more useful when they don't actually exist. That way you don't waste any money on something that may or may not work. Fortunately, legends and rumors don't cost that much."

"Only what you're paying me and everyone who works at the studio back in L.A."

"Like I said . . . legends and rumors don't cost that much." Dolbraith smiled. "Listen, this whole operation cost a *fraction* of an average Nike missile base. It's far more cost-effective to invest in myths. Besides, that studio is going to be busy over the next few years pumping out propaganda that the public's actually going to *see* in their local theatres. Movies trumpeting the military and adventures overseas. So many impressionable young men just waiting for a purpose in life. We'll give it to them, along with popcorn and candy. What little money we pumped into this operation will be returned to us a thousand fold over the course of the next few years. I laid all this out in my proposal to The Committee. And obviously I received the funding . . . therefore, I must know what I'm doing. Correct? So what more do you need to know?"

"This information about McPhillips's mistress, are you going to leak that to the press?"

Dolbraith shrugged. "There's no need to. He's already destroying himself in the media with his crazy alien stories. But all the hoorah about that will die down in a few weeks, he'll take a little vacation to get out of the spotlight, and when he gets back we'll be ready to start blackmailing him. You'll start to see Representative McPhillips voting in a slightly more conservative fashion within the next few years, just trust me. That is, if his whole encounter with the denizens of Wolf 359 haven't driven him totally nutty by then. Anything else?"

"Where did you take McPhillips? You couldn't have had time to fly him all the way back to L.A."

"We didn't need to. We took him to a makeshift set we built in one of our underground facilities beneath the University of Madison."

Curt studied the screen. "Yeah, it certainly looks make-shift. Pretty shoddy craftsmanship. Look at those portholes. And you've got stars twinkling outside. The ship's supposed to be in outer space, isn't it? Stars don't twinkle in space! There's no fucking *atmosphere*! It's ridiculous!"

"Well . . . perhaps you can help us with these piddling details."

"Who gets abducted next?" Dolbraith paused for a moment. "Or do I not have a 'need to know'?"

"No . . . I think you do have a need to know. We'll be show-ing you the film soon enough anyway. There's a CIA agent in D.C. suspected of being a double agent, but no one's been able to prove it, not even our best men and they've been tailing him for years now. So . . . we'll see what he tells our friends from space. If he *is* an agent, our friends will be giving him some juicy information to take back to his masters in Moscow."

"And what if he's not?"

Dolbraith spread his hands in the air. "*Que sera sera*. I view it as simply another chapter in the unfolding text of this elabo-rate fiction you've created, Mr. Adamson. I think most writers would be pleased. Don't all writers seek immortality through their fiction? And the more people believe the fiction, the more successful they deem themselves. Yes? No? Any further queries?"

Curt rubbed his face, wanting desperately to wake up. He sighed and said, "So do I get royalties every time this little operation is performed somewhere around the world?"

Dolbraith chuckled. "I know you think I don't have a sense of humor, Mr. Adamson, but in fact I do. I appreciate your dry asides, your little *bon mots*, I really do. Oh, and do keep in mind that if you ever try to leave the fold, one of us will find you and give you a dose of what we shot up McPhillips with. Now . . . let's get down to brass tacks. Where did we go wrong in the beginning here?"

Curt decided to ignore the threat. The more overt the threat, in Curt's experience, the less threatening it was. So he pushed Dolbraith's crude words out of his mind and felt himself settling back into writer/director mode. And, in spite of himself, it felt good. He recalled the script as he'd written it; he knew they hadn't followed it as precisely as they should have. "Well . . . first of all, astronomy's not your strong point", Curt said. "These aliens don't come from Wolf 359. The aliens didn't identify their planet correctly at the beginning. If you want to create the illusion of a real world, then they have to identify it by the name *they* use. Wolf 359 is just a name Earth scientists came up with for the star their planet revolves around. Get it?"

Dolbraith stroked his beard as he stared at a close-up of McPhillips still crying with joy on the screen. "Momma", McPhillips was saying, "oh, Momma, there's millions of them . . . ."

"I see", Dolbraith said. "Yes, that does make sense."

"The average layman's not going to notice a detail like that, but afterwards—when they've told their story to the media—well, there'll be astronomers and other experts asked to evaluate the tale and they *will* notice something like that."

Dolbraith pulled slightly at his bottom lip, his own personal nervous tic. "The abductees aren't always going to be laymen. It *has* to be right. Why, even your friend Senator Hull might receive a visit from us very soon."

"Hull?"

"That got your interest, didn't it?"

"But why *him*? I thought you and he would be—?"

"Colleagues? Well, we were . . . as long as he restricted his accusations of communism to Hollywood and leftwing 'peace' activists. You've been reading the newspapers, haven't you?"

"To tell you the truth, I haven't been paying much attention to the real world. My head's been up in the stars for so long."

"Well, you *should* start paying attention. All that power's gone to Hull's head. Now he's started accusing the military and various agencies of the government, including the OSI, of being honeycombed with communists. He's making a lot of the *wrong* enemies now. We're not actors and comedians and vaudeville jugglers. He can't push us around in the same way he can push around a symp like Charlie Chaplin. We need to eliminate Hull . . . make him look crazy . . . extract some dirt from him . . . whatever works. We already know he's having an affair with his secretary, but that's not enough. The photos we've taken so far are pretty good, worth a laugh or two. What that little minx did to him at the Cairo Hotel is damn embarrassing for sure, but I'd prefer something a little . . . *grittier* than that." Dolbraith grinned. "So what do you say? Hull's the son of a bitch who destroyed your career in Hollywood. Now, because of me, you might get your opportunity at revenge. No man can turn his back on a good revenge scheme, eh? That makes sense . . . right?"

Curt nodded, accepting his fate. What choice did he have? "You know what else would make sense?" He grabbed a pen from inside the desk and started pointing out gross irregularities about the costumes of the aliens and their movements and certain details about the interior of the extraterrestrial medical room that lacked verisimilitude . . . .

No, this wasn't Broadway,—hell, it wasn't even *off*-Broadway—but it was as close as Curt Adamson was going to get for the time being.

A few days later Curt and Ray stood in an airport lobby waiting for the plane to take them back to Los Angeles. The Committee had gotten their names and Curt's input. Now they were happy. Everybody was happy . . . except Curt.

"Ray", Curt said to fill the silence between them, "do you know what The Committee's up to these days?"

"Nope", Ray said, his nose buried in a newspaper. "Do you?"

"Yes."

"If you're intending on telling me, please keep it to yourself. I don't want to know."

"Do you ever resent it, the fact that they don't tell you anything?"

"No, not really. Why should they?"

"If I were you I would resent it."

"Well, you're not me."

"Is this what you wanted to do when you grew up, back when you were a kid?"

"When I was a kid? I wanted to be a soldier. I've done that. I couldn't continue in the military, so now I'm doing this instead. Either way I'm serving my country. That's all that really matters to me."

"You know what I always wanted to do when I was a kid? Tell stories."

"Isn't that what you're doing?"

"I suppose so."

"Then we should both be happy."

Curt remained silent for a few moments, listening to the rumbling sound of planes taking off just outside the terminal. That and the pages turning in Ray's newspaper.

"Don't you ever want to get married?" Curt said. "Just settle down and have a normal life?"

"It's really hard to make human connections in the business I'm in. I'm often given a new cover with each assignment. Any connections I make while on the assignment are with people who think I'm someone I'm really not. Nothing meaningful could ever result from that. Sometimes I've had to just up and leave someone I cared a lot about because my assignment came to an end all of a sudden, with no warning. It was very hard to just . . . *ditch* them like that, knowing they would think I never cared in the first place. So I stopped trying to form meaningful relationships. With anybody." Ray never removed his nose from the newspaper the entire time he was talking. He appeared to be reading the funnies.

"How's that Charlie Brown doing?" Curt asked.

"Depressed again. Apparently so is Schroeder."

"How many relationships have you had? I mean intimate ones?"

"More than enough."

"Six? Twelve? Eighteen?"

"Why should you care? How many have *you* had?"

"Oh . . . I don't know. I never counted." Exactly eight. And three of those were women the OSI had provided him. "About twenty?"

Ray snorted in derision. "A piker."

"Really? You've had more than *that*?" Curt whistled. Ray said nothing, just kept his eyes on the paper. "How many women have you actually been in love with?" Curt asked.

Ray sighed and said nothing.

"Too personal?"

"Why all the questions all of a sudden?"

"Just trying to fill up time", Curt said. "You must've been in love with at least one of them."

"Maybe. Let's say yes."

"So wouldn't it tear your heart out if you knew you couldn't be with the person you really loved?"

"I know how that feels." Ray turned the page. "I feel it everyday."

"Then maybe you'll understand when I say that I just want to see Tina for a few minutes. I'm not going to say anything to her about the operation."

Ray just shook his head. "She was cheating on you. You know that."

Curt didn't know how to respond at first. "How do *you* know that?"

"We were monitoring your phone calls for months before we approached you. Yours *and* hers."

"Yes, well . . . I *did* know about that. We really hadn't defined our relationship, though. And to tell you the truth, I wasn't paying too much attention to her. What with the Broadway play in the offing and all. It was really stupid of me, I should've—"

"We all have regrets."

"I cheated on her myself." He'd never cheated on anybody in his life. "It was stupid of me. I wish I hadn't, but I did. Why'd I do it?"

Ray shrugged.

"Is she still seeing him?" Curt asked.

"We ceased monitoring her calls after your relationship with her ended. Your guess is as good as mine. What do *you* think?"

"I don't know. There's probably been a couple of guys, but maybe nothing serious."

"Who did you cheat on her with?"

"Vicky Pendleton, this secretary over at Allied Artists. Cute little brunette . . . very sweet. Her fiancée had just left her, so she was very . . . you know, *vulnerable*. It started out with us just having coffee. I shouldn't have taken advantage of her like that. I told Tina about the affair. I thought, you know, I should be honest with her . . . but that was the stupidest thing I ever could've done. Now Tina *and* Vicky hated me. Vicky didn't want me to leave her. She told me she'd do anything for me, but I had to cut if off. I was in love with Tina, so . . . so two guys dumped Vicky in the space of a month. I think it almost killed her. Anyway, even *that* wasn't good enough for Tina. She never forgave me." He'd spoken to Vicky Pendleton about three times in his entire life. He'd asked her out on a date once, but she told him she would be busy that night because she had to do her taxes. It was the worst rejection he'd ever received. "That's probably why Tina . . . you know, did what she did. With that other guy."

"That's rough", Ray said.

"Afterwards, whenever Vicky and I would see each other around town, it was all very awkward, you know. But she'll be fine. Cute girl, but very fragile. She's probably moved on."

"You want permission to see Vicky now?"

"Well, if the Tina thing's totally out of the question . . . ."

Ray shook his head and laughed. "*True love.* Right. Listen, you just stick to Rita and the other girls. That's far less complicated—for you *and* me. Trust me."

"I guess you're right. You know, even though I love Tina I don't think I'd ever go to her if I ever needed any real help. She's too flighty and self-absorbed. Now Vicky, on the other hand, she's a real rock. Very supportive. The more I talk about her, the more I miss that girl."

A voice over the loudspeaker announced that Flight 412 was about to depart for L.A.

"That's us", Ray said. "You go first."

"Okay. See you in L.A. And Ray . . . ?"

"Yeah?"

"Maybe it would be a good idea to call Rita when we get back."

"I'll get right on it. Thank you for coming to your senses."

"Don't mention it."

Curt grabbed his bag and headed toward the plane.

Three days later Rita was lying in bed beside him, still sleeping off the events from the night before, when Curt opened the newspaper that had been left on his doorstep that morning and saw a small headline on the last page of the A section that immediately drew his attention. It was the sort of thing a screenwriter kept his eye out for. A dramatic suicide under mysterious circumstances . . . .

A man named Frederick Olsen, an employee of the Central Intelligence Agency, had leaped out of the ninth story window of a hotel in Washington, D.C. after exhibiting signs of a nervous breakdown. The employees at the hotel claimed he had gone mad, running naked around his room and bouncing off the walls and babbling about bright colors and streaking trails of light. At one point he screamed, said the guest in the room next to Olsen, that he was afraid "*they* were going to come for him again."

Frederick Olsen was survived by a wife and two teenage daughters, all three of whom were baffled. They were quoted as saying that Frederick Olsen had never exhibited signs of insanity his entire life. He'd been in a good mood when he left his Virginia home for a weekend business trip to D.C. He was the *last* person on Earth to ever want to take his own life.

Strangest of all, the window through which he leaped had been closed at the time. It took a lot of balls to jump through a nine-story window. It took even more balls to jump through a *closed* nine-story window. In fact, Curt had never heard of anything like that ever happening at all.

The phone beside his bed rang, making Curt almost jump out of his skin. Rita began to stir, so he grabbed the receiver quick.

"Hey, Curt, you're gonna have to wrap up playtime", Ray said. "We've got another assignment."

"Where?"

"D.C."

"Why . . . why D.C.?"

"As far as I know it's another meeting. This gathering has no connection to the last one, at least as far as I know. I'll give you more details in person. Be ready to leave for the airport in an hour."

"Right. I'll get ready now." Curt hung up the phone, grabbed Rita by the shoulder and shook her awake.

"Mm?" she said.

"Sorry, gotta go, babe."

"What?" Rita looked confused, as if she didn't know where the hell she was. She looked quite different in the morning. He wondered how much, exactly, it cost the OSI to keep her here with him all night. If he wasn't so disturbed at the moment, he might even feel guilty for using the taxpayer's dollar in such a lascivious way. But not really. After all, every year the tax payers handed over their cash to the government and said, "Here, do what you want with it." If this is what they wanted to do with it, why should Curt complain? Besides, wasn't it partly Curt's money too?

Rita closed her eyes and went back to sleep.

He reached out and brushed the back of his hand against Rita's cheek. "Hey . . . hey, Tina", he whispered, "wakey-wakey, hon." He knew he wasn't talking to Tina. But sometimes it was nice to pretend. He used to say the same thing to Tina every morning when she first started spending the night. Those were some of the happiest times of his life. Before it all started to dissolve . . . .

Rita was comatose. Curt sighed, climbed out of bed, let her sleep. What did it matter? He didn't care if she ripped off anything from this place. Now that the manuscript was in the hands of The Committee, he had nothing here he cared about.

So he got dressed, packed, and took off, making certain to close the door behind him as quietly as possible.

He didn't feel it necessary to leave a note.

As they waited for the plane, Ray's nose once again buried in today's paper, Curt said, "Have you ever heard of Frederick Olsen?"

"Not until this morning", Ray said. "You're talking about that guy who did the Esther Williams through the window?"

"Yep, that's him. Did the article strike you as odd in anyway?"

"It struck me as odd that he was an employee of the CIA."

"The window that he jumped through was *shut*."

"Yeah. Sounds like his suicide was a collaborative effort."

"What's the first thing you thought of when you read the article?"

"The first thing? Well, I think it's obvious, don't you?"

Curt's heart began racing. He so desperately wanted someone to confide in. "How so?"

"It's obvious the Soviets probably killed him."

"The Soviets."

"Sure. Who else? He probably stumbled on something they didn't want known and they killed him. But the American newspapers are never going to print that. If they did, it might start World War III. No one wants that . . . at least not right now they don't. So, it'll just be whitewashed. We might never know the truth."

Curt lapsed into silence.

Ray turned the page of his newspaper and began reading the latest installment of *Dick Tracy*.

The sixth official meeting of The Cosmological Research Association met in the back of a library in downtown D.C. the following afternoon. It began at precisely 1:00 p.m. The membership of this particular association wasn't quite as diverse as the last one. Members seemed to consist mainly of teenage boys and older men, almost all of them total gearheads. They seemed obsessed with the nuts-and-bolts aspects of the UFO phenomena. They wanted to know how the things *worked*. They presented graphs and pie charts speculating how a metal disc might be made to fly in the Earth's atmosphere and beyond.

Most of it was way over Curt's head. But he listened intently the entire time, hoping the sweat trailing down his armpit wouldn't interfere with the wires strapped to his chest. As an eighteen-year-old boy stood behind the CRA podium outlining the general principles of anti-gravity, making some sort of link with the work of the late Nikola Tesla, Curt tried to figure out how and when he would make his break.

All he had waiting for him back in L.A. was a long series of empty nights with Rita and her colleagues and a writing career that would never be known beyond a few anonymous eggheads on a Committee whose real names would remain veiled to him forever. Either that, or once his imagination had been bled dry, he'd end up taking a dive through a ninth story window. Communist Screenwriter Takes Own Life. A single column at the back of the A section in the *Los Angeles Mirror*.

It was either now or never. It had to happen between the end of the meeting and his scheduled return back to the hotel room—where, Curt knew, a visitor would be waiting for him. A fat man with a beard and no moustache waiting to show him a film of Frederick Olsen being abducted by characters he himself had created. He couldn't take it. He refused to contribute even a single new idea to this operation.

So Curt sat and listened to lecture after lecture. The man who seemed to be the head of the organization was a silver-haired old gentleman sitting in the front row. He was wearing a flashy suit and tie, as if this were a meeting of important Madison Avenue executives. He was tall and thin, probably about sixty years old. He had introduced each lecture so far in a very formal fashion, and possessed an aristocratic air about him. He seemed to have a British accent, but if so it was rather slight. Perhaps the man had moved to the States a long time ago, or was trying to shed the accent for some reason. His name, he told the audience at the start of the meeting, was Quentin Thesinger.

265

So far no one at the meeting had discussed extraterrestrials at all. The members had only discussed sightings of ships flying in the air, and the possible propulsion methods of these craft.

It wasn't until a gangly teenage boy, maybe about fifteen, stood up and asked the speaker a question did the word "alien" even come up. The boy said to the speaker, "Excuse me, but isn't it possible that these discs don't have anything to do with any sort of physics we're familiar with. I mean, after all, the aliens piloting them might—"

The entire room burst into laughter. The boy turned red with shame. Curt felt sorry for the little guy.

Quentin Thesinger rose from the front row and took to the stage. He joined the Tesla expert on stage and said into the mike, "We don't discuss aliens here. This society is devoted only to back-engineering the craft themselves."

"But . . . if aliens are piloting them, that may not be possible", the fifteen-year-old said. Good for you, Curt thought (even though he didn't really believe life existed anywhere in the universe except on Earth). "Imagine", the boy continued, "a small group of ancient Egyptians, the smartest Egyptians there were in those days, coming across a modern television set that had somehow fallen through a portal in time. Those Egyptians would never be able to back-engineer that television set no matter how many hours they spent taking it apart. They wouldn't have the tools to make the tools to make the tools to make the stupid television set."

A precocious little shit, Curt thought.

"So what's your point?" Quentin said.

"My point is you're all just wasting your time if you're not addressing the issue of who's actually *inside* the craft."

Quentin rolled his eyes and said, "I think we all know who's inside the craft."

"Who?" said the fifteen-year-old.

"Onto the next speaker", Quentin said, completely ignoring the boy's question. "Harold Plimpton has flown all the way here from England to give his unique perspective on how the principles of quantum physics might be applied to the UFO phenomenon. Give a big hand for Mr. Plimpton . . . ."

Curt clapped for a short while, then rose from his seat and approached the front row. He took a seat right behind Quentin. As Plimpton began speaking, Curt leaned over and tapped the man on the shoulder. Quentin turned and Curt said, "Hi, the name's Maxwell Ryder." At first Quentin seemed annoyed, then Curt added, "I'm a screenwriter from Hollywood." At that point the man perked up. "I'd like to talk to you about the organization you have here. Perhaps you could even serve as a paid consultant on the film I'm currently working on for Empire Studios in Hollywood. Would that interest you?"

Quentin nodded. "Certainly."

"Do you have time to talk after the meeting?"

Quentin nodded. "I know just the place we could go. A café just around the corner. I'm eager to speak to you. You know, Hollywood has yet to make an accurate film about this phenomenon."

"Yes, indeed . . . don't I know it."

Quentin then pressed his finger to his cracked lips and gestured toward Mr. Harold Plimpton up on the stage. Curt settled back into his seat and tried to pay attention to a lecture that consisted almost entirely of words he couldn't comprehend. It seemed to stretch on for hours.

Curt and Mr. Thesinger sat in a darkly lit café drinking coffee, discussing the cutting-edge information regarding the UFO issue. Due to all his recent research, the information was fresh in Curt's mind. He could've continued talking to the man for hours, but time was running out.

Curt glanced at his watch. 4:30 p.m. He would have to make his move soon.

Thesinger gave him the opening. "I'm so pleased that Hollywood is now taking an active interest in this subject. I think it has great, untapped box office potential, if handled correctly. And you and I, with your imagination and my know-how, we could handle it correctly. Look at the few movies that have come out about this subject. Have you seen *Night of the Saucers*? Dreadful!"

Curt nodded. He had indeed seen it. He'd written it.

"The worst piece of crap I've ever suffered through", Curt said. He glanced at his watch again. 4:33.

"You know, there's a double feature playing at The Bijou just down the street that you should really see", Thesinger said. "*The Flying Saucer* and *The Man from Planet X*. Now, the first film is horrible . . . in cinematic terms, I mean . . . however, I suspect the basic facts of the film reflect the reality of the subject."

"How so?"

"Well, I think these saucers are being piloted by the Soviet Union based on designs stolen from the Nazis. Of course, our government wouldn't want to admit to that. Why would President Truman want to admit in public that the Soviets are ahead of us technologically? It would cause a panic. Better to disseminate all these silly alien stories, like that little snot-nosed kid was promulgating in the middle of my meeting. Why, I should've—"

Curt had never even heard of *The Flying Saucer* before, but he had seen *The Man from Planet X*. In fact, he'd seen it several times. When the producers over at Allied Artists had asked him to write *Night of the Saucers*, they had screened *The Man from Planet X* for him and specifically requested that he make the script as much like that film as possible.

"Where did you say these movies were playing?" Curt said.

"At The Bijou just down the street."

"You want to see them right now?"

"Now?"

"Sure. You could explain the films to me. You know, do a running commentary. Explain where the filmmakers went wrong. That way I could avoid making the same mistakes."

Thesinger's face brightened. "An excellent idea. I *love* talking through movies, but most people seem to dislike the habit. This is the first time anyone's ever *asked* me to talk during a film." He glanced at his watch. "Why, I think there's a showing at five. We can just make it if we head over there now."

"Let's do it."

Curt wondered what Ray was making of these developments. He couldn't possibly be frowning on them. This was all well within the parameters of his assignment. He was supposed to check out the head of the organization, and that's exactly what he was doing. There was nothing suspicious about his activities. Nothing suspicious at all.

He and Thesinger headed into The Bijou, a small theatre on R Street a few doors down from the Masonic Temple on 16th Street. The theatre seemed to specialize only in foreign films and obscure American films. Later that evening they were showing a double feature of *Metropolis* and *M*, two of Curt's favorite movies of all time. Too bad he couldn't stick around to see them.

Thesinger bought some popcorn. Curt didn't.

There weren't many people in the theatre, maybe about twenty or so. He and Thesinger sat in the exact center of the theatre. True to his word, Thesinger barely shut up during the entire first fifteen minutes of the film at which point Curt tapped him on the shoulder and whispered, "Save my seat."

"The little boy's room, eh?" Quentin said in that annoying, effeminate manner of his. "Don't worry, I'll fill you in."

I'm sure you'd like to, Curt thought. He stumbled around in the darkness, headed back up the aisle, then took a seat in the corner of the back row. He unbuttoned his shirt. During a loud moment in the film, he began to tear the wires off his chest slowly, very slowly. He draped them over the back of the seat and headed for the door. For the next couple of hours all Ray would hear would be the sounds of gunshots and melodramatic background music.

Curt strolled out of the theatre, then began walking briskly toward the Capitol, the very spot where his HUAC inquisition had occurred so many months before.

He glanced at his watch. 5:20. He didn't have much time. He had to hope the man was there. He had to talk to him in person.

Representative Marshall Hull had plagued the nightmares of many writers, directors, producers, actors, and singers over the course of the past few years. He plagued Curt's nightmares even to this day. After all, if not for him—and people like him—he might never have fallen into this mess at all. But he *was* in it. And though Representative Hull was the man who attacked him the most on that fateful morning so many months ago, he was now Curt's only hope of salvation.

Curt knew where the Representative's office was located. He'd seen it on television numerous times, as that was the place Hull generally delivered his live broadcasts to the public about the growing communist menace. Curt had walked right by it on his way into the inquisition.

He arrived at Hull's office just before six o'clock. There was a woman sitting behind a desk, a blonde in her early twenties, gathering packages into her arms as if she were getting ready to go home soon. Curt said, "Hello, ma'am, my name is Curt Adamson and I need to see Representative Hull about an extremely important matter."

"Do you have an appointment?"

"I assure you Hull knows me. I testified before HUAC a couple of months ago. You might remember seeing me on television. I'm a writer in Hollywood." She seemed concerned, as if worried that he might be dangerous. "I'm also a communist", he said. "I have information that's going to blow the roof off this whole town. I need to talk to Hull about his investigation, something he *needs* to hear right now. I need to talk to him before it's too late. Is he in his office?"

The woman glanced at the door a few feet behind her desk. It was closed. An opaque window in the door bore Hull's name. She seemed nervous. "Perhaps I should call . . . ."

He charged past her desk and grabbed the knob on the door. He swung it open and barged inside. Senator Hull sat behind his desk talking on the phone. Curt would recognize that fat reptile of a man anywhere.

The secretary ran after him and yelled, "He just barged in here, sir!"

"Who the hell are you?" said the Senator.

"I'm Curt Adamson, the screenwriter you and your committee interviewed back in January. I took the Fifth then, but now I want to talk. I know the communists have infiltrated the Office of Scientific Intelligence and other government organizations. There's a plot from within that agency to eliminate you, sir, and I don't want to see that happen."

Hull's secretary was growing more and more frightened. "Should I call security?"

Hull waved his secretary away. "Not yet. Let the young man in. I'll be all right."

The secretary reluctantly backed away. Hull gestured for Curt to enter his office.

Curt took a seat in front of the Representative's desk.

"You've arrived at a most opportune time", Hull said, reaching into his desk for something. "A lot of people in this town have been warning me away from investigating the OSI. You're a screenwriter?"

"Yes, sir."

Hull pulled out a revolver and pointed it at Curt's chest. Curt raised his arms in the air. He wasn't entirely surprised. The overzealous Representative *was* from Texas. His most famous photo-op involved the shooting of javelin pigs.

Hull furrowed his brow and studied Curt. "Yes . . . I think I remember you now. We've had so many people testify . . . it's hard to remember. How would *you* know anything about the OSI?"

"I've secretly worked for the Communist Party for ten years. Some of my fellow travelers brought me into the fold of the OSI not long after I testified before your Committee. A reward for keeping my mouth shut, perhaps."

"Is that so? And you're prepared to testify about this?"

"Absolutely. As long as you can guarantee my safety. There're a lot of people who want me dead."

"If what you say is true, boy, I wouldn't doubt it. Can you prove what you're saying?"

"Yes. The OSI has had you under surveillance for some time now."

"So?"

"So you're having an affair with the bouffant blonde in the outer office."

Hull smiled. "You're gonna have to do better than that, boy. That's hardly a revelation."

"Perhaps . . . but how many people are aware of what the little minx did to you at The Cairo Hotel? Pretty embarrassing, wouldn't you say? Particularly if the photos got in the hands of the wrong people."

Hull shifted around in his seat. "All right, you have my attention." He put away the revolver, then gestured for Curt to lower his arms. "By the way, that was entirely *her* idea, not mine. If we're going to move forward, I need names. You need to be prepared to turn in your fellow communists."

"If you attack the OSI they'll attack you back. They'll release those photos."

"Do I seem worried, Mr. Adamson? No? That's because I'm not. It's not as if they can broadcast those photos on NBC during prime time, correct? They'd be arrested for flagrant indecency. My wife and I have an arrangement. She has her life, I have mine. I really don't care who sees those photos. Hell, now that I think about it I'm sort of *proud* of them. Now give me the names."

"Not *all* of them. That would be too dangerous for me. I need to hold onto some of the names . . . you know, for my own protection."

Hull nodded. "Understandable. How many names are you prepared to give up for the time being, Mr. Adamson?"

Curt's brain locked. If he named Dolbraith, a staunch Republican with a conservative pedigree a mile long, Hull would be less likely to believe him, at least at this delicate stage in the game. Besides, Curt knew what Hull was actually asking of him. Hull needed more names to throw to the media wolves that now surrounded his office on a daily basis. Hull had been playing a dangerous game for a long time now. A game that revolved around defeating the ever-shortening, TV-numbed attention span of the country at large. In order to keep making headlines, Hull's revelations had to become grander and grander. There was now a constant demand for new names, new communists, new saboteurs. Hollywood had almost been sucked dry. Where could he go next? What might the new menace morph into before the day was through? In Hull's paranoid world the communists were like shape-shifting aliens straight out of a cheesy screenplay that Curt himself might have written for a quick buck only a few years before, a convenient source of fear that transmogrified from scene to scene depending on the needs of the writer—and in this case, the writer was Hull.

Aliens, Curt thought. His brain unlocked. Of course.

He reached into his inside jacket pocket and pulled out the contact list Pythagoras Invictus has disseminated at the

Orpheum Solutions Group meeting. The form had remained there for days. Names, addresses, phone numbers. Perhaps thirty or more. Just enough to prove Curt's loyalty to Hull's holy crusade. Grist for the media mill Hull had been running out of this office for years. Proof would be unnecessary. Just as it had been unnecessary in Curt's case.

Curt handed the paper to Hull. "This should get you started in your investigation."

Hull glanced over all those names. So specific. Lists always looked good on camera. "My people will have to double check these names and addresses, make sure they actually exist."

"They do, sir. They're part of a very dangerous organization, though they may *seem* benign. Somebody needs to get to the bottom of it before they destroy the country."

"I promise I'll forward this information to the right men in the FBI."

"You *must* protect me from these commies, sir."

"As I said, I'll need at least twenty-four hours to investigate." He reached for the phone on his desk. "In the meantime I'm going to have you arrested." Curt opened his mouth to protest. "Just as a precautionary measure. To keep you safe. You won't *really* be arrested. Consider it 'protective custody.'"

Curt relaxed. "Well, that's exactly what I want."

What did it matter to him? His life had already become a prison. He'd rather be in a real one as opposed to a fake prison where the bars were invisible.

Curt felt a great sense of relief when the D.C. police arrived at Hull's office and slapped the cold metal handcuffs around his wrists.

Within twenty-four hours Representative Hull sent one of his assistants into the jail to assure Curt that his information had indeed checked out. All the people he had fingered belonged to a subversive organization under suspicion by the FBI.

Representative Hull announced a surprise press conference early Monday morning. Hull escorted Curt directly from the jail to his office. During the ride over Hull coached him on what to say.

Curt had written the speech of a lifetime inside his head, one he would never give. He couldn't. He couldn't breathe a word of the truth. Everyone would think he was nuts. Hull would turn his back on him. The OSI would shoot him down dead in the street at the earliest opportunity. No, he couldn't beat the OSI at their own game. The best he could do was create a stalemate situation.

He would say nothing about the fake aliens and the truth serum and the blackmail and the abductions. He would say exactly what Hull and the rest of the country wanted to hear. There were communists under every bed. They had infiltrated Hollywood. Curt had had firsthand experience in that. And now they had infiltrated the U.S. government. Specifically, they had infiltrated the OSI. Sure, there was no proof Curt had ever worked for the OSI. But what did that matter? There was no proof he had ever been a communist either. He knew how to tell a good story—*that's* what mattered. To Hull, to the press, to the public.

With no proof at all, they'd believe it.

You just had to sell it.

Curt was about to pull off the biggest pitch meeting of his writing career.

Hull sat him down at his own desk, the same desk Curt had seen Hull sitting behind a hundred times in the past. The cameras faced him, ready to go live. One of Hull's assistants placed a cup of water in front of him. Curt thought the cameras looked like a firing squad composed of cold glass cyclopses that could stare straight into one's soul. Nervously, he reached out for the cup of water and brought it to his lips and the red lights blinked on and the Senator began to introduce him to the American public.

As the Senator spoke the room began to spin. The effect was immediate. Bright colors. Trails of light darting about in the air before his eyes. *Hyperspace.*

The water.

Something in the water?

Jesus, who had dosed it?

One of Hull's "assistants"?

The OSI was everywhere. They didn't want him to appear sane.

His breathing became erratic. His heart started to race. His head . . . spinning . . . .

He remembered Olsen bouncing off the walls of his hotel room, screaming about "them." What if the same thing happened to him right now? It would all be over.

A truth serum. What Dolbraith gave McPhillips?

It would all come out right here on live television. Qutius. The aliens. The mother ship. Everyone would think he was crazy. In an insane asylum they could do whatever the hell they wanted to him. Shock treatment. A lobotomy. He wouldn't be a threat to anyone. *Tina* . . . .

The Representative finished his speech and gestured toward him. Flashbulbs danced in front of him, the lingering lights merging together into crazy streaks that danced like insects before his eyes. He could feel himself wanting to giggle. It was so funny. The truth was so funny. Just tell the truth . . . the truth . . . .

He felt like vomiting.

The reporters merged together suddenly into one blurry, amorphous mass of hungry flesh and the lights went out in his head and Curt Adamson lost all consciousness . . . .

276

Curt had no memory of his speech whatsoever. Apparently, however, the ratings had been quite high.

He saw the broadcast later, months later. A local L.A. news station sent him a copy in exchange for an interview. His speech was slurred, yes. He seemed pale. Maybe even a little frightened. All of which made his testimony all the more believable. But he didn't appear crazy. Not crazy at all.

Ultimately, the liar—the *writer*—in him had prevailed over the OSI's serum, whatever the hell it was. Even while totally unconscious, he stuck to the fiction. The story that made the most logical sense.

He never mentioned Qutius. Never mentioned aliens. Never mentioned the mother ship.

He wove instead a dark tale of intrigue about the communist secret society that had sent him to infiltrate Hollywood. Once the valiant Representative Hull blew Curt's cover during the HUAC meetings, Curt was reassigned to the office of Kenneth W. Dolbraith at UCLA to help the doctor with his covert behavioral modification experiments. Many of these saboteurs had wormed their way into the corridors of the OSI, thanks to Dolbraith's OSI-connections.

Curt was unable to prove any of this, of course, but the accusation was enough to cast a shadow over Dolbraith's reputation. Besides, Dolbraith was a University professor, and that alone was suspicious no matter what his political associations had been. Eventually the doctor was forced to testify before HUAC. There was talk in the newspapers of removing him from his position at UCLA, but of course that never happened. The University made a big deal of announcing that Dolbraith's behavioral modification experiments had been "temporarily shut down", but Curt knew what that really meant. It meant they would continue under the auspices of some other agency, beyond the scrutiny of the American taxpayer.

The OSI was inconvenienced by the resultant hearings and on-going rumors, but hardly destroyed by them.

Curt now made a living giving lectures all around the country about his many years working for the communists. He hated the patriotic dupes in his audience, but what the hell. He considered the whole affair one gigantic play. Indeed, he had just completed a three-act stage play about his time colluding with the communist menace. It was to debut on Broadway next season. Curt himself would direct. Ziv Productions in Hollywood had already optioned the rights for a regular television series. The title of the TV show had been announced as *I, Communist*. It was sure to be a hit.

Curt tried not to think about his days in the OSI, and for the most part was successful, except when he opened a paper and saw yet another UFO story emblazoned across the newsprint and spotted strange, alien words he himself had created being uttered by a man who claimed to have encountered something horrible on a lonely highway . . . sometimes in the Midwest, sometimes in the Arizona desert, sometimes in another country . . . . Only in this way did Curt know that the operation continued without him. And a brief tinge of guilt mixed with pride would disturb his otherwise contented existence.

All in all, life as a former U.S. intelligence agent posing as a former communist was better than he ever could have imagined.

However, it was made very clear to him during every lecture, in subtle ways unknown to the rest of the audience, that there was an OSI man in the front row for each performance. It had gotten to the point that Curt could spot them before they even made themselves known to him.

A stalemate. If they killed Curt, it would seem as if the "communists" in the OSI had done it. It would simply give more credence to his tall tale. So as long as he stuck to the fiction, as long as he stayed well away from the truth, he was safe from them.

One rainy night, while he and Tina greeted a horde of his admirers after a rousing lecture for the American Legion in Orange County, a bearded man in a heavy overcoat approached Curt and asked for his autograph.

"Can you sign it 'Maxwell Ryder'?" the man said in a voice two octaves lower than it should have been.

Curt looked up into the man's gray eyes. Then he glanced over at Tina who was too busy chatting up his other fans to take note of the exchange.

Ray leaned in close to his ear and whispered, "The only reason we didn't catch you and eliminate you within the first twenty-four hours is because we were too busy harassing Nina Auerbacher and Vicky Petersen. Turns out they never knew you at all. I guess neither did I. You know, you're a very clever fellow, Mr. Ryder."

Curt wasn't certain what to say. So he said, "It's not intentional."

"Do you realize Tina's still cheating on you?"

Curt leaned in close as well. He whispered, "Yes, but I don't care because I love her. Thank you for your concern, though."

Ray tipped his hat toward Curt with deference, then reached out and grabbed the program for the evening on which Curt had scrawled the words *MAXWELL RYDER—TO RAY, FOR LOOKING OUT FOR ME* and blended back in with the night.

Curt knew he would never see the man again.

He and Tina left the performance arm-in-arm.

Since lying had become his fulltime job, their relationship had never been better.

ROBERT GUFFEY's first book of nonfiction, *Cryptosca-tology: Conspiracy Theory as Art Form*, was released by Tri-neDay in 2012. He's published numerous short stories in a wide range of magazines and antholo-gies such as *After Shocks*, *Aoife's Kiss*, *Catastrophia*, *Flurb*, *The Mailer Review*, *Nameless Magazine*, *Pearl*, *Phantom Drift*, *Postscripts*, and *The Third Alternative*. *Spies and Saucers* is his first book of fiction. He's currently a lecturer in the Department of English at California State University—Long Beach.